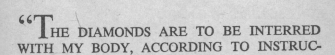

“THE DIAMONDS ARE TO BE INTERRED WITH MY BODY, ACCORDING TO INSTRUCTIONS GIVEN TO MY SOLICITOR. . . .”

An audible gasp was heard. Marcia Milmont fainted dead away in her chair.

“What about Luane?” Gabriel asked. “It was understood that she would get the diamonds. What is to become of her now?”

“The *devil*!” Luane shrieked. “She did it on purpose because I wouldn’t marry Gabriel. She thinks to force me to it yet.”

“It wouldn’t surprise me if someone hadn’t snatched them already.”

The diamonds must be rescued. But how . . . and by whom?

Aunt Sophie's Diamonds

Joan Smith

A FAWCETT CREST BOOK

Fawcett Books, Greenwich, Connecticut

AUNT SOPHIE'S DIAMONDS

A Fawcett Crest Original

© 1977 Joan Smith

ISBN: 0-449-23378-2

Printed in the United States of America

10 9 8 7 6 5 4 3 2 1

Aunt Sophie's
Diamonds

Chapter One

The last will and testament of Sophronia Tewksbury was a document so vile and complex her relatives considered seriously having it contested on the grounds of her having been insane when she wrote it. In following years it was often used as a precedent in cases where bizarre requests were made by the deceased, and when a solicitor was confronted with a particularly difficult legal matter, he would dub it a "Tewksbury Case." When it was read aloud, her neighbor, Sir Hillary Thoreau, threw back his head, laughed, and said it was "just like the old devil to take it with her," till he learned he had been saddled with the unenviable task of being co-executor.

It was a raw, cold day in late March when Sophronia's relatives (she had no friend except Thoreau), assembled at Swallowcourt to attend her deathbed. She had been threatening to die for years, but her companion, Miss Bliss, felt that this time she meant it, so sent out a series of notes to those of the family who were likely to come.

The likeliest ones were Sophie's sister, Marcia Milmont, and the husband's nephew, Captain Jonathon

Tewksbury, the main heir to Swallowcourt. The place was entailed on him, with lifetime occupancy for the widow. They both set out posthaste from London, but as Jonathon made his trip in a curricle, he beat Mrs. Milmont to Swallowcourt by the better part of an hour. He had time to make one last bid to ingratiate himself with the old girl before she died. This was done by some heavy-handed gallantry on how well she looked, with her eyes sunken into their sockets, and by playing a game of chess for ten minutes, at which point it was clear that even a dying Sophronia was more than a match for her nephew.

He had barely rejoined Miss Bliss in the Crimson Saloon, a chamber of impressive dimensions rendered bleak by the faded draperies, dusty furniture, and general air of decay, when Marcia arrived. To his considerable surprise, she was accompanied by her daughter Claudia, a young girl often mentioned but never heretofore seen. They came in, a spritely matron with a carefully painted face, a full but good figure encased in an expensive green traveling suit, and a tall girl of uncertain years. The matron was forty-eight, looked forty-five, and called herself fortyish. It was this duplicity regarding her own age that accounted for the uncertain-appearing age of her daughter. Claudia was twenty-four, but as owing up to this would age her mama so dreadfully, she was treated as a mere child. Except for an unfortunate tendency to tallness, she might have passed for being still in her teens. There was a youthful glow on her cheeks and in her eyes. These were of a clear blue, but with a knack of looking vague as she was a dreamer.

Since turning fifteen, she had spent her time on her paternal grandfather's estate in Devonshire, so that she could officially remain "my little girl" in her mother's conversation. It was decidedly awkward to have her present in London, where Mrs. Milmont had still some hopes of remarrying. Claudia's presence now was due to the beginning of her annual two-week vacation with her mother, timed, of course, to be over before the London season began, and usually spent in such tedious quiet that Claudia was happy to return to her country life. The death of

8

Sophronia had proved a boon to Mrs. Milmont. It would remove Claudia from town, and as Sophie had to go sometime, no time appeared better than the present.

Captain Tewksbury was well known to Marcia. They were friends in London, both inhabiting that uncertain area just on the fringe of society. She viewed him with no more than a stab of chagrin that he had beat her to Sophie's side. To Miss Milmont, however, he was a stranger, and therefore a creature of a little more interest. She saw a tall young gentleman in a dashing red tunic, with blonde hair, curled and smooth, an aquiline nose, and a petulant mouth. He reminded her of a spoilt boy dressed up in a soldier's uniform. Her mama knew him to be a captain in the Foot Guards, and though he had never seen battle and was not likely to as he was attached to the Palace, he made much of being a soldier. No general's buttons shone more brightly; not the greatest hero's shoulders were held back at a straighter angle. He spoke of such weighty matters as "the Corsican's Plans" and "that sly old devil, Boney" as though he were the power behind the Iron Duke. He had, of course, never met the Duke of Wellington. His *real* interest was in his uniform, and the balls and routs he attended in the city. He had also an interest in heiresses, for though he stood to inherit Swallowcourt, he had but slim chances of getting any money to go with it, and it was falling apart. He couldn't sell it, since it was entailed, but it would add to his dignity to have "a country place" to speak of, and the rents would add something to his officer's pay, he supposed. His real deliverance from the confines of poverty lay in marriage, and he never for a moment forgot it.

"Miss Bliss, how is my dear sister?" Mrs. Milmont asked in a grief-stricken voice as soon as the necessary introductions were made.

"She's dying. That's why I sent for you," Miss Bliss replied coolly. "So this is the *little girl* I've heard you mention," she said, looking at Claudia.

"Yes, my little baby," Marcia answered, glancing up at her baby, who smiled apologetically, and seated herself immediately to conceal her height.

The captain gave all single girls a close scrutiny, but he saw nothing to interest him here. A tall, gangly girl, and as she was Mrs. Milmont's daughter, the dowry could not be considerable.

"Mama, should we not go right upstairs, if Aunt Sophie is dying?" Claudia asked.

"I hope we may take two minutes for a cup of tea after jostling all the way from London over bumpy roads. My bones are shaken. Is she really dying, Miss Bliss? Last year when you had me down right in the middle of the Season, it proved to be only a digestive upset."

"That was *two* years ago. This time we're sure. The doctor says so, and she's stopped eating."

These sounded like good omens, and to conceal her pleasure, Mrs. Milmont pulled out a dainty lace-trimmed handkerchief with a beautiful M embroidered in the corner, and held it to her eyes. "Well, none of us lasts forever. She's frightfully old, poor girl."

"There must have been quite a difference in age between you two," Miss Bliss said. "Sophronia is seventy."

Tea had already been ordered, and while it was served, Marcia explained away her ancient sister. "We're of different generations entirely. Sophie was the eldest child, and I was born years later, the youngest."

"There must be nearly twenty years difference," Miss Bliss remarked with a sly smile. She enjoyed humbugs.

"Much more than that! Mama was only seventeen when Sophie was born, and nearly—going on fifty—well into her forties, when I came along."

"How unusual."

"There were the other children, the boys, in between, you know." Disliking this subject, she turned to Jonathon. "I didn't see you at the play the other night, Captain. Shakespeare—so distracting. But then you soldiers are slaves to duty. I daresay you were on maneuvers or making battle plans in case Boney invades us. Claudia, child, pass the captain a biscuit."

"They're stale," he said bluntly, then removed himself from Mrs. Milmont's good graces by saying, "I didn't realize your daughter was a grown girl. I thought she was just a child. Though now I come to think of it, you've been talking about her for close to ten years."

"She is older than ten," she said, shooting fire at him for his question.

"Must be at least twenty," he answered, looking closely.

"You naughty boy!" Marcia laughed. "Why, he's making you out an old maid, Claudia. You ought to give him a good scold."

"Are you making your come-out this year?" he asked Claudia.

"I . . ."

"Too bad. Sophie's death will mean you have to put it off."

"Oh, dear!" Mrs. Milmont gasped. "I hadn't thought of that."

"But I was not to be presented, mama," Claudia said.

"Presented? No such thing. I'm not talking about that. I shall have to go into mourning. For six months too, I suppose—the entire season wasted. I shant be able to go about till the Fall little season. What a pity, and I have ordered four colored gowns."

"I'm dished, too," the captain commiserated, quite cut up.

"That's certainly a pity," Miss Bliss said in her tart way. She looked at Claudia while the other two consoled each other, and thought she saw dismay in those big blue eyes. Without a doubt the girl was ashamed of her mother, and well she might be if she had a bit of decency. She beckoned to Claudia, who arose and went to her side. She engaged her in conversation and found her a quiet, well-bred young lady. Her having spent the last nine years away from her mama would account for it.

"Did I understand you to say you are not to be presented?" she asked.

"There was never any mention of it, ma'am, even when I was at the age . . . That is . . ." She came to a confused stop.

"I see," Miss Bliss smiled and tactfully changed the subject. She believed the girl must be over twenty. In her

11

plain gown and untrimmed bonnet it was hard to tell, but she could not be much more than twenty.

"Do you like it in Devonshire?" she asked next.

Claudia praised the countryside, but her activities, when they were drawn out of her, sounded boring enough. Governess to two brats of cousins was the gist of it, with no mention of balls and parties.

Mrs. Milmont finished her tea and asked Miss Bliss if she would just see if she and Claudia could go up now to see dear sister. No sooner was Miss Bliss out of the room than she turned to Jonathon and began an interview that interested her a good deal more than Sophie's health.

"Have you heard anything about the will?" she asked eagerly.

"She's had her man of business here to make some changes. I couldn't find out what they were."

"You're safe enough, Jonathon. She couldn't take away your portion if she wanted to."

"She could give me a little money to go with it, but it will go to young Gabriel, I expect. I wonder he aint here making up to her."

"He's sly enough for anything," Marcia warned. "But he would be at the university, would he not?"

"Sir Hillary has gone to fetch him home."

"*That* one would stick a spoke in your wheel if he could, and he rich as Croesus himself."

Claudia was at first confused at these names, but as the two bereaved talked and complained on, it became clear to her that Sir Hillary Thoreau was some near-by neighbor who had Gabriel Tewksbury living with him. It seemed Gabriel was also Sophie's nephew by another of her husband's brothers. That one nephew, Jonathon, should get the estate and the other some money seemed fair to Claudia, but she saw pretty clearly it was considered a grave injustice by the captain.

"Don't despair, Jonathon," Mama consoled the captain. "The lot would have gone to Gabriel—the money, I mean—had he married Luane at Christmas as Sophie wanted him to, but as he hadn't the wits to do it, there may be hope for you yet."

12

Here at last was a name with which Claudia was familiar. She knew she had a cousin Luane Beresford. Mama's brother was the girl's father, and Claudia had often wished she could meet her only female cousin.

"Can't think why they didn't do it, for they're close as inkle-weavers, the pair of them. Ever since Luane's been living with Sophie, she's been tossing her cap at young Gab."

"She may have him and welcome, what *I* fear is that she's after my diamonds."

Claudia stared to hear that mama had diamonds and wondered that her cousin Luane should have an eye on them.

"The Beresford Diamonds you mean," Jonathon corrected.

"They were given to Sophie by our aunt; they are family diamonds."

"Well, Luane's a Beresford."

"So am I, or was, and Luane won't be a Beresford when she marries. I see no reason why she should get the diamonds."

"An orphan, and quite like a daughter to the old girl these last years. I take it your brother didn't leave the girl much."

"No, never a feather to fly with—he lost a great deal upon 'Change," she added, lest he take the idea the family was poor, which it was.

"Far as that goes, I daresay your daughter could do with a little something."

"She is well dowered, sir, I take leave to tell you," Marcia fired up. "She has a handsome allowance and is in Mr. Milmont's will."

Claudia stared to hear her pittance of an allowance described as "handsome," and knew very well that her inclusion in grandpa's will was for a roof over her head.

"That so?" Jonathon asked, his interest quickening. "How much . . ."

"Quite a large sum," Mrs. Milmont replied evasively.

"Daresay that's why Sophie is leaving the diamonds to the Beresford chit then."

"I cannot feel she would treat her own sister so shabbily. But there are the other jewels—the long rope of pearls I especially admire, and there are some fine rings . . ."

"All the rest of that junk together wouldn't be worth the price of the necklace."

"You don't have to describe my family's diamond necklace to *me*, Captain. I know it is worth fifty thousand pounds. Why, the large pendant stone hanging off the front is worth ten thousand. And if she wants to be giving it to a niece, I see no reason why Claudia should not get it. She is the elder."

Claudia smiled to herself to hear that she was being allowed to be older than anyone and asked mischievously just how old her cousin Luane was.

"A year or so younger than yourself," she was told by her mama with a silencing frown.

Miss Bliss returned to take the Milmont ladies up to see Sophie, and Jonathon went out for a walk around his estate, an exercise so depressing that he soon returned and had a glass of sherry. Everything was a mess—stonework crumbling, slates off the roof, windows smashed to bits, and the lawn a jungle. It would take a fortune to put the place to rights, and for what? Couldn't sell it. An heiress—there was the answer to his problems, and if Luane Beresford got the diamonds, he'd make a push to attach her. What had Sophie said there, during the chess game? 'Thoreau is bringing Gabriel down from Cambridge in case I should take a pique and leave all my blunt to you. And I'd do it too, if Luane would marry you, which she won't.' Who said she wouldn't though? Be bound to fall for the uniform. He paraded in front of the dim mirror to admire his buttons and lace. He let his eyes wander up to the face, and he saw nothing amiss there either. Bit of a handsome dog actually.

He was disturbed at this narcissistic chore by the sound of flying feet in the hallway. Dashing out to see what had happened, he saw Miss Milmont, breathing hard and stuttering. "She—she's dead!"

14

"By Jove!" the captain exclaimed in a strange voice of which sorrow made up no part.

"They said to tell you."

"What am *I* supposed to do about it? If she's gone, she's gone. You've told me."

"Don't you want to go up?"

"What for? It's the doctor you want, I fancy. Have to sign some certificate very likely. Yes, I'll send for Hill."

Mrs. Milmont was only a minute behind her daughter, the monogrammed handkerchief firmly lodged against her dry eyes. "My vinaigrette, Claudia," she breathed in a dying voice.

The two ladies went into the Crimson Saloon, and were soon joined by Jonathon. "Well, I've sent a boy off for Doctor Hill," he told them and rubbed his hands, unable to control a smile.

Miss Bliss came in, her usually alert face wearing a stunned look.

"Where is Miss Beresford?" Claudia asked. "Should we not tell her?"

"She went down to Chanely—Thoreau's place, to wait for Gabriel's arrival. She should be back soon."

Jonathon was a little worried to hear of his heiress still dangling after Gabriel. He had thought they had a falling out at Christmas, but it could not have been severe.

"What should I do?" Miss Bliss asked the relatives. "We should be letting people know. Jonathon, maybe you'd come with me, and I'll give you some note paper."

Jonathon's chest swelled to be at last master in some house and in a fit of nobility he said, "I don't want you to worry about a thing, Miss Bliss. You can stay right on here and look after things for me. Of course, I wouldn't be able to pay you much . . ." he added, as sanity returned to him.

"No, you couldn't pay me to stay here," she said bluntly and gave him a list of persons to notify.

"I could pay you a little something."

"I'm going to a chicken farm with my sister," Miss Bliss said to be rid of him, and she returned to the Saloon. She then took the Milmonts to their rooms.

When Marcia had attired herself in a black gown and her daughter in an unbecoming dove gray, the closest thing to mourning the girl possessed, they went downstairs to await whatever Fate and Miss Bliss had in store for them.

Chapter Two

They were soon seated in the Crimson Saloon looking at each other in silence. Before talk was necessary, the door flew open and a regular hurly-burly girl came charging in, black curls flying beneath a jaded brown riding cap, and a rumpled brown tweed riding habit, too small for her, covering her body.

"Oh, hello, Aunt Marcia," she said. "Is this your daughter?"

"My poor child!" Marcia said by way of response. She once again produced the monogrammed handkerchief. "Is Sir Hillary with you?"

"No, they're back and coming up after dinner. Why do you call me poor child?"

"You have not heard the sad news," she said with a long face.

"What, did my aunt finally die, and me not here to see her?"

"Indeed, my sister is gone . . ." the last word petered out.

The little face under the brown hat crumpled, and a

tear oozed out of the dark eyes, but in an instant her face resumed its former contours, and a small hand brushed away the tear. "I'm sorry to hear it. Where is she?"

"She—it—the body is still upstairs. We must wait for the doctor to come by, my dear. Sir Hillary is coming, you say?"

"Yes, they are just come home, but don't know Sophie's dead."

"They must be notified."

"They are coming up immediately after dinner. It's not worth while sending a boy down." The stout little voice was trying hard not to break. "Excuse me," she said and turned away to dash up the stairs.

"Rag-mannered," Mrs. Milmont said to her daughter.

"She was overcome with grief, mama," Claudia objected.

"That sassy chit? She hasn't a thought or a tear for anyone but herself. Snatching the diamonds out from under our noses with her conning ways. If Sophie only meant to give them to a niece and not her own sister, I don't see why she shouldn't have given them to you, but you never bothered to make up to her in the least."

"I never saw her till ten minutes ago, and she was dying then."

"You saw her any number of times—at least once or twice—when you were in pinafores. I daresay you don't remember."

"I have not been in pinafores for a good many years, Mama. You forget I am twenty-four."

"You could not have written her a letter, I suppose? Oh no, it never entered your head to be conciliating. You must needs let Miss Beresford walk off with a fortune."

"The will has not been read yet. Mama, why did you keep asking if Sir Hillary was come yet? Do you know him?"

"*Know* him? My dear, he is the Nonesuch!"

"None such what?" her simple daughter enquired.

"Oh, child, don't pester me with your stupid questions. He is one of the leaders of the *ton*, of the fashionable elite in London."

"Is he a friend of yours?"

"No, he thinks he is too highly placed to bother his head with *me*. A toplofty, arrogant . . ."

"Then why are you so anxious to know if he is come?"

"It can do no harm to be pleasant to him. Of the first stare, you must know."

"But if you dislike him, mama, and really he sounds very disageeable . . ."

Such a foolish remark as this recieved the withering glance it deserved. "Run up and see if Luane has anything to say. You might just hint if she is to get the diamonds."

Claudia agreed readily, but she had no notion of quizzing her cousin about the diamonds. She had felt a pang of pity rush out to the girl when she had heard of her aunt's death. So far as she could see, Luane was the only one who did grieve at Aunt Sophia's passing. She must be quite alone in the world now, except for mama and herself. And this Gabriel, of course, but as yet Gabriel Tewksbury was unknown to Claudia. All that was known was that he had refused to marry Luane, so he could not be much comfort to her. The girl's position reminded her uncomfortably of herself when papa had died nine years ago. She had her mama, of course, but no one who wanted her. It was her good fortune that her grandparents had taken her in and given her a home. Miss Bliss directed her to Luane's door, and she tapped twice. Receiving no answer, she opened the door and stepped in. She feared she would find her cousin on her bed in a fit of tears, but it was no such a thing. Luane was standing at a clothespress, flipping over a small selection of gowns. She turned and looked at the interloper out of her big dark eyes.

"Are you my cousin Claudia?" she asked.

"Yes, and I am very happy to meet you at last, for you are the only female cousin I have. My papa's brother has two sons, but they are only rowdy little boys. May I come in?"

"You are in. I am happy to meet you, too. You aren't much like your mama, are you?"

"No, we are not much alike. Are you choosing a gown?"

"Yes, do you think this pale blue ... or should I wear the navy moire?"

"It is chilly downstairs. I'd wear the navy with long sleeves if I were you."

To her surprise, Miss Beresford turned around with her back to her cousin and proceeded to undress herself, with no apparent discomfort or hesitation, though she kept her back to her the whole time.

"I expect you are very sorry to hear of your aunt's death," Claudia said, while she stared at the floor and wondered if she ought to leave.

"Yes, it's inconvenient," was the unexpected reply.

"Inconvenient?" Claudia asked, startled.

"Yes, I had hoped she'd hang on till I was married. I have nowhere to go now, you see."

"I see," Claudia answered, much struck by this plain speaking.

"I can't go to Cousin Gabriel, for he is still at university. Your mama won't have me, because she won't even let *you* live with her, and you can't ask me to your grandfather's place, for they are no relation of mine." There was no hint of a whine or even complaint in this recital, but rather an angry tinge to the whole.

"Well ..." Claudia said and could think of not a single suggestion to proffer.

"Just like Rosalie," Miss Beresford said with a sigh.

This comparison would have conveyed nothing to most, but to a woman much addicted to trashy novels herself in her greener years, Rosalie Dumont was as well known as Queen Charlotte. "Yes, the comparison is striking." Claudia agreed readily. "Very like *The Daughter of Bardon Hall*. I hope you don't mean to solve your case in the same manner, for I think Rosalie was imprudent in fleeing aboard a ship to France, don't you?"

"How else should she have met and married the Comte de Davencourt?" Luane asked.

"Yes, I had forgotten that, but there was no war on in those days and no Bonaparte."

"Yes, it can't be France," Luane said consideringly. "Are the Frenchies in Italy, too?" she asked.

"They are scattered all over Europe and, with Boney escaped from Elba, your best bet to meet a lord is right here in England. And you would do better to remain a girl, too, instead of turning into a boy, like Rosalie."

"It is very vexing, but then I am not so poor as Rosalie. I shall have a diamond necklace worth fifty thousand pounds."

"That is a very respectable dowry," Claudia replied.

"And I'm pretty too," Luane pointed out.

Claudia looked to the little face now turned towards her for examination and was much inclined to agree.

"What I must do is hire some impoverished lady to chaperone me till I make a match."

"What sort of man would you like to marry?" Claudia asked, happy to see the mundane manner of her cousin.

"A titled gentleman," was the unhesitating answer. "I mean to be a great lady."

"Ah, like Rosalie, I collect."

"Yes, and then he'll see . . ."

"That will show him," Claudia agreed quietly. "Who is *he*?"

"My cousin—it is no matter."

"The captain?"

"That toy soldier!" she scoffed. "I mean Cousin Gabriel. He will see I'm not an ill-behaved brat."

"Did he call you so?"

"He certainly did, and only because I asked Hillary if he bought me anything. He usually brings me bonbons," she explained.

"Did he remember the bonbons?"

"Yes, would you like one?" She passed a box of candied gingers. "Have two if you like. These are not my favorite."

Claudia contented herself with only one of the treats and chewed it while waiting expectantly for more news from this interesting creature.

"How old are you?" Luane asked suddenly.

"I am rather old, but you must not tell anyone, for

mama is still young," Claudia answered with a slight tremor in her voice.

"I thought you weren't as young as you let on," Luane said unemotionally. "Would you care to be my chaperone, cousin?"

"It would be excessively diverting," Claudia replied readily, "but I have not yet put on my caps and could not do much to introduce you to great noblemen in any case."

"Sir Hillary will do that. He is a nonpareil. I think you would make a very good chaperone. You are old without being *too* old."

"I am greatly flattered," Claudia said, drawing her handkerchief to her unsteady lips, "but I doubt my grandpa could spare me."

"He will have to spare you when you marry."

"True, but chaperones don't usually marry, especially *old* ones."

"You aren't over the hill quite. We'll find a nobleman for you too, cousin. A widower perhaps, with children, then you won't have to bother having any of your own. I think it must be very uncomfortable, don't you?"

"I have always thought nature mismanaged it very badly. We ought to just lay an egg like the birds."

"Or lay a whole bunch of them at once and have it over with."

"Even better." A small gurgle of laughter escaped Claudia, and she marveled at her lack of decorum when she had come here to console the bereaved. "I expect you are sad at losing your aunt," she essayed once more.

"She wasn't so bad, but she didn't like me. I'll miss her, but she's been talking of dying ever since I came here, and I am used to the idea. Shall we go downstairs? I'm starved," she added prosaically. They left the room, arm in arm and went gaily chatting down into the house of mourning.

Dinner was only an indifferent repast at Swallowcourt, as everyone but Claudia had good reason to know. She wished she had accepted another candied ginger. The captain remained behind after dinner only to taste the port before joining the ladies. One sip informed him he would as lief have tea.

The tea tray was just brought in when the butler came to the door. "Sir Hillary Thoreau and Mr. Gabriel Tewksbury," he announced, and all eyes turned to the door.

Chapter Three

Two elegant gentlemen strolled in, about as different as it was possible for two men to be. Gabriel was young, fair, slight, and appareled in the raiment of a young dandy. His hair was brushed forward in the Brutus do, his shirt points high, and his waistcoat of a brightness bordering on the garish. His companion was taller, older, broader across the shoulders, his hair and eyes dark. His dress was restrained, and his expression, as he observed the mourners, was sardonic.

It was the elder who advanced first into the room. "The vultures gather, I see," he said in a well-modulated voice, with a cool smile directed at random on the group.

Miss Bliss said, "Tch, tch," but the sound blended with the clicking of her knitting needles and went unheard.

"One must suppose Sophie's demise to be imminent, to have lured you two rakehells from the city," Thoreau continued, looking now at the captain and Mrs. Milmont.

"She's dead," Captain Tewksbury said accusingly.

"Don't eat me! *I* didn't kill her," he answered, with no

show of either sorrow or surprise. "How thoughtful of you to have notified us."

Miss Bliss cleared her throat. "It happened late this afternoon just before Luane returned from Chanely. As you were coming over this evening, we didn't think it worthwhile to send a footboy down to tell you."

"I see her clutch-fisted way of managing matters survives her," he said to Miss Bliss, then turned to Jonathon. "Were you on time to be in on the kill, Captain?" he asked.

"By Jove!" the captain answered, and Mrs. Milmont, who had been fulminating since their entry, could contain herself no longer.

"This is a most inappropriate way of behaving in a house of death, Sir Hillary," she said severely. "And you ought to be in mourning, too, or at least wear an armband."

"And so we should be, had we been notified of the death," he agreed. "And I see you brought your black gowns with you, Marcia darling. Up to all the rigs, as usual." He then advanced to Luane and took her hand, saying in a low voice some words of condolence. Gabriel followed him, bowed to everyone, then he too went to Luane, at which point Hillary returned to the others.

"Was it a peaceful passing?" he asked of them all.

"The doctor had just left a while before. She was in bed, of course," Miss Bliss explained.

"You, I take it, were with her?" he turned to Jonathon.

"No, I had been playing chess not half an hour before."

"Ah, that explains it," Hillary said. "It nearly killed me the one time I played with you, and my constitution is quite strong. Something about your manner of moving the pieces is killing."

"I don't see why you must be clever at a time like this," Mrs. Milmont charged angrily.

"No indeed, it will not do me, nor any of us, any good to be clever at this late date. The time to have been clever was before she popped off, *n'est-ce pas*? Were you clever during the chess match, captain?" His eyebrows rose very

25

slightly, and his eyes of a dark penetrating blue looked levelly at Jonathon.

"Not very."

"It was a foolish question; you never are."

"She was beating me all hollow," Jonathon informed him.

"She cannot have been totally unconscious at that time then, one imagines."

"Wasn't unconscious at all. As wide awake as you or me."

"As you or *me*? You must confess there is a large degree of difference."

"I'm awake enough!"

"But, captain, that was precisely my meaning. Awake on all suits, certainly. Our lives in your hands—God help us! What is the news of Boney in London?"

"There's no news."

"No news is good news," Miss Bliss said, with a warning stare at Hillary. She knew him in this satirical mood of old. He smiled at her and winked, then turned back to Jonathon. "Have you got the obsequies in train?" he asked.

"I've been writing letters to everyone. Miss Bliss gave me the list."

Sir Hillary trained his blue eyes on Miss Bliss again. "You notified Fletcher?"

"Yes, he was the first one Jonathon wrote to. It was her wish."

"And who, might one ask, is Mr. Fletcher?" Mrs. Milmont demanded, ready to take offense.

"Now *you*, darling are not nearly so wide awake as Jonathon," Sir Hillary said, wagging a long finger at her. "Is it possible you do not know her new solicitor? Fletcher is the interesting gentleman—er, man—not quite a gentleman I fear—who will stun us all with the reading of the will."

"Mr. Cartwright was always her man of business, and mine too."

"Mr. Cartwright was of no use to her this past year. She needed someone closer to hand than London, for she changed the will regularly. Yes, you may well gasp like a

26

landed fish, my dear, our fortunes were all up and down like a—a suitable simile fails me momentarily." He gestured with a pair of shapely hands on which a handsome ruby ring rested. "It was everything for the captain one day—some vestigial traces of primogeniture consumed her at one time. No, Jonathon, your glee is premature. That was immediately after Christmas, when Gab and Luane refused to be buckled. When you forgot her birthday in February and Marcia so wisely remembered, sending that elegant trifle—what *was* that wisp of lace for, Marcia? We couldn't quite figure it out."

"It was a lace cap."

"*I* suggested to her it was a cap, but Sophie would have it it was a container for her wools. That is what she used it for ultimately. She liked it excessively," he said with a half smile at Mrs. Milmont.

"Did she indeed? So happy to think my little gift cheered her."

"Yes, it was a good idea. Sophie always liked to get something for nothing, but then you both—really how *could* you be so negligent, and Sophie within Ame's ace of sticking her fork in the wall—you *both* forgot Valentine's day, and it was another call for Fletcher."

"I daresay *you* remembered Valentine's day?" Mrs. Milmont asked in a meaningful tone.

"I try to be civil," he allowed modestly.

"She never left it all to *you*!" the captain gasped.

Hillary pursed his lips and shook his head sadly. "My best efforts came to nought. She took it amiss that I twice visited her in a new jacket—that is to say, two visits, two jackets—neither of which she liked, and the lot was destined for Luane."

Two pairs of hostile eyes turned on Miss Beresford, but she didn't notice them. Gabriel also was looking at her, winking merrily. "How he enjoys bamming them," he said.

"Luane is only a niece!" Mrs. Milmont said to Hillary. "No more to her than my own little girl."

"Your little girl was never mentioned in connection with the will. I for one begin to doubt her very existence."

"What nonsense!"

"Why have you so foolishly failed to produce her for inspection all these years, darling?"

"Why, she is right here!" Marcia replied, pointing to Claudia, who sat quietly all the while in a corner, saying nothing but listening to the conversation with her eyes open wide, and a curious expression on her face—something between a frown of disapproval and an upturning of the lips that was not quite a smile.

"Such a quiet little girl," Hillary said, training his quizzing glass on her. Seated, she looked young, for her face was still youthful, and her light brown hair simply styled. "No, no, you fool me," Sir Hillary said, lowering the glass and turning once more to Mrs. Milmont. "This cannot be your little girl."

Marcia flushed with pleasure. "I married very young, and Claudia is big for her age."

"You might pass for—er—sisters? certainly, but so different in looks—style . . ." he trailed off vaguely.

"When Claudia is a little older will be time enough for style," Mrs. Milmont said coyly.

Claudia turned pink at this mendacious discussion of her youth, and in fact turned a mutinous countenance on her mama, who met it with a hard stare and then smiled again sweetly. The quick shift in expression did not escape Sir Hillary's lazy-looking eyes. Though he kept them half closed, they missed very little.

"Do you not mean to present me to your little girl, Marcia?" he asked.

"To be sure, Claudia, this is Sir Hillary Thoreau—your aunt Sophie's husband's . . . Well, it is quite confusing, but Hillary's cousin married Mr. Tewksbury's brother."

"Let us say I am Gabriel's guardian; it is the easiest way," Hillary added.

"He aint really nothing to Sophie," the captain inserted.

"You cut me to the quick," Hillary replied, "I was her closest neighbor, and as close to a friend as she had, poor old girl. Our mutual interest in Gabriel brought us closer together."

"Fact remains," the captain pointed out, "you aint nothing but a connection to her."

"I claim no closer kinship, I promise you. But, of course, it is not the kinship or lack of it that disturbs you. Do you fear I have insinuated myself into her heart, and worse, will? Perish the thought. She promised me her chess set. I doubt she remembered to give it to me, but that is the sole possession of hers I ever coveted."

"You won't get Swallowcourt anyway," Jonathon said.

"I am suitably thankful for small mercies." Thoreau answered.

"Well, and is Luane to get it all then?" Mrs. Milmont asked.

"That only takes us to the end of February," Hillary continued, settling back comfortably, "What was it you did, brat, to turn the tide against you?" he asked Miss Beresford.

"It was the dog," Luane reminded him.

"To be sure, it was. Because of a dog a fortune was lost, if I may paraphrase an old saw. A small spaniel, quite adorable, but with an unfortunate lack of manners which we shall not go into in mixed company. Suffice it to say, he was caught wet-handed, and in this very room, too."

"No, it was in her room, on the new carpet," Luane corrected.

"I *told* you how to train him, Loo," Gabriel said to her and proceeded to tell her once again what she should have done.

"Who does get it all then?" Marcia demanded, becoming impatient with this dallying manner of explaining things.

Again Sir Hillary's hands went up, and he hunched his shoulders to indicate he was at a loss.

"You mean to say you have no idea, and have been wasting our time with this faradiddle?" the captain demanded.

"I was under the misapprehension I was helping you pass this evening of mourning rather agreeably," Thoreau answered, offended.

"Does Luane get the diamonds, that's what *I* want to know," Mrs. Milmont asked him.

"It was one of many versions of the will," Sir Hillary told her. "They were to go to Luane, Jonathon, Gabriel—turn upon turn. Round and round and round they go, but where they stopped nobody knows, as the fortune wheel man at Bartholomew Fair says."

"I don't see why they ought to go to Luane any more than to Claudia," Mrs. Milmont insisted.

"Did your little girl really want the garish things?" Hillary asked. "Have you been pining all these years for a vulgar set of stones in the worst possible taste, little Claudia? I never suspected you of such rapacious leanings for a moment."

"Of course, she wanted them!" her mother replied. "Fifty thousand pounds, and Claudia a poor fatherless child." The monogrammed handkerchief, somewhat rumpled from its many outings, was out once more.

"And virtually motherless," Hillary added, with a quizzing look at Marcia. "But Claudia has not answered." Nor did she, but only sat staring at him with a mesmerized look in her eyes. In her sheltered life in the country, she had never encountered anyone like this sleek person. She felt as though he were a snake charmer, and she a snake, rising up out of a basket. She couldn't take her eyes off him.

"Naturally, anyone would," the captain added.

"And *still* little Claudia has not answered," Thoreau remarked sadly. Then he appeared to forget it and turned to Miss Bliss. "I expect the tea is quite tepid by now. Odd you didn't offer me a cup, ma'am."

"You aren't the only uncivil one in the room," she said sharply. She then put her hand to the pot. "It's still warm," she said. "Would you like some?"

"I wouldn't want you to overexert yourself, but there is a bitter wind outside."

He arose to get his own cup to save Lavinia Bliss the exertion, and when he had it filled, he did not return to his former seat but went to an empty chair beside Claudia.

"You did not answer my question, darling," he said. "Did you truly want the diamonds?"

Claudia had never been called darling by anyone since her papa had died. The smooth-spoken, elegant gentleman bending towards her now, an ironic smile on his face, did not remind her of her papa. Nor of anyone she had ever met in real life. He had stepped straight out of the pages of the lurid marble-covered novels of her young years, and she knew him at once for the villain, hiding his shame beneath a fashionable facade.

"I didn't know there were diamonds in the case," she said simply.

"Less and less can I credit you to be your mama's daughter," he said, his eyes widening a shade. He regarded the quaint creature before him. Utterly unlike the common, encroaching mama in appearance. Less bright, less brittle—a soft-edged water color, set against a hard-edged painting.

"I am thought to resemble my papa," she replied.

"I was slightly acquainted with Henry Milmont. I was only a young fellow when he died—it must have been a decade ago, *n'est-ce pas?*"

"Nine years, actually."

"And in all those years no one told you you had a rich aunt with whom you ought to be on terms? You have been badly treated, my dear."

"Certainly I knew I had an Aunt Sophie. Mama often spoke of her."

"And never of the diamonds? Strange, in *my* conversations with your mama, they were an inseparable pair—Sophie and the diamonds."

"Do you know my mother well?" Claudia asked. Strange that he *seemed* to, yet mama had said they were not friends.

"I believe I know her fairly well," he said, with a speculative glance at Marcia, who was observing them eagerly. She was uneasy to see Hillary in close conversation with Claudia—an artless girl who might go giving away her age or say something indiscreet. She arose and went to join them.

"Now you have met my daughter, Sir Hillary, you must congratulate me on her."

"It is Henry who wants congratulating, darling. She doesn't take after you in the least."

"No, she is a Milmont through and through."

"She has been telling me what a naughty mother you are, you know, and I think you have some explaining to do."

"What nonsense has she been telling you?" she snapped, throwing a suspicious look at her daughter.

"No, mama, Sir Hillary is fooling. I didn't say anything . . ." He looked and wondered at the expression on their faces.

"Now what have I inadvertently stumbled into?" he asked aloud. "Marcia, my dear, have you taken a lover, after all these years of celibacy?"

"How dare you, sir! And in front of my daughter, too."

"But you assured me she is pure Milmont. She won't have a notion what we're talking about. Henry never had. Not a lover then. Well, in that case, I admit the whole affair is beginning to bore me. What I *meant*, by the by, is only that you forgot to tell Claudia about the diamonds. She tells me she hadn't realized there were diamonds in the case."

"I hope I have not raised Claudia to be a grasping sort of girl."

"Whoever raised her for you seems to have led her away from that path. Henry's folks, wasn't it?"

Her bosom swelled with frustration. "Because of her health, it was necessary for Claudia to stay in the country."

"It proves to have effected a miraculous cure," he said, smiling. "Quite a remarkable bloom on those cheeks. No rouge either," he said, peering a little more closely at Claudia, then comparing with a glance at her mother. "Do you know, Marcia darling, I think *you* ought to try a sojourn in the country."

"When I want your advice, I will be sure to ask for it, Sir Hillary."

"And I will be sure to give it, to the best of my poor

ability. But what must your daughter think of us, squabbling as though we were husband and wife—and in a house of death, too. I'll tell you what we'll do. Let us have Luane and Gabriel take your little daughter to see the diamonds and other jewels—the case of reproductions, that is to say, and you and I can get down to fighting in good earnest. I mean to pull a crow with you over the shameful manner in which you have neglected Claudia's education. I mean the diamonds you forgot to tell her about, darling. Don't blanch so—it highlights the rouge dreadfully. Have you neglected her education in other areas as well, you appalling woman? Don't tell me she doesn't waltz and speak French and do those ugly little embroideries the ladies are all crazy for."

"Of course, she does!"

Claudia chuckled and her mother withered her with a stare. "Sorry, mama."

"I'll speak to *you* later, young lady."

"Stand up to her," Hillary advised in an audible aside. "It is the only way with these old tartars."

"Well!" from Mrs. Milmont.

"*Not* speaking chronologically, you understand. 'Old' in the sense of 'damned' you know—or let us say 'cursed,' or even 'blasted.' Come along!" He held a hand out to Claudia. To her mother he said before leaving, "That will give you a few moments to get your temper under control and think up a sharp answer for me."

Claudia arose till her eyes were not so far below the level of Sir Hillary's own, and he looked at her in surprise. "You're a big little Claudia, aren't you, darling?" he said, taking her arm in his and leading her across the room.

"You'll never guess the way this young lady has been maltreated," he said to Gabriel. "While we have been plotting and scheming how to get the diamonds all these years, Miss Milmont has not even been aware of their existence. Really she has been treated abominably, and *I* for one would have written her about them had I known of her ignorance. Well, it's too late to do any good now, but you and Luane can show her the case of reproductions in the armaments room, to prepare her for the shock of the genuine article when she sees it."

"Oh, yes, cousin. You will die laughing to see how ugly they are," Luane replied. "Come along, Gab," she said.

Hillary stood a moment looking at the trio and continued to stare after them as they left the room together. There was a certain maturity about both the face and figure of Miss Milmont, when she stood side by side with young Luane, that argued her being a little older then her mama implied. His mind ran back over the history of her family, and it occurred to him that he had been hearing about 'little Claudia' ever since he was a sprig himself. He looked at Mrs. Milmont, frowning in concentration, then to her great dismay, he turned and followed Gabriel and the girls from the room.

Chapter Four

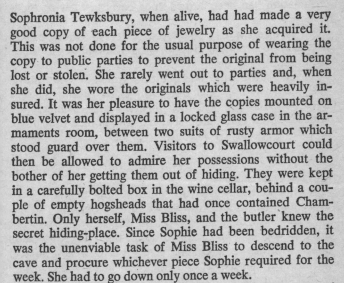

Sophronia Tewksbury, when alive, had had made a very good copy of each piece of jewelry as she acquired it. This was not done for the usual purpose of wearing the copy to public parties to prevent the original from being lost or stolen. She rarely went out to parties and, when she did, she wore the originals which were heavily insured. It was her pleasure to have the copies mounted on blue velvet and displayed in a locked glass case in the armaments room, between two suits of rusty armor which stood guard over them. Visitors to Swallowcourt could then be allowed to admire her possessions without the bother of her getting them out of hiding. They were kept in a carefully bolted box in the wine cellar, behind a couple of empty hogsheads that had once contained Chambertin. Only herself, Miss Bliss, and the butler knew the secret hiding-place. Since Sophie had been bedridden, it was the unenviable task of Miss Bliss to descend to the cave and procure whichever piece Sophie required for the week. She had to go down only once a week.

It was to this glass case, standing between the suits of

armor, that Luane now led Miss Milmont to show her the reproductions. "There they are," she said dispassionately, holding a branched candelabra high to give a view of the ersatz treasures. In the shadowed light, against the dark velvet, they looked magnificent. The diamond necklace was the star of the show—great rock-sized chunks of sparkling stone fashioned into a necklace long enough to lie on the chest. Suspended from it at the very center was a pear-shaped stone as big as a plover's egg.

"It looks for the world like a chandelier," Miss Milmont pronounced, and a throaty laugh escaped her. "Are there candles to go with it?"

"You have an unerring eye in your head, Miss Milmont," Hillary said, coming up behind her.

She jumped, for she had not heard him approach.

"Yes, it is gross," Luane agreed, hardly glancing at it. "But I still hope it's mine."

"It must surely be going to you, don't you think, Uncle Hil?" Gabriel asked. Hillary was not his uncle, but the termination had been agreed upon early in their relationship.

"It is wisest not to count your chickens before they're hatched. According to kinship, Miss Milmont has as much right to it."

"I shall now answer a question you asked me previously, Sir Hillary," Claudia said. "After seeing them, I have no hesitation in proclaiming a total disinterest in Aunt Sophie's diamonds. That red ring is nice though—a ruby I suppose. How oddly it is cut; it looks like a cherry."

"It is called a cabochon—polished rather than faceted," Sir Hillary explained.

"Oh, and that huge rope must be the pearls I have heard mama mention. How very well they look."

"Mama *did* mention the pearls, did she? She was not quite so negligent as I accused her of being. Yes, the glass beads with fish-scale coating give a good likeness of real pearls in the half-darkness."

"Of them all, I prefer the emerald ring," Gabriel said, looking into the case.

"She was wearing it today," Claudia told him. "It is the only one of her jewels I have actually seen."

"I like the little diadem of diamonds," Luane said. "She let me wear it once, and it was very uncomfortable."

"That would be because she screwed it to your head," Hillary suggested. "No borrowing of the jewels was ever taken lightly."

"I wasn't even leaving the house. Don't you remember—it was on my sixteenth birhtday. I thought she meant to give it to me, only she gave me a netting box instead."

Claudia gave her a commiserating smile. "You would not have liked it if it was uncomfortable."

"Pooh, I don't care for a little discomfort."

"*I* do," Sir Hillary said. "And if Miss Milmont has gazed her fill at these pieces of glass, I suggest we leave this drafty room and return to the Saloon, where we might be comfortable with a cup of lukewarm, now almost certainly cold, tea."

"I'll get you a glass of wine instead," Luane told him.

"Thank you, no, brat. I value my health even more than my comfort, and vinegar doesn't agree with me."

They returned to the Saloon and the cold tea, and Sir Hillary went to Miss Bliss. "Have arrangements been set in progress for the funeral?"

"We notified the vicar, and Jonathon wrote notes to several neighbors. As tomorrow happens to be Sunday, the vicar can announce the death and date of the funeral for anyone who wants to come."

"Is Jonathon putting the hatchment up, and doing the knocker in crape? Sophie would have wanted the whole works."

"The butler is seeing to it."

"It's a macabre enough thing to mention at this time, but you must be inured to oddities after ten years' internment in this mausoleum. What I'm talking about is the barbaric necessity for a sort of feast, after the funeral. I suspect, knowing the dear late Sophronia, the cupboards are bare. Tomorrow being Sunday, and the funeral on Monday, shall I bring some things from Chanely?"

"There's a plum cake I was planning to serve Sunday—we could save it."

"Mmm—but I *do* feel, you know, that you ought to feed the guests *something* tomorrow, Sunday or no. I shall risk losing my cook by setting him to bake up the funeral feast on the Sabbath. It will be a nuisance to haul everything over. You'll need some decent wine, too, and very likely some extra glasses and dishes. Do you know, Miss Blissful, I begin to think the easier way is to hold the after-service party *chez moi*. Will it look too very odd?"

Miss Bliss considered it, and though it would certainly appear odd, it would be such a blessed relief that she did not reject the offer out of hand.

"Is it the proprieties that deter you? I can see it is. Never mind, it will be taken for only one more instance of my encroaching ways by the mourning relatives. I have the excuse of Gab's being her nephew."

"It would be no odder than the sort of spread that would be put on here," she allowed reluctantly.

He smiled at her, not the sneering smile recently seen, but quite a warm, engaging expression. "What has kept you here so long, Blissful? You know I have been trying to lure you over to Chanely this age."

"No, you haven't," she said bluntly. "And if this is your roundabout way of offering me asylum now that she's gone, thank you, but no. I have other plans."

"I remember the chicken farm, and what a haven it will seem after this, but I confess my motives were not so philanthropic. I may have need of you, darling."

"Then you'd better stop slumming me with your 'darlings'," she answered curtly, not without a twinkle in her eyes, "What possible need could you have of me? Your housekeeper is unexceptionable, and you have more flirts than you know what to do with."

"You underestimate me. I know what to do with everyone of them, but I am always on the lookout for another unattached Incomparable. Yes, and I fear I am about to inherit one," he glanced to Miss Beresford.

"I've been wondering what is to be done about Luane.

I suppose there's no hope of Mrs. Milmont's offering to take her. If the girl inherits something, I mean."

"She has not seen fit to take her own daughter; I think we may be guided by that. And as far as that goes, she is not the chaperone one would like for such a headstrong hoyden as Loo."

"Dear me, no, she seems a rackety creature."

"Not quite so bad as that, but she don't move in the first circles, to put it mildly. Perhaps some small establishment can be set up for Loo, and I can think of no one with whom she would be so comfortable as you. And you, my poor dear, would be far from comfortable with her."

"I don't mind her, but I could do nothing to introduce her to society, Sir Hillary, if that is what you have in mind. Or was it not London you were thinking of?"

"Yes, it was, and *I* would undertake to introduce her, as my ward, if that is what she turns out to be."

"Surely Sophie hasn't served you such a trick as that. You're barely even connected to the girl."

"Who else is there? Besides, I'll be connected if she marries Gab. I like the little beggar anyway. We can't just turn her loose in the world with her fists full of diamonds for some bleater to grab. But I'd like to bring her out in London and give her a chance at some other gents. Wouldn't you like a Season? You'd be all the crack, Blissful."

"I can think of nothing more uncomfortable," she said primly, but an unsteadiness of the lips betrayed her amusement at the idea of a fifty-year-old matron of very plain appearance setting the *ton* on its ear.

"Put on fifty pounds and you might even nab Prinney. He likes 'em pleasingly plump."

"You forget yourself, Sir Hillary," she said, feeling this dalliance had gone further than was seemly.

"I never give myself a thought from cock's crow till dark," he returned, unphased. "My mind is always occupied with caring for the less fortunate."

"Nothing can be decided till after the will is read. We'll speak of this again."

"A good deal must depend on the will. But you are not

to worry about the funeral party. They will come to Chanely."

While Captain Tewksbury was secretly delighted to hear of the arrangement, and Mrs. Milmont similarly thrilled to be at last getting a toe into Chanely, they both felt some show of reluctance to be called for.

"Seems to me," Jonathon said, "people ought to come here. Looks as if I'm slighting the old girl, foisting the party off on you."

"You are only a connection," Marcia reminded him.

Sir Hillary examined his fingernails and said nothing.

"As the new owner of Swallowcourt, the honor ought to be mine," Jonathon declared. "Her nephew, too."

"Well, so am I her nephew," Gabriel pointed out, "and I live at Chanely."

"That is a point well taken," Marcia allowed, not wishing to push this objecting too far.

"You aint her heir," Jonathon retaliated.

"You don't know that," Gabriel replied. "You only get Swallowcourt because of the entail. There's no saying you'll get anything else."

"There is no food for the guests here," Luane pointed out.

"Well, I wouldn't want to put on a shabby do," Jonathon backed off, knowing when to give in.

"That's what I thought," Hillary replied quietly. Then he and his nephew made their adieux and left.

The announcement of the death and funeral were made at chapel on Sunday. It was an unusually brief period between death and burial, but it had been her wish, and everyone seemed happy to get it over and done with. Some callers came to Swallowcourt on Sunday, despite a dismal, cold rain. In fact, there was a good deal of peculiar traffic to the old mansion. Such various persons as the solicitor, Mr. Fletcher, the steelmonger, Mr. Peoples, bearing a large covered box on his wagon, Jed Flaro, the blacksmith, also in a lumbering, heavy wagon, and the local midwife, Widow Heppersmith, who also performed the unhappy chore of 'laying out' the dear departed. Tewksbury had suggested that Miss Bliss and Luane should perform this homey chore, but both roundly declined, the latter saying she wouldn't touch the corpse with a pair of tongs.

Sir Hillary and Gabriel came, too, in the late afternoon. As a sop for undertaking the arrangements for the funeral feast, Jonathon offered them the hospitality of the house for dinner, but this was an offer declined as frequently as it was made, for they were well aware of the sort of meal served at Swallowcourt. They remained only half an hour, which was sufficiently long for Sir Hillary to come to cuffs with the captain on the conduct of the campaign against Napoleon, and with Mrs. Milmont over the custom of damped gowns for ladies. Thinking to toadeat him, Marcia had inveighed against the new fad, and Sir Hillary, who thought it the crudest idea in a decade, decreed that it was unexceptional, providing the figure of the wearer warranted such exposure.

"What a contradictory man he is," Mrs. Milmont said to her daughter after he had left.

"I thought you liked to wear your gowns damped, mama." Claudia reminded her.

"Well, if the figure warrants it," she allowed, smiling and pulling in her stomach.

"Why did you say you disapproved then?"

"I made sure he would be against it. Those *fast* men are so contrary. There is never any saying what will please them. They are usually very strict about the conduct of *ladies*, and never mind what they tolerate or encourage in the other sort. He holds himself as high as may be in society and looks down his nose at any hint of impropriety. How I wish he would invite me to one of his parties."

"You are invited to Chanely for the funeral party."

"Ninnyhammer! *That* is not a party in the least, though I am curious to see what the place is like. All the crack, I daresay, and it will be fine to mention in London that I was at Chanely. But I meant one of his *ton* parties in the city. One may meet everyone there."

"Does he never ask you? How very odd, when he calls you 'darling'."

"He calls everyone that, though when he happens to meet me in London, it is 'Good morning, Mrs. Milmont,' especially when I am with anyone. He is so contrary there is no bearing it. He will never call one 'darling' when she wishes it. So very friendly," she finished up with a little sniff.

"He is certainly odd," Claudia confessed. "But Gabriel is nice, is he not?"

"He is well enough, or will be if he inherits the money. Otherwise there will be nothing but for him to take a position, and that, you know, will set him down sadly."

"How will he manage if he doesn't inherit anything?"

"Sir Hillary will get him some sinecure. He will be a member of Parliament or a minister's secretary, or some such thing."

"He is very young."

"That has nothing to say to it. *Pull*—that is what it takes. And Sir Hillary quite dotes on the boy. That much is obvious. Run over and make up to the captain, love. He is very taken with you, I promise you."

"I cannot like him, mama."

"Silly creature, what is that to the point? Swallowcourt is his for a certainty, and till we see where the money and jewelry go, there is no point being unfriendly. There, he's smiling at you. Go and give him a game of chess."

There was no necessity for Claudia to go to the captain. His charms were evenly divided between her and Luane till the will should be read. In fact, Miss Milmont received something more than half his attentions, for her handsome allowance and inheritance were a settled thing in his mind, and the girl, while not a dasher, was not ugly in the least, only a little plainer than he really liked. She wouldn't turn any heads, but he could get her rigged out in a higher style than she now wore. He declined a game of chess, but offered to show her over his place, an offer that was accepted and occupied most of the time till dinner was called.

Sophie's corpse was left at home till the funeral, but by the wish of the deceased it was not exhibited. The casket was not only kept closed, but out of sight entirely. Its resting place, oddly enough, was the stables. The captain did not offer to take Miss Milmont to view that portion of his estate because of the weather, nor did he have the faintest notion what was going on there himself. Only Fletcher, the ironmonger, and the blacksmith knew. They attributed it—at least the latter two persons—to some eccentricity in the deceased, a fear of worms consuming her body maybe, and thought only that it was a grisly chore to perform on a Sunday afternoon.

Chapter Five

The funeral on Monday morning was uneventful. The family went together to the church, and the ladies directly to Chanely afterwards, while the gentlemen repaired to the burial grounds for the interment. The pallbearers, Sir Hillary, the captain, Gabriel, and three local gentlemen, all of husky build, struggled under the weight of the casket, but none of them were much accustomed to carrying coffins and suspected nothing amiss. Mrs. Milmont was suitably impressed by the grandness of Chanely—a large, stately home that might have been a castle. An expanse of marbled floor in the hallway laid out in black and white squares like a chessboard first caught her eye, and before any close scrutiny of the surroundings could be completed, the guests were ushered into the Blue Saloon by the housekeeper, Mrs. Robinson, a woman of genteel birth and impoverished background. Mrs. Milmont had hoped to scout around downstairs before the arrival of Sir Hillary, but her hope was thwarted. She was given a seat in a needlepoint chair, handed a glass of sherry, and forced into polite conversation with the rest of the group.

The richness of the room before her led her to suspect untold glories in the remainder of the building, but as her comments in London would have to be limited to the Blue Saloon, she took a careful inventory of its furnishings and accessories that she might point out a similarity in a friend's decor to some feature of Chanely.

It was not long before the arrival of the others, and after eating, drinking, and merrymaking of a more restrained sort than usually prevails at a wake, the party was over.

"Fletcher will be waiting at Swallowcourt," Sir Hillary said, and watched with a rueful smile the haste with which his little party broke up.

All those with any particular interest in the will were duly assembled a half-hour later in Sophie's Crimson Saloon. Mr. Fletcher, a saturnine man with dark eyes and the black suit of his calling, frowned at the document under his hands, cleared his throat, and began to read. The smaller bequests to old family retainers were read first, and these underlings were then given to understand they might go and resume their customary business. The captain was not so nervous as the others, yet he breathed a sigh of relief when it was confirmed that Swallowcourt went to him, entailed to his son, with the possibilities all covered in case of his death before producing an heir, and so on. Miss Bliss received a thousand pounds for long service faithfully rendered. Sir Hillary was not surprised to become the official guardian of Miss Beresford, though Luane seemed to find it quite amusing. The next item mentioned stirred the auditors to some interest.

" 'The Tewksbury jewelry collection, with the exception of the Beresford diamond necklace, is to be disposed of as follows: the pearl necklace, the emerald ring, the ruby ring, the diamond diadem, the bracelet of various stones, and the sapphire pendant are to be present at the reading of my will. In the following order of predominance, each of the after-named people are to choose one piece: my sister, Mrs. Milmont; my elder niece, Miss Claudia Milmont; my younger niece, Miss Luane Beresford; my younger nephew, Gabriel Tewksbury; my elder nephew

Jonathon Tewksbury; and my companion, Miss Lavinia Bliss.' "

"We will proceed with the selection now," Mr. Fletcher said. "It was her wish." He drew out a bolted metal box—the one usually hidden in the cellar—and unbolted it. The named pieces were laid out on the surface of the desk.

"But what about the diamonds?" Mrs. Milmont enquired immediately. "They are the most valuable piece in the collection. Surely they should be here, too. I should prefer to choose the diamonds."

"They are to be disposed of separately," Mr. Fletcher said firmly.

"Well, upon my word, I hardly know what to choose," Mrs. Milmont said, smiling greedily at the whole assortment.

"You always liked the pearls, mama," Claudia mentioned.

"So I did, love. I like them excessively, but I am not sure the emerald ring is not more valuable. What do you think, Sir Hillary?"

"The pearls are large, and perfectly matched," he replied. Everyone got up and gathered around the desk to view the treasures and silently pick out his own favorite.

"Very true, they are, and then Claudia can have the emerald ring."

"I prefer the ruby," Claudia said.

"Nonsense, my dear, the emerald is larger, and I much prefer it. Or you might take the tiara. It will set off my little diamond clips to a nicety. Though really the diamonds in the tiara are very small, and they do not shine very brightly either. I daresay they are inferior stones. You will do better to have the emerald."

"First, you must choose, ma'am," Mr. Fletcher said.

"I *think* the pearls—but one can get such very good imitations for an old song, and there is no imitating an emerald. But Claudia can have the emerald if I take the pearls. Which do you think is the more valuable, Mr. Fletcher?"

"I should think the pearls, considering the length of the

rope and their size, but I cannot give you a positive answer. It is a very fine emerald."

"To be sure it is. I have never seen one so large. But Claudia . . . Well, I could be here all day deciding. I'll have the pearls then." She snatched them up and immediately put them around her neck. She was so enraptured and so busy testing them with her teeth to verify their authenticity that she hardly remembered to urge the emerald on Claudia. "Take your emerald, Claudia," was all she said.

"I like the ruby, mama."

"Silly chit. It isn't worth a thing. It is done up so oddly, with no facets to it. I hate red stones. Anyone would take it for a garnet or some such thing." She interrupted this tirade to try another pearl with her teeth. "Yes, they are nice and rough," she said to her daughter. "The glass pearls are as smooth as may be to the tooth. It is a good thing to remember, my dear. You must always test a pearl against the teeth."

"Well, I'll have the emerald then," Claudia said, a little reluctantly.

Her mother reached out her hand for it, but Claudia slipped it on her own finger and liked it pretty well.

"I'll take the ruby and we'll trade," Luane whispered to Claudia.

"No, take the tiara. You like it." Luane took up the diamond tiara.

"I'm next I think," the captain said, coming forward.

"Mr. Gabriel Tewksbury is next," Mr. Fletcher corrected him.

"I'm the elder. Better have another look at your paper, my good man," Jonathon said.

Fletcher looked and repeated the order of predominance.

"What should I have, Uncle Hil?" Gabriel asked.

"Have the ruby."

"*I* wanted the ruby," Jonathon said, with a look at Claudia that startled her.

"Gabriel has next choice, however," Hillary said carelessly. The young man took the ruby.

47

"Well, I'm next then," Jonathon announced, shouldering forward. "Which do you prefer, Miss Milmont?"

"The sapphire is prettier, but I daresay the bracelet may be more valuable. There are a few quite good-sized stones in it."

The captain hesitated, with some thought that whichever he chose might be a wedding gift to his bride, who might possibly be Miss Milmont. His hand hovered over the pendant, but greed won out in the end, and he picked up the bracelet.

"That leaves the sapphire pendant for me," Miss Bliss said, satisfied. "I didn't expect anything like this, after the thousand pounds. She did promise me that." Not that I ever thought to see it, she added to herself.

"Now let us get on to the diamonds," Mrs. Milmont said eagerly. Aside to her daughter she added, "I'd like to try on the emerald, dear."

"I can't get it off, Mama. It's stuck," Claudia said.

"Let me try," the mother said, and reached out for Claudia's hand, but as the ring was not at all tight, Claudia whisked her hand beyond reach.

"The next few items may strike you as a trifle out of the ordinary," Mr. Fletcher said, rather understating the matter. " 'The collection in the glass case, exactly as it now stands, goes to Miss Beresford, to be held in trust by Sir Hillary Thoreau until her eighteenth birthday or until she marries, whichever comes first, at which time they are to be examined by myself and given to her. The tiara is similarly to be held in trust.' "

Luane hunched her shoulders and made a moue.

"And the diamonds?" Marcia pressed.

" 'The diamonds are to be interred with my body, according to instructions given to my solicitor, Mr. Fletcher,' " he read, in a calm voice and with a wary eye.

An audible gasp was heard—a joint reaction from the group—and Marcia Milmont fainted dead away on her chair. Her daughter grabbed at her, but she tumbled toward the captain, who caught her in his arms and called for brandy. Before it could be fetched, she had revived, and the first words to leave her lips were "the diamonds."

There was a good deal of excited babbling from all corners of the group and one quite loud guffaw from Thoreau. Miss Bliss directed an admonishing look on him and said, "Tch, tch."

"Just like the old devil to take it with her," he said and resumed his laughter till his shoulders shook.

"This is an outrage!" Jonathon shouted.

"She was clearly deranged!" Mrs. Milmont seconded him. "Something must be done."

Gabriel looked a question at Hillary, who smiled back at him and hunched his shoulders.

"What about Luane?" Gabriel asked. "I thought—well, it was generally understood she would get the diamonds. What is to become of her now?"

"Never mind about her now. Let's hear if Sophie buried her blunt with her too," Thoreau answered.

"She wouldn't!" Marcia gasped.

"Optimist," Hillary replied.

"The *devil*!" Luane shrieked, stamping her foot. "She did it on purpose to annoy me because I wouldn't marry Gabriel. She thinks to force me to it yet."

The racket eventually subsided, and Fletcher frowned at the will while his auditors observed him impatiently, fearing more outrages to be in the offing.

"What about the money? Surely she is not burying that, too," Mrs. Milmont declared.

" 'The money—cash, mortgages and investments, mostly in Consoles . . .' " Mr. Fletcher began, then stopped dramatically.

"Let's hear the worst," Hillary prodded him.

" 'The disposition of the remainder of the estate, with the exception of a few small personal bequests, will be read one year from this date, in this room, when the same people as are now present re-assemble to have the arrangements explained in detail. In the interim, the monies will be in the control of my solicitor, Mr. Fletcher, and my co-executor, Sir Hillary Thoreau, who will handle said monies as they see fit.' "

"But how is this!" Marcia Milmont immediately burst

into speech. "You mean we must wait a whole year? This is absurd."

"We should have had her committed long ago," Jonathon said in a supporting manner.

"Certainly, and I only wish we had thought of it," Marcia added.

"She was perfectly sane in my opinion," Mr. Fletcher announced.

"What do *you* know about anything?" Marcia charged. "I daresay you were in cahoots with her and are only planning to slip away with all the money."

He had expected some opposition and pointed out that Sir Hillary was co-executor.

She turned her wrath on him. "*You* are at the bottom of this, Sir Hillary."

"How can you say so? I've been diddled out of my chess set by this arrangement."

"The chess set goes to Miss Bliss, to dispose of as she sees fit," Fletcher added.

Miss Bliss nodded to Sir Hillary in an understanding fashion. The set was for him, obviously, but not directly as that would invalidate him as an executor.

A silver tea service was bequeathed to Mrs. Milmont, who immediately proclaimed it was only silver plated, and she didn't want the ugly old thing in her house.

"Can leave it here then," Jonathon offered.

"Certainly not! You only mean to sell it, and it is worth a good deal."

A pair of dueling pistols went to Gabriel—not a part of the entailed estate by law, as she had purchased them herself at an auction. Claudia was the joyless recipient of a Sèvres vase from the same auction, which had in the interim become severely cracked from a fall to the hearth. Luane was given her personal effects and wondered what she would do with a bunch of well-worn gowns suitable to a seventy-year-old invalid. The captain got nothing else.

The will finally read, the pent-up ferocity of the mob was unleashed.

"We must have this abominable will overset," Mrs. Milmont began immediately.

"Seems devilish odd. Can't think it's legal to go burying diamonds," Jonathon took it up.

"They are *my* diamonds!" Luane said furiously.

"No such a thing!" Jonathon returned. The girl had inherited only a rusty old tiara and a caseful of glass junk and was thus rejected.

"Yes, they are. They were always to go to me. It was understood. She *promised*."

"Well, she was crazy," Mrs. Milmont decreed. "Now, captain, how should we go about getting the will set aside?"

"See a solicitor, I suppose."

"That would be unwise," Mr. Fletcher told them.

"Very inconvenient for you, Mr. Fletcher," Marcia turned on him. "Yes, indeed, you will end up in Newgate for your part in this affair, or I miss my bet. There was coercion at work here."

"Nonsense," Sir Hillary scoffed.

"There is no nonsense about it. She was clearly mad, to go burying a fortune in diamonds, and not to tell us who gets the money."

"The remainder of the will is to be read one year from this date," Mr. Fletcher pointed out. "The money is not buried, but is to be disbursed according to how events fall out."

"What does that mean?" Jonathon asked, confused.

"It means the money is to be distributed according to what happens in the intervening year," Mr. Fletcher explained vaguely.

"That tells us nothing," Mrs. Milmont exclaimed. "Do you mean we must do something in the meanwhile to get it? Then you must tell us what it is that is to be done."

"No, that is not the way she wanted it. She wishes you all to go on as though there were no money, and then when a year is up, the conditions will be read, and the money dealt out accordingly.

"Yes, you silly man, but according to *what*?"

"It just occurred to me," Miss Bliss said calmly, "it might be according to who *doesn't* try to have her declared insane. Just an idea," she added deprecatingly.

"Sounds exactly like her," Jonathon said, much impressed at Miss Bliss's insight.

Mrs. Milmont was sent reeling at this horrendous possiblity. "Well, I am sure you all know *I* was only fooling! As though I would ever seriously say such a thing about my own dear sister." She then fell silent trying to figure what other implications the phrase "according to what happens in the intervening year" might conceal.

Sir Hillary said aside to Gabriel, "She might have had in mind your marriage to Luane. It was what she always wanted."

Gabriel frowned and nodded. The same idea had occurred to him. Luane had the identical thought and expressed it aloud. "She is trying to make me marry Gabriel again."

Jonathon looked startled. That too sounded exactly like Aunt Sophie. It was not long in striking him that the terms might be more generalized than that. Maybe if either himself or Gabriel married her in the interim . . . What had she said? Something about she would leave her money to him if Luane would have him. Or if neither of them took her, *he* might come into the blunt himself. On the other hand, Luane might. Or even Claudia. With such a surfeit of possibilities, he was at *point non plus*, and went and sat alone in a corner to think.

Various other interpretations of the wording of the will were spoken of. Maybe if any of them lost or sold their inherited jewel it would cut them out. Possibly she wanted the captain to do something with Swallowcourt—to bring it into shape, in which case he would have proved himself able to handle the money. The awful idea even darted into Mrs. Milmont's head that what was meant was for her to take Claudia to live with her. Sophie had never approved of keeping the girl with the Milmonts. Or was it conceivably Luane she was expected to take on? She was the girl's aunt and only living relative of the proper age and sex to chaperone her. But then, to take her and have the will mean something else entirely . . . Her brain, like the captain's, was reeling. The only thing perfectly clear was that none of them were to get the diamonds. They were to rot away in the ground.

"That seems oddly unlike Sophie, to go wasting a fortune," Hillary remarked when someone mentioned the fact. "She was too well aware of the value of money to throw it away."

"Maybe something different is to be done with them at the end of the year," Miss Bliss suggested.

"That sounds more like it," Hillary agreed, thinking the mystery was solved, for he could not credit her intending them to remain buried forever.

Captain Tewksbury, after cudgeling his brain for ten minutes, determined that the wisest course was to remain on very good terms with both the nieces, and to this end he rejoined the party. "Seems to me she's creating a lot of mischief," he said, going on to make it perfectly clear he didn't mean to imply she was crazy, but only thoughtless. No harm in that. "Mean to say, if the story gets about there's a fortune buried in the grave, there'll be any number of robbers after it."

"It would be wisest to keep the fact to ourselves," Fletcher advised them.

"Even so . . ." Jonathon looked at Gabriel in a suspicious manner.

"No doubt another term of the will is that the grave is not to be tampered with in the intervening year," Sir Hillary commented.

"Who's to know who did the tampering?" Jonathon asked. "If one of you makes off with the diamonds, he's got a cool fortune, and won't care a peg about the rest of the blunt."

"One of *us*, shall we say?" Sir Hillary corrected with a lazy smile.

"For the sake of argument say one of us then, though I shall be in London."

"You are the owner of Swallowcourt now," Hillary reminded him. "Do you not mean to sell out and set up as a country gentleman? Much more the thing, Jonathon."

"What about my uniform?"

"Yes, you would lose the advantage of your regimentals. That is certainly a point against the scheme. But then you might have them put into a glass case in the armaments room to replace the reproductions of the jewels."

Jonathon sensed a little irony at this point and reverted to the real item of interest. "Fact remains, *I'll* be in London, and you and Gabriel will be here—right on the doorstep of the buried diamonds."

"The graveyard is *not* on my doorstep," Hillary replied. "Really, you cannot think I would tolerate so funereal a view. The prospect from my doorway is of gently rolling lawns, well manicured, with discreet groupings of trees at well-placed intervals. Relieves the monotony of just grass without impeding the long-range view."

"That's all very well, but you're *here*," Jonathon said.

"Well, so are you at the moment. Will it be shovels and spades at midnight, captain?" he asked in a quiet undertone laden with significance.

Jonathon's eyes widened, and he was conned for a moment into thinking Sir Hillary was serious. "You may laugh and joke about it, but *someone* will dig her up before the year's half out, and if you don't know it, you aint such a knowing one as I take you for."

"Very true. I expect the traffic will be heavy in the graveyard the next few nights. I'll speak to Fletcher about setting up a guard."

Jonathon was silent a moment, frowning, but soon added, "Yes, by Jove. Ought to be done."

Luane was recovering from her first spasm of anger and beginning to formulate plans for the retrieval of her diamonds. Her eyes scanned the room, going more than once to Gabriel and Claudia. She went to Gabriel and tugged his sleeve. "I must see you alone before you leave. Come to the armaments room with me. We'll pretend we're looking at my paste jewels."

They slipped out at once, and in the general confusion and noise, which were still at a high level, no one noticed their exit except Miss Milmont. Once they were safely alone, Luane put her plan to Gabriel.

"I mean to dig up the grave as soon as may be and get my diamonds," she said.

Gabriel looked at her, not in surprise certainly, but not quite in agreement either. "They are bound to be stolen long before the year is up," he said. "I don't trust Jonathon for one, and the story is bound to get about locally, too. I can't imagine how Sophie came to do such a corkbrained thing. They must be meant for you at the end of the year."

"Of course they are, and this is just spite because you—we wouldn't get married at Christmas."

"Of course it is, the old devil. I wish we *had* gone through with it then—though I'd feel a fool being married and leaving my wife behind while I go back to school like a boy. Hil wants me to take my degree, you know."

"I had no wish to be pushed into it, and I know you didn't want to do it . . ."

"I told you, Loo, after I graduate. Hil thinks that is the event referred to in the intervening year. I daresay he's right."

"I haven't said I'll have you."

"I haven't asked."

She sniffed. "Never mind *that*. Will you help me get my diamonds?"

"I don't think we can, though I'd love to have a go at it. Hil says he and Fletcher will have a guard set to watch the grave. That must be done, I think."

"I bet you it won't be done *today*."

"You mean we should go after them tonight?"

"The sooner the better. What time shall we meet there?"

"Late. About twelve, I suppose. Can you get out?"

"What is there to stop me?"

"You can't go down there alone. I'll come here and get you. I'll have to make some excuse to Hil."

"He'll be asleep long before that, but I'll take Cousin Claudia with me."

"Don't be a sapskull, Loo!"

"No, she's all right, and she hates the diamonds herself. Besides, she needs some excitement, poor old thing. I feel sorry for her, with that horrid old mother."

"She don't see much of *her* from what I hear. Are you sure she's trustworthy?"

"Oh yes. We'll meet you at the graveyard at midnight then. How exciting it will be. I can hardly wait. What about shovels and things?"

"I'll take care of that."

"It isn't *stealing*, you know," Luane said, in a questioning voice.

"Stealing from the dead—there's no harm in that. I suppose it's illegal, however."

"We must be careful not to get caught. Hush, someone's coming."

It was Sir Hillary and Fletcher, come to take Luane's case of paste jewels. "Would you like to see them?" Fletcher asked her.

Not two steps behind the gentlemen came Captain Tewksbury, to see what was going on.

"No, I see them every day," Luane answered.

"That the reproductions you're talking about?" Jonathon asked. "I've never seen them out of the case. Like to have a look at them before they go."

Mr. Fletcher, rather curious himself, was willing to open the case and did so. "Try on your diamonds, Loo," Gabriel said, with a secret smile at her.

She reached out and took them but didn't bother trying them on. Jonathon's hands reached out and lifted them from her fingers. "They're very real looking," he said.

"The reproductions are works of art in themselves," Mr. Fletcher pointed out. "In the rings, for example, the mountings are made of gold, and it is only the stones that are false. The reproductions altogether are worth a couple of hundred pounds. That's why the case is kept locked."

"The workmanship is very fine," Jonathon said, handling the diamonds, then giving them back to Luane.

She flung them angrily on the lid of the glass display case. "Poo, who cares for a bunch of paste stones," she declared.

"Not you apparently," Hillary replied, picking up the necklace and replacing it in the velvet setting.

Jonathon looked at the glass case where she had

thrown them, then looked again closely. He then reached once more into the case and lifted out the necklace. "Of course, the stones don't sparkle like the real thing," he said, holding them up to the weak light filtering in through the window. There was a distraction at the door, for Mrs. Milmont entered at this point and demanded to know what everyone was doing. While she was being shown the reproductions, particularly the pearls, which she hinted she could put to very good use, Jonathon set the diamond necklace on to the lid of the display case, and carefully arranged it. Mrs. Milmont had then to compare the fake pearls to her real ones and even test both with her teeth.

"Yes, there is no mistaking the real thing," she said, and handed the ersatz ones back to Mr. Fletcher.

He put all the reproductions back in their allotted places, locked the case, and gave it and the key to Hillary. "They are to be kept in trust by you for the present." He gave him Luane's tiara, too.

"Shall we be getting back to Chanely?" Hillary said to Gabriel.

"Welcome to stay to dinner," Jonathon offered mechanically.

"Until you have had time to restock your cupboards and hire a new cook, we must decline," Hillary replied and went to take his leave of Miss Bliss and Claudia.

As soon as the gentlemen and Fletcher left, Luane approached Miss Milmont and requested her company for a walk about the garden. As it was cold and windy with no sign of the sun outdoors, Claudia went with some curiosity to get her pelisse. She could not believe a desire for fresh air formed any part of the reason for this walk. From the excited eyes and high color of her cousin, she thought an adventure was in the offing. The minute they were safely outside, she said, "*Do* tell me we are to dig up Aunt Sophie and take the diamonds! I have been hoping you didn't mean to exclude me from the adventure."

"Oh, cousin, how did you guess? I told Gabriel you were a right one. Will you come with us?"

"Oh, is Gabriel to come? I thought it would be more

dangerous if we went alone at midnight, just the two of us."

"Yes, so it would, and I shouldn't have bothered asking him if I had been sure you would come. But one can never be sure with old people."

"Very true, there is no saying we won't take an attack of gout or an ague at just the crucial moment, but I shall wrap myself up well."

"Oh, cousin, you are not *that* old! I've been thinking about what we should wear, and I believe trousers will be more comfortable."

"Trousers, to be sure. An excellent notion, but I'm afraid I didn't bring any with me. Do you happen to have two pairs?"

"We will steal old livery. There are several suits in camphor in the cedar closet, all eaten with moths, but we shant mind that."

"Certainly not, it will lend us an airy quality."

"We are to meet Gabriel at the graveyard at midnight. It is two miles; shall we ride or walk?"

"I have no mount, though I confess a two-mile hike in the pouring rain—it is best to plan for the worst, and the sky is very cloudy—is a little more excitement than I bargained for. Is there a farm animal I might ride?"

"There is Casper—the gig horse, but I've ridden him."

"He sounds just the thing. Will it be possible to get the horses out without being discovered?"

"We can always hit the groom on the head."

"Now why didn't *I* think of that?"

"I don't expect you have had many adventures, cousin, but I shall contrive all the details."

"I am very grateful you let me in on it. I'll do my bit with the shovel and—should we not take a crowbar to pry open the casket?"

"Will it be nailed shut?"

"It is the custom, I believe."

"How vexing. Gabriel said he would take care of the tools, but I bet he doesn't know we shall need a crowbar."

"Let us take one along, just to show him how wide awake we are."

"And if we can't find one, we'll take the axe."

Claudia recoiled slightly at the picture conjured up of them chopping through a wooden coffin, possibly right through to the contents thereof, but she didn't demur an iota.

"*I* can get away quite easily," Luane said, "but perhaps your mama will check your room at a late hour?"

"No, she won't."

"Good, I didn't really think so. Does she *like* you at all?"

The startled exclamation this question called forth was coughed away. "Yes, in her own way. She is not an effusive person."

"She was effusive about the jewelry. She means to get your emerald ring from you."

Claudia looked in wonder at this artless girl with the knowing mind of a woman, and not yet the guile to conceal it. "She shant get it," she said.

"I have been thinking of a famous stunt, cousin, only I daresay Hillary won't let us do it, he is such a prude."

"A prude! That is certainly not the word I would have used to describe him."

"He was only showing off yesterday and a little today. He is really very straight and stiff, and never lets me or Gab do anything at all. He acts satirical like that sometimes when he doesn't like people."

"I see," Claudia answered, marveling anew at her companion's blunt speech.

"I don't mean *you*. It is Jonathon and your mama. He doesn't like them because of the way they neglected Sophie, then came pacing down the minute they heard she was dying."

"Yes, now where shall we meet, and at what hour?"

"I'll take the livery to your room after dinner. You get dressed and slip downstairs around eleven. Agreed?" She stuck out a little hand, like a man, and gave a violent shake to Claudia's hand.

"Agreed."

"I'm glad I decided to let you come."

"I'm very grateful," Claudia said, hiding a smile at this condescension. "By the way, what was the stunt you mentioned?"

"I should love to give you the paste emerald ring, and let your mama take it back to London. She'd not likely ever know the difference, and then wouldn't be pestering you for the real one."

"You don't begin to know mama. The first thing she'd do would be to take it and have it evaluated."

"I suppose she would. Hillary said she was sharp as a tack." On this flattering speech, the cousins returned to the house.

Chapter Six

Two very different sorts of dinners were suffered through and enjoyed by the inhabitants of Swallowcourt and Chanely respectively. While Captain Tewksbury and Mrs. Milmont were settling in for a hand of piquet and Claudia and Luane were chatting quietly in a corner with Miss Bliss, Sir Hillary and Gabriel sat over a glass of ale, discussing the day's events and particularly the will. "Do you plan to marry Loo within the year?" Hillary asked.

"I always intended to marry her as soon as I was through college—well, and as soon as I have some means of supporting her of course."

"I'm sorry if it was my influence that caused you to put it off at Christmas. You both seemed so young."

"We neither of us wanted to when Sophie started her pushing. There's nothing like being told you must do something to make you sure you don't want to do it."

"There's no guarantee that your marriage to Luane is the event she refers to in the will. Unless you are determind to have her, I shouldn't do it on the expectation of inheriting. Not do it just for that, I mean."

"No, no. That has nothing to do with it. It would put us in easier circumstances, of course, but I can get a position of some sort. Lots of the fellows plan to do so. What do you think I should apply myself to, Uncle?"

"A seat in Parliament eventually, but you're a bit young for that yet. A few years as secretary to some member would be good experience. I'll speak to some friends. I can tide you over financially till you're in a better paying job."

"I can't take any more from you. Paying for my education . . ."

"At the moment you're my heir, cawker. A fine skint I'd look, with the pair of you begging on a street corner while I live the high life in my various mansions."

"It goes against the grain."

"It's bound to, but we weren't all born shod and hosed, Gab. Thank your stars you have some family. That's what families are for, you know."

"Some families. That Mrs. Milmont is a rum touch, aint she, Uncle?"

"You're too kind in your choice of words."

They talked on in this manner till ten, with never a sarcastic or nasty remark leveled at Gabriel. Sir Hillary was fond of his charge, and in fact considered him as something very like a son. He had felt alone, though not lonely, in the world after his father's death ten years previously, till he had been saddled with Gabriel. He was always fond of Gab's mother, his cousin Anita, and though he wasn't the closest relative, he had taken the boy willingly. By insensible degrees he had regulated his life so that it revolved around his cousin. He made it a point to be home at Chanely when Gab was on holiday, and for his racier friends not to be. He took a more than avuncular interest in the boy, but was determined not to be so bound to him that he interfered unduly in his life. He and Loo were a good match—were as at home with each other as an old married couple despite their youth. Odd their relationship had developed along these lines rather than as brother and sister, but Gab was just enough older so that Loo had always adored him.

As the hands of the clock circled past ten, Hillary and his nephew both began stirring restively. Gabriel was waiting till his uncle mentioned retiring, failing which—and ten-thirty was pretty early for Hil to go to bed—he must start yawning himself. Hillary was wishing Gabriel would invite him along on the diamond hunt. He half hoped he wouldn't, too, for he supposed it behove him to put a damper on the scheme. He was ninety-nine per cent sure Gabriel meant to go and ninety-eight percent sure Loo would be with him, but hadn't even a suspicion that Claudia would be along. Added to this, he was about ninety per cent plus sure Jonathon would have a go at the grave-digging. Yes, it would be an interesting night, one way or the other.

Gabriel was not happy that Miss Milmont was to be of the party and risked sounding out his uncle on the girl. "How does Loo's cousin strike you—the Milmont girl?" he asked.

"As not quite a girl," was the sardonic reply.

"What do you mean? Of course, she's a girl."

"Oh, she was once, no doubt of that. I didn't take her for a man in disguise."

"Well, do you think she's *old*?"

"Older than seven," he answered cryptically.

"She seemed quite young to me, but older than Loo, of course. I meant though, do you think she's trustworthy?"

"She hasn't had any opportunity to inveigle herself into the will. Never met Sophie till two minutes before she cocked up her toes and wasn't aware there were diamonds in the case, or so she told me. I am inclined to believe her."

"I didn't mean that exactly," but what he did want to say proved difficult to put into words. "Do you think she would do Loo a mischief if she could?"

"I don't see how she could, unless she is attempting to set up a flirtation with yourself and alienate your affections."

"She certainly isn't doing that! I don't think she's much interested in men, do you?"

"No, she'll turn into a fine maiden aunt in another decade. Be just the one to lend a hand with your houseful of brats. You want to be nice to her."

Gabriel smiled at his playful rejoinder and then began yawning, stretching, and exhibiting all the gestures associated with the onset of sleepiness.

"If you're turning in already, I'll go to my study and go over some accounts," Hil said. This would give Gabriel privacy to sneak out of the house, suitably attired in some old dark clothing, and also be an excellent vantage point from which to watch his ascent to Swallowcourt, as the study windows looked in that direction. Not knowing Loo had found a different escort in Claudia, he assumed Gab would go to get her. He became impatient when half an hour had passed and still no dark figure was seen going up the hill.

Surely he isn't letting her come all alone, he thought to himself, then slipped quietly up to Gab's room to ensure that he was in fact gone. The bed was empty, of course. *Now how the hell did he slip past me?* Going quickly to his own room, he dressed silently and swiftly in dark clothing. Knowing the night to be chilly, he threw a long black cape over the outfit, grabbed a hat, and went to the stable. He was not in the least surprised to see Gab's mount gone, but wondered whether he ought to go directly to the graveyard, or head up towards Swallowcourt. Getting such a late start, he went directly to the graveyard. He tethered Lady, his bay mare, at the gate, and went silently on foot towards the east side, where Sophie had that same morning been interred.

His eyes accustomed now to the gloom, Hillary surveyed the gothic scene before him. The trees, still thinly leaved, formed a black skeleton background at the yard's edge. A wind came howling down from the north, flailing the branches. The stones and marble grave markings erupted from the earth at irregular intervals, like ghosts rising from the dead. Sir Hillary was not a fanciful man, yet the hair lifted on the back of his neck when a fox barked in the distance—three eerie howls.

He had spoken to Fletcher about a guard, but he noticed that the man had not yet assumed his duties; the grave was not guarded. Concealing himself behind the granite slab of some long-gone gentleman by the name of Alexander Coughlin, he peered over toward Sophie's last resting-place.

Then he heard the soft sound of metal being judiciously applied to loose earth. He recognized Gab instantly with the shovel, while Loo stood lookout for other comers. There was no moon, and if she had missed his own careful approach, she might have missed the captain as well. Hillary took it upon himself to help her observation. After looking around, he returned his intent gaze to the scene before him. He now saw that there was a third party present—a tall person in trousers. Surely to God they hadn't invited Jonathon and left himself out! He took an angry pace forward, then stopped as a soft, feminine voice came from the shadow he had thought to be Jonathon.

"It's my turn now, Gabriel. I wish you had brought two shovels. We shall be here half the night."

"I'm winded," Gab replied and handed the shovel to Miss Milmont, the possessor of the soft voice. She began digging away like any man. She tired pretty soon, and Gabriel took over again. For half an hour they dug away, while Hillary watched in silence from his place of concealment. He disliked that a third party had been brought in. During his vigil, it occurred to him that Gab's questions about Miss Milmont had been because she was to join the dig. Oh, yes, and that's why he hadn't seen his nephew go up to Swallowcourt, too.

The lid of the coffin was finally unearthed. He could hear the harder slap of the shovel against the wood when this happened. There was some excited discussion among the group, and Miss Milmont handed a crowbar to Gabriel.

"I *told* you the lid would be nailed down. Now aren't you glad you asked me? Just think if you got this far and had to turn back for lack of a crowbar." The squawk was clearly audible when Gab succeeded in prizing off the lid. Some other sound seemed to occur as well—some half-human preternatural sound, as of a banshee howling.

"Good God!" Gabriel shouted loudly.

"You cannot mean someone's beaten us to it!" Miss Milmont answered.

"No, there's a steel box welded shut under the wooden coffin. No wonder she seemed to weigh a ton."

"Oh, the wretch!" Loo complained, but Miss Milmont went into a very girlish fit of giggles, and Hillary too found himself stifling a laugh into his fist.

Getting herself under control, Miss Milmont said in a matter-of-fact voice, "What a bother! We shall have to return tomorrow night with a welding torch. I expect we should fill back in the earth, in case someone happens to come by tomorrow."

"Damnation!" Gabriel exploded, and began to shovel. "Whoever heard of such a stunt. Burying yourself in a steel box, sealed shut, I think she *was* crazy."

"It was to protect the diamonds very likely," Miss Milmont told him.

"I don't see how we are to get a welding torch here," Gabriel complained on. "What we ought to do is take the coffin along home, and open it there in the stables, then bring it back tomorrow night."

"That odious Sir Hillary would not let us use his stable for Aunt Sophie," Miss Milmont answered unhesitatingly, and Thoreau's eyebrows rose in the darkness. *Odious, am I*? "But a steel coffin would be too heavy in any case," the soft voice went on. "And we didn't think to bring a carriage—only our mounts. As I may very likely have to carry Casper home on my back, I don't see how it can be contrived," Lord, had she pulled that sluggard of a Casper all the way from Swallowcourt?

"It can't, of course," Gabriel agreed. "The six of us men today could hardly lift it. Well, what a waste of time!"

"I was never so gammoned in my life," Miss Milmont agreed mildly.

"It is exactly like Aunt Sophie," Loo told then both in an angry tone.

"She sounds a positive beast," Claudia said, "I am becoming quite happy I never met her till she was at death's door. And the one look she cast on me was very disap-

66

proving, too, now I consider it. She would have liked to light into me for not coming sooner, I bet."

"You're lucky she was dying," Loo replied.

"It will serve her well to have the diamonds ripped from her rotting corpse," Claudia continued.

"Will it be decomposing already?" Gabriel asked, in a voice trying to conceal the horror he felt.

"I daresay it will have reached an advanced state of putrefaction before we get the steel box open," Claudia answered readily and with satisfaction. "Though it is quite cold, and that preserves flesh. In fact, Loo, I don't know about you, but I'm freezing in this ventilated suit you found for me. Shall we all help replace the earth and go on home?"

"We might as well," Loo answered, "but I'll never forgive her for this. Never."

"No more you should," Claudia replied, and began kicking earth into the hole with her booted foot.

While he gazed and listened, Sir Hillary was trying to figure out what the young ladies were wearing. Trousers it seemed. He was not surprised to discover Loo in such a prank, but it amazed him that the placid Miss Milmont should have consented to such a scheme, and to enter into the whole with such good humor. He had thought Marcia had squeezed all the life out of her; he was rapidly revising his first opinion.

The night, already dark, cold, and windy, now took the final step and began to lash the conspirators with rain. "I wish we had another shovel!" Claudia remarked. Failing this, she began pulling the earth into the hole with her bare hands and urged Loo to do likewise, or they'd be there all night.

Hillary then stepped forward. "Trouble?" he asked, in a normal, friendly voice.

"Uncle Hil!" Gabriel gasped and dropped the shovel.

"Oh it's *you*," Luane exclaimed, and Miss Milmont just looked, quite unconcerned.

"As you see," Claudia answered, "we came to retrieve Miss Beresford's property but ran into a slight hitch." The water streamed down her face, plastering a stray wisp of hair over one eye as she spoke.

Seeing that his uncle was not angry, Gabriel rallied and said, "The worst luck, Hil, the old fool has got herself buried in a steel box, welded shut, under the wooden coffin. Did you ever hear of such a thing?"

"I heard the whole from behind a tombstone. Take the ladies home, Gab, and I'll fill in this hole."

"It's nearly done," Gab pointed out.

"Do as he says," Loo commanded her lover. "I am freezing to death, and so is Claudia."

"So am I if it comes to that," Gabriel retorted. "I'm soaked clean through."

Claudia began to sneeze, and a shudder shook her. "Go on, take them home," Hillary repeated.

The three prepared to leave, and as they gave Hillary the shovel, Miss Milmont turned and said, "Thank you for your help, Sir Hillary. It is very kind of you."

"You're very welcome, Miss Milmont," he returned with a nod that sent water cascading from the brim of his hat over his face.

She sneezed again, and he could see she was trembling. "Better stop at Chanely and give the ladies some dry clothes," he said to Gabriel. Chanely Hall was about half-way between the graveyard and Swallowcourt. "And something hot to drink. Go in by the library door; I left it on the latch."

"You're a great gun, Uncle," Gab said, and shepherded his charges off to their mounts. It was a miserable, slow walk in the rain and dark to Chanely, made no swifter nor pleasanter by a recalcitrant Casper, much inclined to dawdle.

Between the hole being nearly filled before they left and the slow gait set by the ancient gig horse, Sir Hillary reached the stable as soon as the others, and all four went together around to the library door.

"Now that's strange," Hillary said to himself. "I left the door on the latch, but I'm certain I didn't leave it wide open." It was open now about three inches, but as there was a rose trellis in the garden to break the wind, the storm was not lashing the door so violently as it might have. He opened it wide on oiled hinges and stood thinking.

"Shall we consider the mystery *indoors*?" Claudia suggested, sneezing again.

"Yes, come in, all of you. You must be freezing in those wet clothes."

A single brace of candles was burning in a branched holder, and from them Hillary lit others to reveal a pleasant book-lined room, with a small fire burning in the screened grate. He pushed the grate aside and stoked up the fire as he suggested they all remove their wet garments. His idea was speedily carried out, and still their shirts were wet under their sodden jackets. Sir Hillary put off his hat and threw aside his cape.

"How very elegant you are, even when you go gravedigging," Claudia said, looking at his tidy dark sweater and unruffled hair.

"Good lord!" he shouted, observing closely for the first time the girls, who stood revealed in the full squalor of moth-eaten trousers, well spattered with mud, once-white shirts now yellowed and frayed, for clothing even in half-repair was never discarded at Swallowcourt. Their sodden hair was flattened against their heads, their faces and hands muddy from refilling the grave without shovels. "What on earth are you girls wearing?"

"Old livery from the cedar press," Luane told him nonchalantly. "We couldn't go there in our skirts."

"You're filthy! Go upstairs and get cleaned up at once," he said like a father scolding a batch of naughty children. "And leave your boots here if you please. They're soaked with mud. Loo, you know where to go—take Miss Milmont." Gabriel went along to his room, and during their absence Hillary went to order some cocoa to warm them up.

It was a little while before they felt themselves presentable, and even then they were not so much presentable as relatively clean, with their hair toweled dry, combed back, and pinned into a knot behind. When they came back to the library, hot cocoa was waiting by the kindling fire, with their jackets put to dry over chairs. An old blanket had been placed over the sofa to protect its covering from their damp trousers.

"This is more like it," Loo said, picking up the cup of cocoa and warming her hands on the cup.

"If you haven't taken your death of cold, it's a wonder," Hil said.

"Never mind that," Gabriel brushed it aside. "The deuce of it is it was all for nothing. We couldn't even see the diamonds, let alone get them out. How shall we go about it, Uncle?"

Claudia cleared her throat in a meaningful way and frowned heavily at Gabriel who ignored her. She was obliged to express herself verbally. "Am I to understand Sir Hillary is to be included in our adventure?"

"If he *wants* to . . .", Loo looked a question at Thoreau, whose eyes flickered to Miss Milmont.

"I cannot think he would enjoy it in the least," Claudia objected. "A dandy cannot wish to be digging a coffin out of a . . ."

"A *dandy!*" he shouted.

"Out of a muddy grave," she continued, as though he had not spoken. "It will be pea soup by tomorrow if this deluge holds up. Then, too, there is the welding torch. What we really need is a blacksmith, I think."

"No, we can't get Jed Flaro to come along—he's the smitty in the village, Claudia, and he is *not* the sort for an adventure," Loo said sadly.

"Well, then," she answered, "we may have to do as Gabriel suggested and take the coffin away to perform the deed."

"We can't bring it here unless Sir Hillary is one of us," Loo pointed out.

"The *odious* Sir Hillary." he added, but all pretended not to notice.

"And we cannot take it home to Swallowcourt because of Jonathon," Loo continued.

"If necessary, I might cause a diversion within, while *you* are doing the deed in the stables," Claudia con-

70

sidered. "I am very good at hysterics, or I could let Jonathon make love to me."

"Lucky Jonathon," Hillary said aside and was again ignored.

"Cousin!" Loo smiled in admiration. "Didn't I tell you she was all right, Gab? Yes, let us do it at Swallowcourt. I wish I could be both places at once, to see Jonathon make love to you."

"Yes, but really, Uncle Hil could help us enormously if he would *like* to join us," Gabriel said hopefully.

"I shouldn't like to deprive Miss Milmont of her love-making, or hysterics, as the case may be."

She smiled at him vaguely, unruffled, but it was Gabriel, eager for his guardian's help, who spoke up. "The thing is, even if we manage to get the coffin to Swallowcourt, and it is very heavy, we three could never lift it, I wouldn't know how to get it open."

"Would *you* know how, Sir Hillary?" Claudia asked.

"Certainly."

Luane and Claudia exchanged questioning looks. "A sign of good will is usually required before admitting a new partner to a venture," the elder said.

"You might take my filling in the grave for good will," Hillary mentioned.

"It was nearly filled before you came," Loo pointed out.

"Then I have a more practical contribution to suggest. How had you planned to dispose of the diamonds? Much good they would do you—a stolen necklace. It would have to be broken up."

"Actually, *I* am very good at breaking things," Claudia offered. "I broke two jugs just the day before I left Devonshire."

"The individual stones separated from the metal for selling," he said.

"You underestimate us, sir," Claudia said, offended, "That promised to be the most exciting part of the adventure in my opinion. Going to Amsterdam . . ."

"What did you plan to use for money?"

"Nothing. We mean to work our way aboard a tramp vessel, as crewmen."

"And have taken to wearing trousers in advance for practice. You know, till tonight I took you for a fairly sensible woman, Miss Milmont," Sir Hillary said.

"That is quite a common mistake with people who are first making my acquaintance. I am really a person who craves excitement and danger."

"Cousin Claudia hasn't had an adventure before," Loo explained.

"I can see she was ill prepared for it. Would you ladies like to change into some dry—livery?"

"I doubt yours would be so interesting as this," Claudia said. "Besides the exciting aroma of camphor, we have all these moth holes, in the most unusual places," She poked a finger through a hole in the knee, and out the other side as she spoke.

"Unlike Sophie, I don't keep every worn-out rag about the house. I can't vouch for the holes. Those old woolen liveries make a feast for moths. It only encourages pests to hang around if you feed them."

"Do you suppose that is why he has given us no more than a cup of cocoa after our night's labor?" Claudia asked Loo in a loudish voice.

"Would you care for a biscuit, Miss Milmont?" Thoreau asked.

"No, thank you. To tell the truth, I am ravenous after the meager crumbs they feed us at Swallowcourt, and a biscuit would only serve to awaken my appetite, which I am trying to keep in abeyance till I get home to Devon."

Thoreau's lips quivered slightly, and he pulled the bell cord. "Some cold meat, cheese and bread, please," he said when a servant came.

"And a biscuit?" Claudia asked in a small voice.

"Biscuits," he said to the waiting servant.

The victuals were welcomed by all, most especially by the inmates of Swallowcourt, and when a luncheon more tasty and filling than their dinner had been tucked away, Claudia said to Luane, "If he continues to feed us in this fashion, I am all in favor of letting him join us. But one

72

detail—actually two—we have forgotten. Besides the necessity for a quite heavy wagon and at least a team of horses to pull it to bring the steel box here, there is the problem of the guard Sir Hillary so stupidly arranged to have hired. Or will you just hit him on the head, Loo, as you had planned to do to the groom at Swallowcourt if he hadn't been sleeping so soundly?"

"But of course—that is no problem," Loo said immediately. "Besides, he will likely hire Tim Larriman, and he will be dead drunk by midnight. Perhaps you ought to slip him a bottle of wine, Gabriel, to make sure."

"You know I can't do that."

"What a poltroon!" Claudia said to Luane, to whom she addressed most of her remarks, rather as though they two were alone in the room. "Are you quite sure you once planned to *marry* this fellow? Well, like everything else, it will be left up to *us*. I daresay if we just leave a bottle lying about close to the grave, Tim Larriman will have the wits to see it and get drunk for us."

"You are rushing matters, little Claudia," Sir Hillary said, assuming his nasty character and tone. "The broaching of the grave will not be tackled in one night. Arrangements will have to be made. The welding equipment, getting the stable cleared of men on some pretext or other."

"Somebody will beat us to it if we wait," Loo interjected.

"We have got ourselves stuck with a very stupid pair of conspirators," Claudia said to her cousin. "Speed is clearly of the essence. How long will it take you, Sir Hillary, to hit your groom on the head, and break into the blacksmith's shop and steal his equipment? I should think one day more than sufficient. Ought we not to nip down to the village right now, tonight, and steal the torch thing we require?"

"You may leave those arrangements in my hands," he answered.

Gabriel had been listening to this conversation in a little confusion. He didn't know quite what to make of Miss Milmont—whether she was serious or not. "She's right about one thing, Uncle. Jonathon will be there having a go at the diamonds before he leaves. I wonder he wasn't there tonight."

"I was wondering the same thing myself. A strange lack of initiative on his part."

"It was a nasty night with all the rain. His uniform, you know . . ." Claudia remarked.

"I was sure we'd see him there and had the crowbar all ready to hit him," Loo added. "And he wasn't asleep, for when I tiptoed past his door at eleven-thirty, the floor squeaked, and I ran on very fast, but round the corner I heard his door open, and he came out. And he didn't have on his uniform either, for I peeked. He had on a funny old jacket, or maybe it was a dressing gown."

"His nerve must have failed him at the last minute," Claudia said. "Well, shall we get on home, Cousin? I don't hear the rain lashing so heavily now, and I see our jackets have stopped dripping."

"It's long past time you were going," Hillary said.

"I have felt all evening we were no more than half welcome," Claudia remarked, ostensibly to Luane.

"Come on, Gab, we'll accompany the ladies," Hillary said.

"No, no! You deprive us of half our adventure! We have some hope of being befriended by thugs or villains en route and beaten before we get home. The evening has been a total loss so far," Miss Milmont objected.

"You may have the pleasure of a thrashing before you leave the premises," Hillary replied dampingly.

"You told me he was a prude!" Claudia said to Luane.

"He's showing off again," her cousin replied.

"I suppose that means he has taken *me* in aversion, like mama."

Despite the argument, the gentlemen donned their capes and hats and accompanied the girls to Swallowcourt. But as they were in the hall about to leave, a footman beckoned Sir Hillary aside and with an excited face told him something that lifted his eyebrows. "Excuse me," Hillary said and dashed off quickly. They waited a few moments, then Gabriel went to fetch him. As he too

74

failed to return, the girls went off after them both. They followed the path taken by the men down a hall to an open doorway with light streaming forth.

"Have you changed your minds about coming with us?" Luane asked.

"We do feel it would be better if we got into our beds before dawn," Claudia added, entering the room—a small study. She stopped short, for two men were standing looking at an open window, and all about them lay a scene of wreckage. Chairs were upturned, pictures askew on the wall, and papers littered about the floor.

"How interesting!" Claudia continued, walking in and looking all around. "Do you frequently enjoy the company of housebreakers?" she asked Thoreau.

"This is the first time," he answered, a pensive look on his face.

"And it happened while you were at the graveyard, I collect? What a pity! You would have had a more exciting evening had you stayed home. Was there anything stolen? A chest of gold perhaps, of the family heirlooms? You wouldn't—no, it is too much to hope for a treasure map."

"Nothing," he replied, looking more mystified than ever.

"It was a disappointing night all around," Claudia consoled. "Really, we have had a remarkably flat adventure. Is there any significance to his choosing this particular room? I do not mean to criticize, you understand, but I see nothing of much value here." She gazed at a rather indifferent desk and a couple of chairs, two pictures on the wall of uninteresting scenes, the same view of a dreary castle, one in summer and one in winter.

Gabriel glanced at his uncle, who considered a moment, then spoke. "The only significance I see is that it is in this room I have my safe."

"Aha! The plot thickens. Who would have known this?"

"My servants, ergo, the whole damned countryside," Hillary replied angrily.

"That gives us an interesting group of suspects," Claudia continued. "I trust you kept no great sum of money in it."

"No, I never keep anything of value in it. It's behind that winter scene of Blaize Castle. You'll notice the picture is slightly askew."

"You don't keep your valuables in your safe," Claudia repeated. "No, of course not. My grandmama always keeps her egg money in the sugar bowl, and I personally plan to keep my valuable—my emerald ring—in the toe of a pair of slippers I have which don't quite fit anymore, only they are too good to throw out. Would it be—no, it is really none of my business to enquire where you *do* keep your valuables."

"In the bank, like any rational person," he snapped.

"I think he is insulting me. And my grandmama," Claudia offered to Luane. "Though really it would be too nonsensical to have run to the bank every time I wanted to wear my ring. I plan to wear it for all festive occasions—visits from the vicar, meetings of the Bible Society . . ."

"It was my tiara he was after," Luane decreed, after considering the matter a moment.

"Possibly," Hillary said, "and that narrows our interesting group of suspects considerably, don't it?"

"No one knew you had it but the family," Gabriel said aloud what was in the minds of all.

"And Mr. Fletcher," Miss Milmont added. "Mama had no good opinion of *him*."

"That's foolishness," Hil scoffed. "He's as honest as the day is long and in no need of stealing a paltry little tiara. He's loaded with blunt."

"Now he's taking his ill humor out on you," Claudia said to her cousin. "I think your tiara is very fine. By the by, Sir Hillary, have you looked to see if the tiara is safe?"

"No!" He turned and dashed from the room, returning in a moment with the news that both tiara and replica case were untouched in the bottom of his clothespress, where he had left them.

"You may be sure it was Jonathon after my tiara," Luane told them, "and I hope you mean to take it to the bank tomorrow for safekeeping."

"Yes, but why the deuce would he go trying to steal the tiara when there was a fortune in jewels in the grave, and he knew it?" Gabriel asked.

"To be sure, I never took him for a clever fellow, but I had not thought him such a fool as that," Claudia agreed. "I wonder if he knew, somehow, about the steel-lined casket, and just decided to pick up the tiara while we, like ninnyhammers, were out digging up a sealed metal coffin."

"You may be sure he knew," Luane announced, her little chin jutting at an angry angle.

"How and when was the body sealed in the metal box anyway?" Gabriel asked. "Was it possible he knew?"

"It must have been done on Sunday in the stable," Hillary replied. "The coffin didn't leave Swallowcourt except to go to the church. Certainly he might have discovered it easily enough if he chanced to be there, taking a look at his horses or some such thing."

"Oh, who were the fools in the case?" Claudia repined. "If only *we* had chanced to the stables, what a lot of bother we might have saved ourselves."

"I mean to charge him with it the minute I get home," Luane said, still furious.

"Haul him right out of bed?" Claudia asked her. "I should wait till breakfast if I were you."

"No, he will have thought up some excuse by then."

"Don't say anything," Hillary cautioned. "There's no saying it was Tewksbury."

"If you charge him with it before Sir Hillary or Gabriel call on us tomorrow, there will arise the embarrassing question of how we came to know of it," Claudia added.

"He'll *know* how we came to know," Luane answered. "He said we would be trying to dig up the diamonds, and he would have done the same himself if he hadn't known about the steel box."

"Very likely, but I wouldn't give him the satisfaction of knowing we had such a miserable task in vain," Claudia told her.

"Do as Hillary says," Gabriel directed, and Luane accepted the advice with a sniff.

There was ample food for conversation all the way home, and as the rain had let up and talk was possible, they discussed any aspect of the case that occurred to them. The girls and Gabriel learned that the footman had discovered the break-in just a moment before calling Hillary. No one had been in the room since ten o'clock, so there was no knowing exactly when it was done.

"I know what I *will* do," Luane said. "I'll find out if Jonathon had his horse out."

"You won't, you know," Claudia pointed out. "The groom, you recall, was sound asleep. He didn't even awake when Casper bit me, and I yelled a little. And his own groom, who is also his valet, though he goes by the termination of batman, is an ugly little customer whom I wouldn't even dare ask the time of day."

"You mean there's someone in the world you're afraid of?" Sir Hillary asked.

"If you ever saw Tuggins you'd know what I mean," Claudia said with feeling. "He is dashing all over the house, in places where neither a groom nor a valet has any reason to be, and Jonathon dotes on him. I asked him—Jonathon—what Tuggins was doing coming out of one of the empty guest suites, and he told me he was taking an inventory for him. I could swear the batman was hiding something behind his back, but when I mentioned it to Jonathon, he merely laughed it off."

"They've been thick as thieves for years," Gab explained. "Very likely he had set Tuggins to pick up some small things he could take to London to pawn. Jon is always in the suds, you know. Well, there's nothing wrong in his selling off a few gewgaws. The estate is his now."

"It is entailed on *you* if he doesn't have any children," Loo reminded him.

"Every snuff box and mirror in the place isn't entailed," Gabriel replied. "Besides, Jonathon will certainly marry, now that he's a man of property."

"What you might do," Sir Hillary said to Claudia, "is see if any horses in the stable are wet. That will give us an idea whether they've been out."

"I meant to do so though, of course, if the animal was rubbed down an hour ago, there will be no telling."

Claudia examined all the horses in the stable, but as foreseen, if any had been out, it had been rubbed down and no evidence remained. She and Luane let themselves in by the kitchen door and got to bed with no difficulty.

Chapter Seven

On Tuesday the young ladies slept in late after their busy night, and it was not until after ten that they met in the breakfast room. Claudia was not surprised to see that her mama was not up yet; she knew her to be a late sleeper. Nor was she surprised to see Jonathon awake and dressed in his scarlet regimentals, the buttons gleaming. What did offer her not only a surprise but a severe shock was to observe him bending over backwards to make himself pleasing to Luane, who fought off his every advance with an irate retort.

"I have been giving a good deal of thought to you," he attempted coyly to Miss Beresford. "Some arrangement must be made for your welfare now that your aunt is gone, poor old girl."

"Sir Hillary is my guardian," Loo replied. "*He* will look after me."

"Yes, but you cannot go to a bachelor's house. Not the thing. I have something else to suggest." Luane didn't even bother to ask what, but Claudia was so curious she asked the question.

"Why, to be sure, she must stay on here. I'll speak to Miss Bliss, and I'm sure she'll agree to chaperone you."

"This is a bachelor's establishment, too," Luane pointed out.

"No such a thing! I'll be in London nine-tenths of the time, and with Miss Bliss to play propriety, I might visit my cousin from time to time."

"I am not your cousin," Luane said curtly. "We are only slightly connected through Sophie."

"Dear Aunt Sophie. *She* would have wanted you to make your home here."

"Much I care what *she* wanted."

"Heh, heh, what a little minx she is, eh, Miss Milmont? Tell her she must stay here."

"I cannot think it is for me, or indeed anyone but her guardian to decide that," Miss Milmont replied.

"We shall discuss it another time. Think about it. You know you are welcome—more than welcome, both of you, for so long as you wish to remain. You too, Miss Milmont."

"Thank you," a dazed Claudia replied. She had made sure Jonathon's first aim would be to get rid of them all as soon as possible. It seemed forthcoming for them to go on billeting themselves on him, now that Sophie was dead and buried. She had dreaded the prospect of leaving, for she hadn't so enjoyed herself in her whole lonesome life since papa's death. In Devon she had been the only young person in the house for several years, till her papa's younger brother came to live with them, bringing his two young sons with him. Grandpapa was becoming too old to run the estate. The brother's wife was not an engaging woman, and while the boys were well enough, they were of the wrong age and sex to be any company to a young lady. Grandmama was a dame of strict principles which she tried to inculcate into her granddaughter. One believed she really wanted to be a Quaker, only her husband forbade the official adopting of the religion. So far as any fun or partying went, she was as good as a Quaker. Life was tedious for a girl still youngish, and the two weeks with mama were not much better, though she looked forward to them annually with hope.

Mama was as different as it was possible to be from the Milmonts, and no favorite in that quarter. She led a gay, partying life with dozens of beautiful gowns, but the visits took place in late winter when the city was asleep, and Claudia, as she got older, was kept as much in the background as possible. On two occasions the annual vacation had been spent in Bath, but there, too, social outings had been sadly limited. Visits to the Pump Room, the circulating library, drives, and walks were the entertainment. Mama did not think she would like to visit the Assembly Rooms and, as she was not going anywhere, there was no reason to buy gowns. Every year she looked forward to the visit, but by the end of the two weeks, she was usually looking forward to getting home again.

She had never had a young girl friend. Loo was not only that, but a cousin, someone of the family with whom she could talk and laugh and, most of all, share an adventure. She was determined to do all in her power to help Luane get her diamonds and, if it were possible, which it was not, she would very well like to be the girl's chaperone. So she was pleased, if curious, to hear Jonathon urge her to stay on at Swallowcourt. She hoped mama would agree to remain for the entire holiday. She couldn't think she'd object, for the visit had been spoken of as for the two-week holiday. In fact, the London servants had been given a vacation and, if they left here, there would be a problem where to go.

"I have been thinking how to amuse you young ladies," Jonathon continued, very much the host. "As we are all in mourning, I cannot have a ball as I would otherwise like to do, or a party, but we must do something to entertain you. Would you both like to take a drive into Maldon—that is the closest town, Miss Milmont—and do a bit of shopping? See the sights, such as they are, and have a neat little luncheon at an inn. What do you say, eh?"

Claudia was much inclined to say yes and jump up and down in glee, but her cousin turned a cold eye on the offer and replied, "I must wait till Sir Hillary and Gabriel come. They may have other plans."

"No need to wait on them. All the time in the world to arrange things with Sir Hillary," Jonathon urged.

"I wish to know if he has deposited my tiara in the bank. I have the idea someone may try to steal it," Loo returned, quite pointedly.

Claudia gulped on her coffee and rushed in to save the day. "It is a worry having all these valuable jewels just lying about. I ought to do something with my emerald too, and mama should take some precaution for her pearls. It is no wonder you are worried, Luane."

The three retired to the study where a small fire was lit in the grate, and for a quarter of an hour they discussed the renovations that were necessary at Swallowcourt, with Jonathon professing a great interest in what Luane considered desirable. Gold satin walls and white marble fireplaces met with no objection, and ripping out the great staircase and installing a new one with gold leaf trim was greatly admired. Even replacing the orchards with a pavilion was considered appropriate.

"It will cost a great deal of money," Luane said. "I cannot think how you will pay for the half of it, unless you marry an heiress."

Jonathon blushed, his pink face echoing the red of his tunic, and mumbled, "No such a thing," just as the butler announced the arrival of Sir Hillary Thoreau and Mr. Tewksbury.

"At last!" Luane said, running to the door. She waited for nothing but rushed right in with a report of the morning's doings. "Jonathon wants me to stay on here with Miss Bliss," she said, "but I told him *you* would decide what I am to do."

Sir Hillary's eyebrows rose an inch. He said nothing for a moment, and when he spoke surprised everyone in the room. "An excellent notion," he said. "I confess some such arrangement had occurred to me, but I was by no means sure the captain would oblige us with the offer."

"She can't stay here!" Gabriel shouted.

"It is the last place in the world I want to be," Loo said bluntly.

"Seems very reasonable to *me*," Jonathon said to Hillary, ignoring the uproar from the younger members. "Been her home for some years now. Daresay she'll be getting married pretty soon. No point in having her move; besides, where should she go?"

"Where indeed?" Hillary asked. "She has some little monies from her mama, enough to pay for her chaperone. Miss Bliss is agreeable, is she?"

"Haven't asked her. You might be the one to handle that quarter. Seem to have some influence with the old girl."

"Shall we ask her?" Hillary said.

"Yes, by Jove. Let's get the matter settled," the captain rejoined and went off to look for Miss Bliss.

"I do not at all want to stay here," Luane challenged Sir Hillary the moment Jonathon had left.

"No, Uncle Hil," Gabriel added his entreaties. "If she is to be in a bachelor's home, she might better be at Chanely."

Claudia edged her way to Hillary's side and said in a low voice, while the other two discussed the matter, "Something very strange is afoot here. Before you arrived, the captain was exerting himself to be agreeable to Loo. Was he always interested in her?"

"No, he never had an eye for anything but an heiress."

"A small tiara and a caseful of glass stones doth not an heiress make."

"There was that interesting phrase in the will you recall, something about depending how events fall out in the intervening year. He has reason to believe, or believes in any case, that if he marries Loo, he gets the blunt. He may even be right."

"She'll never have him."

"He can but try."

"I'm surprised you lend yourself to this scheme. You must know he'll camp on her doorstep—do all in his power to win her."

"Jealous, little Claudia? Is he not making love to you,

84

as you had hoped? Don't worry. She wouldn't have him if he were the last man on earth."

"She may have no choice. This set-up lends itself very well to compromise, and I'm surprised you hadn't noticed it."

"And so should I be surprised at myself, if I *hadn't* noticed it."

"What do you mean to do, then?"

"To keep you and your mama here to watch over her till I make some other arrangement."

"He has asked us to stay."

"Has he indeed? Am I incorrect in my surmise that he hasn't been making up to you then?"

She tossed her head and glared. "I am only on a two-week holiday, and already half of one week is gone. There's no counting on mama to stay beyond the two weeks."

"I'm amazed she has consented to rusticate so long, but two weeks should be more than sufficient."

"Sir Hillary, have you a Plan?" she asked, her eyes sparkling.

"You may leave the matter in my hands."

"And the other matter—the coffin. Have you completed arrangements for its remove to Chanely?"

"I am not at all sure it is necessary."

"You mean to cut the box open at the graveyard?"

"That too may prove unnecessary."

Captain Tewksbury came back with Miss Bliss in tow before this cryptic phrase could be explained, and the plan devised for Loo's keeping was put to her.

She proposed a dozen reasons for its ineligibility, including a chicken farm and the impropriety of a lady's staying in a bachelor's home, but it was borne in on her by a significant glance from Thoreau that he wished her to remain, and she eventually capitulated.

Luane was in the sulks, and Gabriel in a state not far removed from the same. "I suppose you didn't take my tiara to the bank either," Loo said, to show him her opinion of his guardianship.

"Certainly I did."

"I wouldn't put it a bit past someone to try to steal it," she said, shooting a black scowl at the captain as she spoke. He looked out the window, and ruined his seeming nonchalance by clearing his throat nervously.

"As a matter of fact," Sir Hillary replied, "someone did, last night."

Everyone except Gabriel and Miss Bliss had to feign surprise at this, but the latter's very real surprise saved it from becoming an embarrassment. She demanded an explanation, which was given tersely and simply.

Just as the explanation was completed, Mrs. Milmont entered the room, and it had to be given over again. She was as indignant as if it had been the pearls that had been attacked and demanded immediately to know what Sir Hillary meant to do about it.

"I took them to the bank this morning for safekeeping," he told her.

"I trust you also reported it to the constable."

"I did not like to do so when it was only ourselves—exactly the small group here—who knew I had the tiara."

"I hope you are not accusing *me*!" Mrs. Milmont responded angrily. "Nor my daughter, for I assure you *we* did not budge an inch from the house the entire night, did we, Claudia?"

"No, mama."

"Certainly not, and we shared the same bed, didn't we, Claudia?"

"Yes, mama."

"I scarcely closed an eye all night long."

"Did she, Claudia?" Hillary asked with a twinkle. She frowned heavily at him.

"I can assure you neither Claudia nor myself moved all night. I daresay Luane just decided she wanted to keep the tiara herself and ran over to bring it home. I shouldn't blame her in the least. I don't see why *you* must have the good of it till she's eighteen."

"It doesn't suit me at all," he agreed reluctantly.

"There is no need to report the matter," Marcia Milmont went on, oblivious to sarcasm. "It would only create mischief."

"Just what I thought myself, ma'am," Hillary agreed.

"I did not take it!" Luane bristled at Mrs. Milmont.

"Hush up, you silly girl. Do you want to have someone thrown in jail? These matters are best kept within the family. Your tiara is locked up now safely enough, and no one can steal it."

"It may be *now*, but I have a pretty good idea who tried to steal it!" Luane said, with an angry look at Jonathon.

"Yes, well *I* have a pretty good idea who went sneaking out in the middle of the night to try to rob the grave of diamonds too," he retaliated. "And don't think *I* was the one who tried to steal your old tiara, for it's nothing but a bit of tin with diamond chips not worth a groat in it."

"You don't mean the diamond necklace has been *stolen*!" Mrs. Milmont shrieked and seemed in danger of swooning. "We are surrounded by sneaks and thieves."

"No, it wasn't taken," Gabriel assured her.

"Wasn't it though?" Jonathon asked, looking baffled.

"As if you didn't know perfectly well there was a sealed steel box inside the coffin," Gabriel charged. "And that's the only reason you weren't there trying to get the necklace yourself."

"A steel box! Good God, that's why the coffin was so heavy," Jonathon shouted. And if he's acting, he's giving an excellent performance, Hillary said to himself. He stood looking on quietly, observing everyone carefully.

Mrs. Milmont recovered from her semiswoon and was immediately screaming. "My pearls! My emerald! Claudia, do you have my emerald? Run up at once—no, I must go myself and see if my pearls are safe. Where is my emerald?"

"I am wearing my emerald, mama," Claudia replied, holding out her hand, on which the large emerald shone magnificently. "I can't get it off, you recall I told you."

"Well, that is a blessing in disguise. They can't steal the emerald unless they cut off your finger. I must see to my pearls." She was off, huffing and puffing up the staircase.

"You'd never miss just *one* finger, would you, Claudia?" Hillary asked with a smile.

"So someone tried to steal the tiara," Jonathon said, and was treated to a description of how this had been discovered by Hillary, who was careful to give the impression he never for one moment connected the captain with the theft, whatever Luane might say.

"Very wise to put it in the bank," Jonathon advised. "I think Miss Milmont and her mama should do the same with their jewels. All the real ones should be put away for safekeeping. Of course you won't bother having the glass case of reproductions put into the bank. Ought to put them away safely though."

"I shall."

"Sophie used to keep her real jewels in the basement, Fletcher said. Not a bad place for the replicas. No one would be looking in a basement for them."

"The damp might turn them rusty," Hillary answered.

"Well, the settings are gold. That don't rust."

"Not the necklace, just the rings. An attic would be better."

"Yes, in the bottom of a trunk they'd be safe. Why don't you do that?"

"That is really not what I am come here to discuss," Sir Hillary said in the tone of announcement, which won him the attention of the group. "I would like you all to come to Chanely for dinner this evening. Your hospitality is being strained, Captain, while I do nothing to entertain the relatives, of which I am of course only a connection, as you all delight in pointing out to me. Still, I would be honoured if you would come to me en masse this evening. Say about six. We shall dine at seven."

The invitation was accepted eagerly and, when Mrs. Milmont descended wearing her pearls, she was more delighted than any of them to return to Chanely.

"We should be back in plenty of time if we leave soon," Jonathon agreed.

"Back from where?" Marcia demanded.

"Offered to take the girls to Maldon for a drive," he explained.

"An excellent idea!" she immediately included herself. "I did not come prepared for long mourning and have only this one black gown. I shall see if I can't pick up a few things—black ribbons and a dark shawl. Claudia too might need black gloves."

"I have no proper mourning clothes either, mama," her daughter said hopefully.

"My dear, so far as *I* can see, your grandma dresses you in half-mourning all the time. You haven't a bright stitch to your name, and that gown that you are wearing is close enough to gray to make no difference."

"It *used* to be blue," Claudia explained.

"Well it is gray now. What time do we leave, Captain?"

"As soon as you're all dressed."

"*I'm* not going," Luane announced. "Gabriel, what are you and Sir Hillary doing?"

"Nothing," Gabriel answered, looking to his guardian.

"Why don't you ride along and escort the party?" Hillary suggested. "The carriage will hold the captain and the three ladies, and you can go mounted."

This plan pleased everyone except Jonathon but, as the King's highway was free to all citizens, he could not well prevent Gabriel from going along.

"Why don't you come, Uncle?" Gab asked.

"I have some business in the village."

"Aren't *we* going to the village?" Claudia asked.

"No, we are going to Maldon," Loo told her. "Sir Hillary is going to Billericay—it is only two miles away, and is just a little place. Maldon is bigger."

The gentlemen left, and the ladies went to prepare themselves for the trip.

Luane was happy to be having an outing with Gabriel, Mrs. Milmont in alt to be going to dinner at Chanely, and Claudia very excited indeed to be doing anything festive. Marcia came into her daughter's room, demanding to know whether Claudia had gloves to protect her emerald, and to ask whether she ought to wear the pearls—much too dressy, of course—or risk leaving them behind.

"Wear them under your gown, mama."

"Why, so I shall, an excellent idea. Yes, and I have

had another excellent idea, too, my dear, and tell me what you think of it. You recall Mr. Blandings, that nice gentleman we met at Bath two years ago?"

"The big man with dark hair? I remember him."

"I daresay you didn't know, for I haven't mentioned it to you, but the fact of the matter is, he has become very particular in his attentions to me over the past two years. Yes, indeed, he has several times hinted he wants to marry me, only he is not quite . . . not to say he isn't a gentleman, for he certainly is, and loaded with money too."

"Why don't you have him?" Claudia asked.

"The fact of the matter is, he got his money in trade— owned an ironmongery, but in Somerset, so far away no one need know. But marrying him was not the idea I had in mind, though I might very well . . . What I meant was, I shall ask him here."

"Here?" Claudia asked, stunned at the ineligibility of the scheme. "What on earth for?"

"To steal the diamonds for us. What could be better? He will know precisely how to open up the steel chest. It will be like opening a hat box for him, for he is so clever, especially with metal. Someone will take them before the year is up. You may depend on that. Already young Gabriel has been after them, and the captain would have too, if he hadn't been busy trying to steal the tiara. That was very bad of him, was it not? And hardly worth his while, I should have thought. But if they are to be stolen by just anyone, we might as well have them as not. They were given to Sophie by her great aunt, Lady Mary Withers, and she was *my* great aunt too, and it seems to me if anyone is to get them, it ought to be *me*."

"If Mr. Blandings is so rich, mama, you shan't need them, and really Luane had nothing."

"Pooh, she has the tiara, hasn't she? It is extremely valuable, very likely, and besides, the necklace will be yours eventually, so I should think you would be willing to help us."

"Help you!"

"Help Jerry—Mr. Blandings and myself, to steal it."

"Oh, mama, I could not!"

"What a gapeseed you are. I should have known more than to expect you to lend yourself to anything the slightest bit irregular, with the way your grandma Milmont has raised you, like a blasted saint, but at least you must be quiet about my plan."

"How do you plan to account for asking him here?"

"I have it all thought out. He lives in Essex, you see, that is just what is so convenient about it. He's bought a country seat near Colchester and is setting himself up as a country gentleman, though he hardly ever goes there. And if he should be driving from London to Marcyhurst—that is what he's called his place, after me of course, Marcia . . . Well, as I was saying, if he should be passing by, what more natural than that he should stop off to say 'how do you do' to me? Then we have only to arrange a little invitation, and I'll say I'm lending you my carriage to return to Devon, so *he* will have to wait and take me back to London."

"But he was coming *from* London to Colchester."

"Well, the other way around then; what's the odds? He will have an excuse to stay over, and there you have as neat a scheme as you could care for."

Claudia was overcome at the complexity of it all and wished to eliminate the whole. "Sir Hillary has hired a guard for the grave. I can't think you will succeed with your plan."

"A guard? My dear, have you forgotten Mr. Blandings is over six feet tall? And a bruiser, too. He will knock over any guard with one hand tied behind his back, and could lift the steel casket out of its hole all by himself."

"Jonathon will not invite him to stay. Indeed it is already a great deal for *us* to be staying so long."

"No, he and the captain are good friends. I see a deal of Jonathon in town, you must know. We were all together at the play only last month, and the two of them frequently dine at my place. Besides, Jonathon will do as I tell him, now that I know he tried to steal Luane's tiara. And another thing, Claudia, Jerry has taken the absurd notion that you are not my daughter at all, but only a

91

stepdaughter. I can't imagine where he got such an idea. But in case he should mention anything about it, you might just tell him you *call* yourself my daughter since we are so very close, but really you are your papa's daughter by his first marriage, and that is why you are staying with your Devon grandparents."

"And also why I am twenty-four?" Claudia asked with an innocent gaze not quite authentic.

"Your age need not come into it."

"Yes, mama. When do you expect Mr. Blandings to arrive?"

"I have just written the letter and will post it in Maldon today. He should have it tomorrow and, if I know Jerry, he will dash down here immediately."

"How nice," Claudia said in a dying voice, and turned to the mirror to adjust a very plain navy bonnet over her brown curls.

She then went to Luane's room and disclosed the whole story to her, urging her to get her diamonds as soon as possible, for Mr. Blandings was a giant who could pull the steel box out of the earth with his bare hands.

"We *must* do it tonight—or tomorrow at the latest."

"We'll talk it over with Gab and Sir Hillary tonight."

"Yes, and I should prefer you not tell them about mama's plan."

"Why?"

"Because she's my mother."

"They'll think it's Jonathon we're afraid of."

"Yes, and *he* will be after them, too, since your tiara is safely out of his reach."

Chapter Eight

The trip to Maldon was a pleasant variation in the dull lives of the young ladies on the expedition. Mrs. Milmont, too, derived some pleasure in driving a sharp bargain on a piece of very nice black lace that would lend her mourning weeds an elegant touch, and found a fine white satin rose that trifled with the rules of mourning without quite rupturing them. No purchases of any significance were made by the two younger girls, both with their pockets to let. Claudia's handsome allowance was only a fiction, and of Luane's there was not even a fiction; she had a guinea a month while her aunt lived, and nothing upon her death. When Sir Hillary spoke of her having some little money from her mama to pay for her chaperone, he planned to pay for it himself. Marcia very nearly bought her daughter a pair of black gloves, till she remembered she had a similar pair at home in London that she could send her when she got back to town. She would have them then for Devon, and wouldn't be going anywhere to speak of while at Swallowcourt. She pointed out quite a few handsome articles she would have liked to buy Claudia but for this sad, sad mourning that was upon them. No point in buying her the bonnet with the primroses, for she couldn't wear it, and very likely it would be out of style by next year.

It had been the captain's hope to let the ladies fend for themselves during the shopping spree and meet them for lunch, but as Gabriel made no move to leave, he stuck with them as well, jostling elbows with Gab in an effort to walk beside Luane. Mrs. Milmont put him to good use, however, by ladening him with her purchases and later sending him off to post her letter. Claudia, used to no more than a weekly visit to a very dull local village, thought she had a marvelous time and was inordinately pleased when her mama bought her a yard of blue ribbon, that she might not go back to Devon completely empty-handed. The captain had not thought to include Mrs. Milmont and Gabriel in the luncheon treat when he had initially made his offer, but as they were there and he had enough money, he paid up without complaining and even urged Luane, though no one else, to have some fruit after she had already consumed a full meal and two cream buns, and he was positive she couldn't hold another bite. She fooled him and accepted a nectarine that cost a shilling. He consoled himself that it ofttimes took a sprat to catch a mackerel, and the number of bits of rubbish Tuggins had rounded up to take to be pawned would see him through till quarter day.

As if one singular outing were not enough to enliven the dullest week, which this one was not by a long shot, Claudia had still the dinner at Chanely to look forward to when they got back to Swallowcourt. Her mama, looking very fine with the black lace over her shoulders, the white satin rose tucked into the neck of her gown, and the pearls worn over the whole, came into her room to check her ensemble before leaving. Plain. The girl looked decidedly plain. She did her no credit in the eyes of Sir Hillary Thoreau, on whom she was desirous of making a good impression, for he could catapult one to the heights of society if only he could be brought round the thumb. She had her own woman in to see what could be done with the hair, of a natural curl but no particular style. She pulled it back, and it looked better, but there was no passing Claudia off for anything but a young lady in her twenties with such a do, and so it was again pulled down round her cheeks. The loan of her own violet shawl also proved unsuitable as it clashed with the pale blue gown, which was to be gray in the evening light. So Claudia went to dinner looking like an upper-class servant to her mama's majestic matron. It was some slight consolation that Luane looked very little better. A navy serge suit was what she considered suitable for evening wear. She explained that her "good" dress was pink and she couldn't wear it because of Sophie's death.

The captain, who had come to Swallowcourt in his dashing curricle and pair, had had Sophie's ancient traveling coach scrubbed up for the trip to Maldon, and this was again the means of conveyance to Chanely, since there were five of them to go. Miss Bliss was invited as well. Whatever the deficiencies of toilette and transportation, there was nothing lacking in the house and feast prepared for them. Candles burned in all corners, dispelling the gloom of a dismal March evening, and the fires in the grates took that nip from the air that sank into the bones at Swallowcourt. Mahogany furniture glowed richly, and the sheen of silver candelabra flickered welcomingly, to be taken up in the mirrors and multiplied.

"How very charming!" Marcia said to her host in a gushing manner.

"Thank you," Sir Hillary replied. "But you have seen Chanely before."

"Oh, yes, after the funeral, but that was afternoon. It looks much better at night. There is something so romantic about candlelight."

He looked at her elaborate get-up and at Claudia's near rags, and the familiar sneer settled on his features. "I have often observed elderly ladies prefer candlelight," he answered and turned to make the others welcome before she had time to recover. They were taken to the Blue Saloon and seated, and Marcia immediately began hinting for a tour of the other parts of the house.

"I thought you would all like a glass of wine before dinner—after your drive," Hillary suggested, turning a deaf ear to her hints.

"We can have a glass of wine any old time, but it is so seldom we get a chance to see Chanely," Marcia insisted.

He put his hand on the bell to call for wine, then suddenly reconsidered, and said, "Am I correct in assuming you would like to be shown around, Marcia?"

"I'm sure we would all enjoy it."

"Miss Bliss is familiar with the house, as are Luane and the captain, but perhaps Claudia . . ."

"She would love to see it," Marcia answered unhesitatingly, without a single look toward her daughter.

With the host thus forced to absent himself from the majority of his guests, the party was off to a poor start till Luane decided to join the tour, which brought Jonathon at once to her side.

"Well, Blissful, you might as well join us," Hillary said, and she too arose and tagged along with them.

They were conducted through different rooms—library, portrait gallery, various parlors, armaments room, and music room with a compliment for everything from Mrs. Milmont. Sir Hillary then tried to return his guests to the Blue Saloon for their wine, but pointed questions about the chambers abovestairs revealed to him that he was not to get off with showing only the downstairs. With a resigned bow he led them up the grand staircase. They were shown the green guest suite, the blue guest suite, the gold, and the chambers that had been honored long ago by sleeping Charles II—but still the insatiable viewer not satisfied.

"How about the part of the house that is being used?" Marcia asked.

"My guest suites are in frequent use," Thoreau told her.

"What a jokesmith you are, Sir Hillary," she laughed. "I mean *your* chambers, of course. I am sure you have taken the very best suite for yourself."

"I have taken the master bedroom, certainly. Must you see it too, Marcia?"

"We would not want to miss the best room," she said

coyly, and with his tongue between his teeth, Hillary led them to his own room. His butler was just clearing away the garments shed by Sir Hillary half an hour before and looked up in surprise to see the party being shown in.

"Surprise, Blicker," Hillary said. "Company, and you caught with your chores undone." The valet bowed wordlessly and left with the shirt and spoiled ties in his hands.

There was nothing extraordinary in the room after all. It was fine, with a huge four-poster bed hung with gold brocade curtains, the replicas of which hung at a pair of windows. There were the usual pieces of furniture: dresser, clothespress, a few chairs scattered about. Mrs. Milmont complimented him with every adjective at her command and then turned, satisfied at last. Luane, who had never been in this particular room, walked around and stopped in one dark corner.

"Why have you left my jewels here?" she asked. On a dresser stood the replica case.

"I didn't bother taking them to the bank," Hillary told her. "My vault is not a safe place, as we have reason to know, and I haven't quite decided what to do with them."

"You should not leave them here."

"Blicker is never far away."

She peered into the glass case, then said suddenly, "I'd like to wear my diamonds."

"What, with a serge suit?" Mrs. Milmont took her to task. "Entirely inappropriate, my dear. You should look a quiz. You might wear the little sapphire pendant if you wish to dress up. Why, you and Miss Bliss will be twins, for I see she is wearing hers too."

"No, I want to wear my diamonds," Loo insisted.

"Said you didn't like them," the captain reminded her.

"Never mind, they are mine, and I shall wear them. You are wearing your pearls," she said to her aunt.

"And I my emerald," Claudia augmented. "As you have been robbed—I mean deprived temporarily of your tiara, I am sure Sir Hillary will let you wear your ersatz diamonds."

"Why not?" Hillary said. He opened the case with the key he had with him and handed her the diamonds.

They looked every bit as ludicrous as Mrs. Milmont had prophesied, and the sapphire pendant was replaced in their stead.

"You wear my diamonds, cousin," Loo said, "I'd like to see them on someone."

"No, thank you. They would clash with my emerald ring."

"Try them on, my dear," her mother urged. "Let us see how they will—would look."

Claudia put them on and wrinkled her nose in the mirror. "Gaudy!" she declared and reached around to undo the clasp.

"No, they look nice on you, don't they, Gabriel?" Loo asked. "An older woman can wear them."

Gabriel looked unconvinced, and Mrs. Milmont took up the cudgels in her little girl's defense.

The captain wore a considering look on his face. "Give you a bit of dash," he decreed.

"Come on, let's have our wine," Loo said and turned to leave, so Hillary locked the case, and everyone trooped from the room, Claudia weighted down with the unwanted necklace.

"Would you care to go upstairs and see the cheese room and attics?" Hillary asked Marcia in a perfectly civil tone, only slightly marred by a half-sneer.

She detected an edge of irony and declined with yet more compliments on what she had viewed already. They were finally allowed to have a glass of wine, and within minutes dinner was called. Mrs. Milmont had at last the glory of not only being at Sir Hillary's table, but seated in the place of honor on her host's right side. She had also the honor, as the meal progressed, of being called first 'Marcia', then 'darling' as she became ever more officious. Everything was of the first stare, as she knew it must be. The finest of china, silver, and crystal, a meal obviously prepared by a male chef, with interesting ragouts and other French dishes to offset the plain English fare. Her approval of every detail was given to the host. After two courses and two removes, the company from Swallowcourt was stuffed, for their stomachs had shrunk during their visit, but still there was more to come. Chantillies and cream pastries and fruits were set on the boards, and in spite of their satiety, a little corner had to be found for these unaccustomed treats. Conversation was general and lively. Marcia was seldom silent and hoped by her gaiety to make herself a frequent guest during her stay at Swallowcourt. How stunning if she could wangle an invitation for Mr. Blandings!

"Have you managed a good meal for once?" Sir Hillary asked Miss Milmont, seated on his left.

"Yes, I am *gorged*."

"You see how well advised you were to allow me to join your adventure? And you may take home a basket, too, in case you are reduced to crumbs again tomorrow."

"Is that why you asked us?" she smiled.

"Only partially. I can't have my conspirators failing away from malnutrition, but I have been trying to get your mama to come to me this age, only she doesn't bother with me at all in London."

"What a whisker! She was as pleased as punch to receive the invitation. Oh, by the by, did Loo tell you we must speak to you privately before we leave?"

"No, have there been further developments in the case?"

She nodded. "We must move quickly. Will it be possible for us to talk?"

"Of course, but not here. I'll show you my—ah, collection? after dinner."

"Collection of what?"

"What are you interested in that we might use as an excuse."

"Coins?"

"You are not *pure* Milmont after all. There is a little something of your mama crept in. Let us make it sermons. That should scare off the others."

A little later he turned to her again. "You are looking very elegant in the diamonds," he said.

"Aren't they ghastly? And with this horrid old gown too."

"Now you are offending me, Miss Milmont. Do I not rate a better gown? Your mama, you will see, is looking as fine as fivepence."

"This is my best," she told him, a little apologetically.

He looked at her gown, then a few moments later at her mama's. He had always disliked Marcia Milmont excessively. A toadeater, a pusher, and a dead bore. He now despised her. That a young girl should have not one decent gown while her mother was a walking clotheshorse was the outside of enough. The girl was attractive too, beneath the austerity. Lovely eyes and a well-shaped face. But when he turned to address a remark to Mrs. Milmont, he was smiling blandly and was very polite.

Dinner over, the ladies went to the Blue Saloon and after a short interval, the gentlemen joined them. Sir Hillary carefully avoided taking up a seat beside Mrs. Milmont and went to sit with Miss Bliss, but before they could exchange two words, Marcia came mincing over and joined them.

"I can't tell you how much I have enjoyed myself this evening," she began.

"I have noticed, darling, but really you have *tried* to tell me often enough. I take your word for it that you have had an evening of unsurpassed joy."

Miss Bliss 'tch'd, tch'd' disapprovingly and brought out her knitting.

"Such an elegant home, and all done in the best of taste."

"Thank you once again, ma'am."

"Your chef, I am sure, must be French."

"His name is Gallagher." He was in fact a Monsieur Beaupré.

"Well, he *cooks* like a Frenchie. But then, do you keep a different cook in London, for I know your chef there is French. Everyone says so."

Caught out in his lie, he had now to pretend he had

a different chef in each place, which extravagance raised him even higher in her eyes.

"We shall be quite spoiled for the simple little dinners Miss Bliss arranges for us," she continued in a playful tone.

"Miss Bliss was hired as Sophie's companion, you recall, and cannot be blamed for the paucity of food at Swallowcourt. Why don't you take the captain to task for it? I see he is sitting there all alone."

"Yes, and I told that foolish Claudia she should . . . But that is always the way with daughters. They never know enough to look sharply about them for a good match."

"They don't learn a thing from their mamas, do they?" he agreed mildly.

"Oh, naughty! Isn't he naughty, Miss Bliss?"

"I'd use a stronger term myself," Miss Bliss said without looking up from her knitting.

"Tell me, Sir Hillary, for it is a matter that has been troubling me, and I am sure you will know just how I should go on—what degree of mourning do you plan to undertake as a result of Sophie's death?" Marcia asked.

"I plan to wear my armband for a month."

"But what I really mean is in London, for the Season, you know."

"I do not plan to go into mourning at all. I have a fairly full calendar planned already."

"Not at all! Why, how wonderful. I daresay you are right. Not a soul there will know of Sophie's death, and we might just keep it mum and not even go into half-mourning. It would be a shame to miss all the routs and balls."

"I don't plan to miss one, Marcia. They will be but dull affairs with *you* absent, however."

"But I shant be absent. I shall not say a word about her death and go everywhere, just as you said."

"I merely said what *I* should do. *I* am only a connection of Sophronia, as has so often been pointed out. You are her sister."

"But you are Gabriel's guardian!"

"True, and certainly Gab shall not attend any balls for the next six months."

"That is a very good idea. The young ought to be made to tow the line, and there is no saying, too, that he won't come into the money, when the will is read next year. You wouldn't want him to be gallivanting all over, and then get her money. It would look so very disrespectful."

"Yes, there is nothing gives one so sorry an opinion of people as to see them disregard the proprieties. Had it been my brother who died, I should certainly go into full mourning."

"Yes, but . . ."

"Miss Bliss," Hillary turned to her. "I leave you to console Mrs. Milmont on the necessity of missing the routs and balls. I have just recollected I wanted to show Miss Milmont the collection of sermons in the library. She is particularly interested in them."

"Sermons!" Mrs. Milmont said in wonder. "The girl is a changeling, I swear. It is all the fault of her grandparents, stuffing her head full of nonsense. Mrs. Milmont, you must know, is Quakerish . . . ," Sir Hillary heard her spiel as he went across the room to Claudia.

"Sermon time," he said, holding out his hand.

Claudia arose and went with him. Her mama watched them leave together and was struck by the charming couple they made. If only Claudia could be her right age, she might make a stab at Sir Hillary. This thought was banished as soon as it was born. For years past numbering, she herself had been trying to cajole him into mere friendship and knew him to be a tough nut to crack.

In the library he said directly, "Now, tell me what has happened."

"We must make an early try for the diamonds—tonight or tomorrow," she replied eagerly.

"Impossible. What is the reason for the haste?"

"We have discovered that someone else means to steal them."

"Jonathon will make a try, but I doubt he'll succeed."

"No, not Jonathon. Someone else—pray don't ask me, for I can't tell you, but . . ."

"Marcia? Your mama is not so foolish. She knows about the steel box and couldn't possibly . . ." He stopped as he noticed the strange expression on her face.

"Good God! You haven't by any chance had a visit from Mr. Blandings!"

"Oh, you know about him!"

"Everyone knows about him. He's been laying siege to your mama any time these two years. The wonder of it is that she doesn't capitulate. Not a bad-looking fellow and loaded with blunt. Is he here then?"

"No, he's coming."

"How do you know this?"

"That's not important. The thing is, we must get them before he arrives, for he is *huge*, you know, and an ironmonger, so he knows all about metals, mama says."

"I never knew him to be a felon."

"A felon! But he would be doing it for mama, and I suppose she is no more a felon than we are, for she only wants to get the diamonds for herself, as Luane does," Claudia defended.

"My dear girl! Are you really so green as you seem?" Sir Hillary asked. "You must know Luane cannot *keep* the diamonds, even if she manages to get them out of the grave. Till the year is up, they must be held in trust by Fletcher and myself to see what Sophie had in mind to be done with them. I can understand your craving the adventure of going after them, and in fact it's not a bad idea to get them put away safely, but I made sure *you* knew Loo couldn't keep them."

"You only meant to hand them over to Fletcher?" Claudia asked, her eyes like saucers. "I can't believe you to be serious. I took you for our friend."

"I hope I am."

"Well, you are not, Lord Turn-about. Like all inhabitants of Fair-speech, you are nothing but a deceiver."

"I *beg* your pardon?"

"I daresay you never read a Christian book! Well, I have taken up enough of your precious time," she said, making to push past him to the door.

"One moment, please," he said, grabbing her wrist. "I had no notion you were serious, but I can at least assure you that no one else, including Mr. Blandings, will get the diamonds. The guard has been hired, and he is *not* Tim Larriman, but a very reliable fellow, who will patrol with a gun and a pair of ferocious dogs."

"You *beast*! How are we to get past a gun and *two* dogs?"

"You cannot mean to try, just you two girls. I assure you Gabriel will not accompany you another time."

"Another Lord Turn-about!"

There was a sound at the door, and Luane entered. "Did you tell him?" she asked her cousin.

Claudia cast a fulminating eye on Sir Hillary and said, "He does not mean to help us, but rather hinder us by having set an armed man with two wild beasts to guard the grave."

"Sir Hillary, you have not done anything so shabby!" Luane declared.

"He did, and furthermore he never intended to let you keep the diamonds if we did get them, but only to hold them till the year is up and then meekly hand them over to whoever was supposed to get them."

"I can't believe this is true," Loo said, staring. "Tell me it's not true, Sir Hillary."

"Do you think I want to see you both in Newgate? What do you think would be the penalty for stealing fifty thousand pounds?"

"Stealing from a grave!" Luane retorted.

"Sophie can never have meant for them to remain there permanently. You may be sure she has some other end in mind for them. They may be intended for Miss Milmont, for all we know."

"I don't want them," Claudia said immediately. "I

think they are excessively ugly." She looked down at the set she wore round her neck as she spoke.

"And excessively valuable. If you think for one moment your mother would allow you to disclaim your interest in them, I must believe you to be more foolish than seems possible."

"She would never have left them to *me*," Claudia stated firmly. "I never met her till two minutes before she died. She didn't even *know* me."

"She only meant to make mischief," Loo snapped.

"And how well she has succeeded," Hillary remarked, frowning. "We can't stay here any longer. We'll discuss this again tomorrow."

"Before you go," Luane said, "who is the man hired to guard the grave?"

"His name is Bronfman, an ex-soldier, retired from Wellington's army because of losing a leg. An excellent shot."

"He no longer lives in the village."

"He will, starting tomorrow. Fletcher was in touch with him in Maldon, and he has agreed to take the job. And I cannot think you two can manage the job in one night, with no preparation." With this speech he turned and left the room, feeling he had in some manner treated them very badly, though he had only done what was right and sensible.

"I was never so deceived in anyone in my life," Luane said to her cousin. "The man with the dogs comes tomorrow, so tonight it will be only Tim Larriman, or maybe even no one. How are we to do it? We cannot possibly get the coffin out."

"No, we'd have to open it there, and we have no equipment."

"I shouldn't have the least notion how to manage a torch in any case," Loo fretted.

"Is the blacksmith a possible ally, if we paid him?"

"We have nothing to pay him with, and anyway he is a friend of Sir Hillary's, and has naturally no imagination. He would report us to the constable the moment we approached him."

"How then? Could the lock be filed open, I wonder? If it is only one of those bolts that shoots across like the kitchen door at Swallowcourt it could be done. Did Gabriel say how it was sealed?"

"No, he said only that it was a sealed coffin, and if I try to find out from him now, he will go running to Sir Hillary."

"We must give it a try. We'll take an axe and file, and see if we can't get it open."

"Sir Hillary has all kinds of tools in a workshop off the kitchen. If we could sneak down there we might find just what we need, if only we knew what the thing looked like, that we shall need—the torch thing."

"It would be justice if we could use his tools. How does one get to this workshop?"

"There's a little stairway at the far end of the corridor just outside this door. The workshop is right there at the bottom of the stairs," Loo said.

"Would it be locked?"

"No, why should he lock up a bunch of hammers and saws?"

"Let's go right now and see if we can find something."

"Yes, and we can just chuck the things outside the door, for there is a door leading right into the backyard, and we can pick them up on the way to the graveyard later tonight."

Their discussion was interrupted by Gabriel, come to ask them to play some music for the guests.

"Are you against us too?" Luane asked him, ignoring the mention of music.

"Sir Hillary is right, Loo. He always is, you know. It would be illegal, and . . ."

"And you are afraid of him," Loo scoffed. "What a coward! You were right, Claudia. How could I have considered marrying this poltroon?"

"Dash it, Loo, you know I'd help you if it would do the least bit of good. But with that Bronfman fellow coming . . ."

"I understand," Loo said in a frigid voice, her face hard as granite.

"No, you *don't* understand! You couldn't keep the diamonds if we did manage to get them, and anyway I don't see how we could."

"The coffin was *all* sealed up, was it?" Claudia asked, attempting to make it sound nonchalant.

"There was a lock an inch around. I never saw such a one in my life before."

"A bolt-type lock?" she asked.

"Yes, and welded shut."

Miss Milmont could not envisage exactly what this meant, but a lock, even an inch in diameter, could be filed through with time and patience.

Annoyed at their prolonged absence, Sir Hillary came to the door. "Everyone would like to hear some music," he said. Three irate pairs of eyes turned on him. "Are they seducing you, Gaby?" he asked. "It is quite futile, ladies. Gabriel agrees with me on the folly of your scheme. Come along."

Their compliance with this request was of so dallying and sullen a nature that the music coming out of it promised to be indifferent at best. They were accompanied to the music room, where Miss Bliss and Mrs. Milmont were already seated. "I'll slip down to the workshop while you play," Claudia whispered to Loo. Then turning aside to Thoreau she asked, "Could you direct me again to that chamber we used to wash up in the other evening? I see I have spilt some cream on my skirt and would like to sponge it out."

He took her to the hall and pointed out the way. "Shall I call a maid?"

This offering a great conflict to her true errand, she immediately recalled the exact location of the room and thanked him. She waited to see him walk off in another direction, wondering why he didn't return to the music room. No matter, he was gone, and she nipped smartly to the corridor Luane had pointed out. The captain, sitting near the door of the music room saw her turning down the corridor towards the library. He slipped silently from the room and followed her at a little distance.

The main portion of the house was well lit, and Miss Milmont was not prepared for the sudden plunge into nearly total darkness that confronted her when she was half-way down the staircase to the lower floor. She turned and went back to the library to get a candle. Across the hall, a door opened a crack and she fled to the staircase, but no one came out the door. A servant seeing what's going on, she thought, for she had made no effort to be silent, thinking herself alone in that part of the house. Glancing back, she saw the door remained closed, and she tiptoed silently now back down the stairs with her lone taper flickering in the breeze. Her heart was in her throat as she pushed open the door at the bottom of the stairs. She thought to find herself immediately in the workshop, but she was not. She stood in a long flagged area, with three doors opening off it, everyone closed. Luane had not explained that other activities than repairs were carried out here. The whole was dark and frightening. Her first inclination was to run back upstairs as fast as her legs would carry her. Surely Swallowcourt must have a file. This was madness to lurk about a cavernous, unknown, extremely dark corridor, hiding unimagined horrors behind every portal. The echo of lurid fiction reeled in her head; the skeleton behind the black veil, the eerie hand, not connected to any human form, the disembodied miasma of evil empowered with magic properties. The taper in her hand trembled and she turned to leave, took one step, then heard a rustle behind her. Her heart rose from throat to mouth, and with every nerve on edge she peered fearfully over her shoulder. A slinky ginger cat glided from the shadows, brushed past her skirt in a supercilious manner, and scooted upstairs. It was such an anticlimax after expecting to see a ghost at least that her spirits raised a little, and he decided to try one door—the one closest to the bottom of the stairs, since Loo had said the workshop was there.

She pushed the door in, slowly, and held her taper

108

high. She saw garden chairs and tables, empty flower pots, and long strings of Japanese lanterns, and realized she was in the storage area for the happy paraphernalia of summer. She closed the door. Should she try one more? They would be soon looking for her; she had thought it would be the work of a minute to throw a file out a door, but already several minutes had passed. With this poor shred of an excuse for her cowardice, she literally ran to the stairs, bolted up them to the corridor and safety. Yet it did not appear so safe as formerly. Since her descent, someone, a servant presumably, had been around to extinguish the hall lights, and the darkness was still all around her but for her own single taper. She went to the study to return the candle, and it too was in total darkness. She chose a resting place near the door for the candle, blew it out, and reached up to put the holder on top of a pedestal holding a marble bust of some philosopher of yore. With a sigh of relief that the ordeal was over, even if a total failure, she turned to leave. And then it fell—a crashing blow on her left temple, and she crumpled to the floor. Just at the doorway to unconsciousness, she felt a strong pair of hands go around her neck.

Chapter Nine

In the music room, Luane sat at the pianoforte and Gabriel stood beside her, looking through music which they might perform together, for he had quite a fine tenor voice. Everyone was ready and waiting except Miss Milmont. Sir Hillary had taken up a seat beside Marcia and Miss Bliss, and Jonathon lounged in a chair at the end of the row.

"Now what can be keeping that girl of mine?" Marcia said, looking towards the door.

"She spilt something on her gown, and went to clean it off," Hillary told her.

"The clumsy child! It is well she didn't wear her best gown. With this mourning come on us so unexpectedly, she hasn't a decent stitch to wear, I swear, for her gowns are all bright and lively, as becomes a young girl."

Thoreau stared at her with an unblinking eye and said nothing.

"What can be taking her such an age?" her mother demanded petulantly after another moment. "I'll send

Luane after her." She went to the pianoforte. Luane was not in the least averse to go after her cousin, and as no one observed her direction, she naturally headed towards the stairs leading to the workshop. As she passed down the dark passage she decided to return for a light, and as she once again proceeded down the corridor, she heard a low moan coming from the library. In an instant, she had discovered its source and ran for help.

"She's had an accident!" she shouted, hurrying into the music room, and from the excited state of the bearer of the news, no one took it for any minor mishap. Everyone jumped up and ran to the door.

"Oh, my poor baby!" Mrs. Milmont moaned, pulling out one of her monogrammed handkerchiefs. "What did she do, the silly goose, stumble on the stairs?"

"No, she's in the library."

"The library?" Thoreau asked and led the way towards it, with the others hustling after him. "Why are all the lights out?" he asked. "Gab, get these lamps lit."

Miss Milmont had achieved a sitting position by the time her helpers reached her, and had a hand to her throbbing head. Simultaneous enquiries from everyone sent her into a relapse, and she leaned against the shoulder closest to her. Sir Hillary had gone down on one knee and supported her.

"We must get her to a sofa," he said, and lifted her from the floor. "Loo, fetch some wine," he said over his shoulder, and he was given room to jostle past the onlookers. Deeming the Blue Saloon unsuitable, for they would all be hovering around and pestering her, he took her to a smaller parlor formerly used by his mama as a reading and sewing room. When Loo returned with the wine, Hillary told Gabriel to call for Dr. Hill.

But Claudia was rallying by this time, and said, "I don't want a doctor."

"Call him, Gab," Hillary repeated.

"He aint at home, uncle. You remember Mrs.

111

Grosvenor is in labor. Cook said he went after dinner, and he'll surely be there the night."

As Grosvenor's was an inconvenient seven miles distant, Thoreau said to Claudia, "Drink this wine, and tell us how it feels."

She took a sip, then put her fingers gingerly to her temple and said it hurt like the very devil.

"But how did it happen, my love?" her mama demanded.

"I was attacked," she said.

"Nonsense! You slipped and hit your temple against the edge of the pedestal in the dark," Sir Hillary objected. "I can't think why the lights were extinguished so early. You were lying right at the foot of the pedestal. How did it come you were . . ." There was a general babble from all present, and he said, "You'd better go and leave us. All this racket can't do her any good."

"No!" Claudia said, trying to sit up. "Let Luane stay with me."

"My dear, surely it is my place to stay with my little girl," Marcia said, deeply offended.

With a truly deceitful expression of concern, Claudia answered, "Your poor nerves, mama. I'm sure you must be in worse state than I am myself. You will want a glass of wine and a rest."

"To be sure I am as nervous as a kitten with all this commalia. My nerves . . . But I shant leave you, darling."

Miss Bliss surveyed the scene of confusion before her and said to her rosy-cheeked companion, "You look white as a ghost, Mrs. Milmont. Come with me, and I shall get you a cordial. You will want all your strength to tend your little girl when she gets home."

"That might be best," she said in a weak voice, her interest already waned upon seeing that the foolish girl had only tripped, and likely broken something valuable besides, when the whole truth should come out. She allowed herself to be led away, supported by Miss Bliss. Tewksbury and Gabriel were strongly inclined to remain behind, but Miss Bliss gathered them up also on her way, and led them all to the Blue Saloon to discuss in total ignorance how the accident had come about, and what Claudia had been doing in the library when she had gone upstairs to clean her gown.

When Luane, Claudia, and Thoreau were alone in the small parlor, he said, "Are you well enough to tell us what happened now?"

"As if you didn't know!" she flashed out angrily.

"I haven't the least idea what you're talking about. And how came you to be in my library in the dark?"

The girls exchanged a guilty glance. Miss Milmont chose to defend herself by the time-honored method of attack. "You *hit* me, and were about to strangle me as well." She reached to ease her strained throat with her fingers, and the diamond necklace came off in her hands.

Thoreau stared at her in patent disbelief. "Your brain is disordered with the blow."

She handed him the necklace. "This has come loose. You might as well take it."

"Claudia, did someone truly hit you?" asked Luane, a much more believing auditor than Sir Hillary.

"Yes, I had just gone into the library to put back the candle. The whole place was in total darkness, and just after I blew out the candle, I felt a stunning blow on my temple."

"You slipped and rapped your head against the edge of the pedestal. Was it you who blew out all the candles?" Hillary asked.

"No, they were on when I went down . . ." She pulled herself up short. "I didn't slip and I didn't bang my head on the pedestal! I had to reach *up* to put down the candle, and I'd like to know how I come to have this bruise where there are no sharp edges on the column."

Thoreau thought about it for a moment and had to acknowledge to himself that the top of the pedestal was a good foot higher than Miss Milmont's temple. The bruise indicated having been hit with a sharp edge—it was a straight line, red, turning purple around the

113

edges. It looked very sore. "You'll want a cold pack for that bruise. Loo, would you . . ."

"No!" Claudia said sharply. "Don't leave me, cousin. He means to hit me again and will likely succeed in strangling me this time."

"You are not rational!" Hillary said angrily, and went to the door himself and summoned a servant by hollering loudly, while Miss Milmont winced at the noise. Returning he said, "Why should I do anything so foolish?"

"Because you mean to prevent us from getting the diamonds!" Loo charged. "And I daresay he will too," she added to Claudia. "You will be in no shape to go grave-digging tonight, and by tomorrow the soldier will be there with his dogs."

"Good God! You can't mean you're still harping on that!" Hillary looked down at the necklace Claudia had handed him and stuck it into his jacket pocket. "I can't believe you're so insane as to think two girls could unseal a steel casket, welded shut."

"There is only a latch," Loo told him. "And your file . . ."

"I don't keep my files in the library." Comprehension dawned on him. "So that's where you were going *down* to—the workshop!"

"I was only getting a book from the library," Claudia said, shamefacedly.

He looked at her, frustration lending an angry hue to his countenance. "A Bible, I daresay. There is no making any sense of this business. Why should anyone attack you? Who could have done it?"

The cold compress arrived, causing a diversion. "I think *I* know *why*," Loo said significantly, "and as to *who*, I can only say you were very late in coming into the music room, Sir Hillary. Gabriel and I were waiting ages for you to show up."

Claudia directed an accusing stare at him and rubbed her temple.

"Don't be absurd!" Thoreau sneered at Luane. "Did

you happen to notice whether Jonathon was in the music room the whole time?"

"No, not the whole time. He went to get a shawl for Aunt Marcia; it was rather chilly in the music room, you recall, and he said she would take a chill."

"*He* suggested it?" Thoreau asked.

"He may have suggested it, but she was shivering, and I was rather chilly myself, too. You didn't have any fire in there. And besides, he was back long before *you*."

"What is *your* alibi, Sir Hillary?" Claudia demanded.

"My *alibi* is that I was speaking to my housekeeper about packing you two waifs a lunch basket to take home."

"I hope you put in the left-over cream buns?" Luane said with a question in her voice.

"And the rest of the Chantilly," Miss Milmont added weakly. "If it is not too difficult to carry."

"Mrs. Robinson could put it in a covered bowl," Loo suggested. It began to seem as though the attack had been forgotten. Hillary could only stare at their guilelessness.

"You are forgetting there was an alleged attempt on your life, Miss Milmont," he said ironically.

"I am not forgetting it; it is exactly why I think I shall require more nourishing sustenance than I am likely to get at Swallowcourt."

"You don't fear a little arsenic in the Chantilly?" he asked.

"Well, I don't suppose you meant to kill me. But I bet he'll put laudanum in it," she said aside to Loo. "We'd better not eat it till after we have the diamonds safe. Then I shouldn't mind a good night's sleep."

"You are staying here the night," Hillary announced. "You are not well enough to travel. And don't think your mother will rescue you. It will give her an excellent excuse to stay and have a look around any cupboards or attics she missed out on this evening."

"You can let me go back to Swallowcourt. I am not ripe for any digging after this. I'm sorry, Loo."

"It's not your fault," Loo admitted grandly. "And besides, I have had an excellent idea. We shall pack a fine lunch for Bronfman with some of Sir Hillary's leftovers and put laudanum in it, as Sir Hillary meant to do to us, and then he will fall asleep tomorrow night, and we shall steal the diamonds. Oh, and we must be sure to give something to the dogs too."

Sir Hillary stared in disbelief, but he refrained from commenting on the plan. He was coming to the conclusion that the girls were in dead earnest, and every precaution would have to be taken to keep them from trying to get at the diamonds. Glancing at Claudia, who still lay back against the pillows, rubbing her throat, he said, "I see your emerald is safe. I wonder if that could have been the object of your attack."

"Jonathon, he means," Loo explained to Claudia. "He tried to steal my tiara; I daresay he would snitch your ring if he could. You must keep it in a safe place. That Tuggins is all over the house, sneaking into all our rooms when we are not about."

"I wonder," Claudia said, rubbing her ring, with a speculative expression. "But he might have had it off my finger in a moment, without strangling me."

"I thought you couldn't get it off," Loo asked.

"Oh, no, it slips off easily. I only tell mama it is tight, so she won't take it from me."

"Surely this matter of your strangulation is imaginary," Thoreau said, believing with Luane that they had hit on the true explanation of Miss Milmont's attack.

"No, I could *feel* fingers around my neck before ever I hit the floor. Well, very likely that is what loosened the clasp on Loo's necklace. You recall it fell off, and it has a safety clasp."

"Yes, it is an exact duplicate of the original," Sir Hillary replied, drawing the necklace from his pocket. "In fact, I fail to see how it came undone, for it has

116

the little gold chain and hook besides the regular clasp."

"I'm not sure I bothered to do up the safety hook," Claudia told him. "I was only trying it on, you know, then we left the room rather suddenly."

He returned the necklace to his pocket once more, but was obviously dissatisfied. "Are you feeling better now?" he asked Claudia.

"Yes, and I should like to go home. What I want above anything is a good night's sleep."

"I wish you and your mother will stay here the night. I'll take you to Swallowcourt first thing tomorrow."

There was no reason not to stay, still Claudia was reluctant. She no longer believed Sir Hillary had attacked her. Jonathon was a much more acceptable villain. It would be pleasant just to go to bed now, in a room with a fire, which Swallowcourt would not have, and a surfeit of servants to fetch and carry, and likely bring one hot cocoa in bed in the morning. Still, she did not want to stay. "I should prefer to go to Swallowcourt," she said.

"You still think it was I who attacked you," he said matter-of-factly. "I did not, and if you insist on going back there, promise me you will take good care of yourself and your emerald."

"Of course."

"You must promise me one more thing. You will not go to Sophie's grave tonight."

From confusion and pain and nervousness after her ordeal, Claudia felt suddenly ill-used. A warm tear started in her eyes, and she groped for a handkerchief. "My reticule is in the Blue Saloon," she said. This seemed like the last straw. "I daresay my poor lonely guinea has been stolen by now," and on this childish complaint she burst out crying.

"Now see what you've done," Loo accused Hillary. "As though she is fit to go digging tonight. There, there, cousin," she patted Claudia's shoulder comfortingly. "I'll fetch your reticule." She went off to the

Blue Saloon, where Miss Milmont's little black patent bag lay unmolested in the corner of the settee.

Sir Hillary pulled out his handkerchief and handed it to Miss Milmont, who took it and wiped angrily at her tears. "I can't think why I'm crying," she said. "I never cry."

"It is a delayed reaction from your attack," he offered. "Finish your wine." He took up the glass and held it to her lips. She sipped, then sniffed, and wiped her eyes again.

"I *was* attacked, you know," she insisted, her tear-stained eyes looking at him disconsolately.

"I know you were, and I am sorry it happened in my home. I hope it will not give you a disgust of the place."

"Oh no, it is the Palace Beautiful," she replied.

"It is not a palace."

"It reminds me of Bunyan's Palace Beautiful. You remember—'and behold there was a very stately palace before him, the name whereof was Beautiful.' That is what I thought when I first saw it, on Monday. Palace Beautiful was where Christian met the saints and virtues, and was strengthened to go and fight the devil on the way to heaven. Grandmama Milmont is very fond of *The Pilgrim's Progress*. We have readings from it two nights a week. The rest of the time it is the Bible."

"I am not much familiar with Bunyan's book. I started to read it once."

"It is not so very interesting, but he has wonderful names for everything. The Slough of Despond is my favourite. I'm sorry I called you Lord Turn-about."

"Another of Bunyan's characters?" She nodded. "I am sorry if I did a turn-about on you, but after giving the matter consideration, I thought it best, and I hope you will, too, when you have thought about it."

Miss Milmont appeared to accept the apology, but she made no rash promises.

"We shall have a good long talk about all this when you are better. I'll call on you tomorrow."

"Yes," Claudia said sadly. She couldn't say quite

what saddened her, for to tell the truth, she was relieved not to have to go to the graveyard that night.
Leaving the comforts of Chanely had something to do
with it, yet it was not precisely that either.

Sir Hillary regarded her silently a moment, then
asked suddenly, "Why is it you are going to such
lengths to help Luane get the diamonds? You scarcely
know her, and it seems to me you have as much need
of them, and as much right to them, as she has."

"No, I have neither the need of them nor the right
to them. It was understood Sophie would provide for
Loo, and she has not done it. Another inhabitant of
Fair-speech, you see. It was wrong of Aunt Sophie to
make her fair speeches, then serve Loo a cruel blow
like this. I have a good home with my grandparents
and had never any thought of inheriting them. Indeed,
I didn't expect my emerald." She looked at her ring in
a loving way as she spoke.

"Do you like jewelry?" he asked.

"I have a heathen weakness for pretty things," she
confessed readily. "But I am not allowed to indulge it.
Grandmama says a woman's finest adornment is virtue.
She won't want me to wear this ring. I might as well
give it to mama, I suppose." She cast a wistful glance
at her ring as she said this and rubbed it lovingly.

"Don't be absurd!" Hillary said in a harsh voice, to
hide the emotion her pathetic speech had raised.

Loo came in with the reticule, and Miss Milmont
was aided to the door with a supporter on either side.

"It is foolishness for you to be going home," Hillary
scolded as they went along to the Blue Saloon, but
knowing she did not wish to remain, he said nothing
when the others came out, or Marcia would make her
stay whether she wanted it or no.

A few moments were spent in Loo handing her pendant back to Thoreau, in the basket of food being
given to Jonathon to carry, and in adieux being exchanged between host and guests. With a final volley of
compliments from Marcia, they were off.

Mrs. Milmont was loud in her praise of the evening

all the way home, with only a few adjurations to her daughter for being so clumsy as to slip and bang her head. As Miss Bliss discovered as soon as they were inside the door that Mrs. Milmont had no thought of helping her daughter get to bed, she went along with Claudia to her room and got her into her nightdress.

"Have you got your emerald in a safe place?" she asked before leaving.

"Under my pillow."

"It would be better under your mattress," she advised. "That's where I keep my sapphire while I sleep. Has it occurred to you that whoever hit you might have been after it?"

"Yes, that has occurred to me," Claudia answered.

Nothing more specific than that was said, but there was a fair understanding between them that the hopeful thief wore a scarlet tunic.

Gabriel and Hillary sat alone in the Blue Saloon having a single glass of wine before retiring. "What do you make of this attack, uncle?" Gab asked. "I think Miss Milmont must be a trifle hysterical, don't you?"

"She is overwrought certainly, and no wonder."

"What I meant was, she must have slipped and imagined she was attacked, don't you think? Who would attack her in this house? You? Me? The servants? It doesn't make any sense."

"There were others in the house. She didn't imagine it. There was a welt on her temple."

"You mean Jonathon, I suppose, but why should he risk attacking her here, when it had to be a very rushed job? He might steal her ring any night while she sleeps, without so much risk of getting caught. Or have Tuggins do it for him."

"That has been puzzling me considerably. He must have done the whole in a flash, and how did he know she was in the library when she said she was going upstairs?"

"Far as that goes, what the deuce was she doing in the library? I find her an unaccountable woman, but I expect it had something to do with digging up Aunt

120

Sophie if the truth were known." A youthful smile parted Gabriel's lips, and he was soon laughing merrily.

"What's eating you, cawker?"

"I was just thinking what you said about Miss Milmont. Said she'd be a fine maiden aunt in ten years, or some such thing, and just the one to mind my and Loo's brats. I tremble to leave Loo alone with her, let alone a bunch of kids."

"I said nothing of the sort!"

"Yes, you did. You don't think they'll tackle the grave tonight, do you?"

"Poor Miss Milmont could scarcely walk. I can't imagine why she insisted on going home. No, they'll not go to the graveyard tonight, and much good it would do them if they did."

They discussed the matter for some moments, then Gabriel went to bed and Hillary spoke to his butler, who informed him that no order had been given for the lights in the study corridor to be extinguished. The attack was no secret to the servants by that time, and the butler added with a meaningful look that the captain had been seen in that area, but sometime before the attack, and he was not making any accusation, mind, but just telling what was seen.

"That confirms it then," Sir Hillary said, and went to his bedroom. He removed the two necklaces from his pocket—the sapphire pendant and the diamonds—and put them back in the case. He then sat down, lit a cheroot, and sat smoking it in silence for fifteen minutes, a frown of deep concentration on his face. Arising, he went back to the replica case and examined it carefully, first the glass box, then each piece of jewelry individually. "So that's it!" he said at length. "The old devil, making a May game of us all. I could happily kill you, dear Aunt Sophronia, if you weren't already dead."

Of course, he only imagined that echoing laugh that sounded from the corner of the room. He locked the case, put it under his bed, and went to the dresser.

121

From the bottom drawer he extracted a black leather case, opened the lid, and lifted a silver-barreled dueling pistol from it. Carefully he charged it, and put it under his pillow, before he undressed, locked his door, and went to bed.

Chapter Ten

It was raining the next day. Claudia awoke with a nagging headache, and when she touched her temple, she remembered the preceding evening. She had no idea what time it was. The sun, her only time piece, not being visible, she had to guess, and from her lack of fatigue, she guessed it to be time to get up. Her regular hour of rising was a puritanical seven a.m., and she knew it to be well past that, but in the holidays she was allowed to sleep in as late as she liked. Mama seldom rose before noon. At mama's house, the mornings were the best part of the day. She had a lavish breakfast with a servant to tend her, then sat lolling on a heathen velvet settee with a whole pile of satin pillows, looking at fashion magazines, and eating as many bonbons as she liked, for mama had always a box of them on the table. None of these luxuries were available at Swallowcourt, of course, still there was a hamper of treats from Chanely to be indulged in, and she arose and dressed hastily, forgetting her headache once she was out of bed.

Downstairs she discovered it was nine-thirty, and already Luane sat at the table, eating cream buns and drinking coffee.

"How are you feeling this morning, cousin?" Loo asked, and looked at her bruise. "Pity we have no plaster for that."

"I feel all right."

"Isn't it heavenly having such a breakfast? Better than Christmas. When I'm rich I'll have them every morning—in bed," she said, passing the plate along. Claudia took off two and poured herself a cup of coffee.

"Loo, we must make plans," Claudia began at once, fearing their privacy might be interrupted. "This rain will make our job miserable."

Luane sat chewing her cream bun, her little face alive with interest, her dark eyes shining. "And not only the rain," she added. "We were very foolish to let Sir Hillary know what we meant to do. You may be sure he'll be watching the graveyard every night to stop us. He's like a dog with a bone when he gets an idea, and he thinks it's wrong of us to steal the diamonds. I warned you what a prude he is."

"It is wrong to steal in the general way, but I cannot consider this stealing, when our aunt only means to leave the diamonds in the ground to turn to dust."

"Goodness, how long will it take?" Luane asked, worried.

"Ages and ages, but they are no good to anyone buried. Of course, if she really means them for someone else at the end of the year, I suppose it *is* stealing to take them. But we could always give them back."

"She meant nothing of the sort," Luane assured her, licking a finger on which some whipped cream had become lodged. "I considered that when Sir Hillary said it, for he is generally right, you know. One of those horrid people who always know what is best, but this time he is mistaken. It just reminds me of a plum velvet gown Aunt Sophie had, and she was going to throw it out. I asked her for it, to have it made over for myself, but she was angry because my little spaniel wet on her carpet, so she had Rankin throw it into the grate right in front of my eyes. She was *spiteful*, cousin—you have no idea. This time she was angry that I didn't marry Gabriel, so she burnt the diamonds—buried them, I mean, and you can be sure she never meant for anyone to have them."

"She sounds truly wicked!" Claudia gasped, much impressed with this tale.

"Oh, that's nothing!" Loo continued, sipping her coffee between words. "Another time she bet Sir Hillary her Persian chess set he couldn't beat her at chess, for she thought she was quite good, though she cheated when no one was looking. Well, I was sitting right there in the room the whole time, and it was very boring, too, since she always took forever to move her pieces; and when he had her in check, she lifted her knee and sent all the pieces flying about the bed, pretending it was an accident, and *then* pretended she had a move all figured out to save herself from checkmate. That was the day she promised Sir Hillary her set when she died, because he said the devil would get her for it. And she didn't give it to him either, the sneak."

"But Miss Bliss means to give it to him. She says that was the intention."

"Sophie promised it to him, and she didn't give it to him, and she promised me the diamonds, and she didn't give them to me, but I mean to get them, only I don't see how we shall ever do it."

"And I have to leave in ten days," Claudia worried.

The butler came to the door and announced Sir Hillary and Gabriel, who came in brushing water from their faces.

"You are just in time for breakfast," Luane said. Sir Hillary looked and smiled to see the girls so soon into their hamper of food. It seemed they actually were starved here at Swallowcourt.

After greetings were exchanged, the gentlemen were seated and given a turgid cup of coffee, from which even three spoonfuls of sugar did not take the bitter edge. "How is your head this morning?" Sir Hillary asked Claudia. "You should put something on it."

"No plaster," Loo said.

"It's tender," Claudia answered, not wishing to belittle the nature of the wound she had sustained under his roof. There being no plasters in the house, she pulled a curl down over it.

"Are you come to discuss my diamonds?" Loo asked.

"Let us call them by their proper name—the Beresford Diamonds," Sir Hillary corrected her. "No, I am come to see how Miss Milmont goes on but, of course, there is no setting a toe in this house without discussing the diamonds. I hope you two have come to reason on the subject and decided they must be left where they are."

"To turn to dust in the ground!" Loo charged. "No, indeed, we have not decided that."

"We really should see about sending this girl to school. She is ignorant as a swan," Hillary said to Gabriel, who smiled at his sweetheart to show he disagreed with this comparison.

"Maybe Sir Hillary is right," Claudia said, with a narrowing of her eyes at her cousin.

"Cousin! You cannot mean *you* are going to desert me too," Loo squealed.

Claudia continued to narrow her eyes and dart little sidewise looks at Thoreau, intending to convey to Miss Beresford that their plans had best remain secret from this obstruction in their path. "We do not wish to set Sir Hillary on edge, and have him haunting the graveyard every night to stop us," she said in a voice laden with significance. "It will be better for us to forget the plan, since he has taken it in such aversion."

"Oh, Oh, yes, *I* see," Luane answered, smiling triumphantly, and fooling neither gentleman that she had the least intention of abandoning her quest for the gems.

"That sets my mind at rest considerably," Hillary announced in a wooden voice.

"It's too bad it's such an awful day," Luane said to Gabriel, looking out the dusty windows to the rain drizzling down outside. Then she remembered she was angry with him, and turned aside to take another cream bun, passing the plate around the table till it stopped at Miss Milmont.

"I hope tomorrow will be better," Thoreau said. "I plan to go on a little trip."

"Are you taking Gabriel back to Cambridge?" Miss Beresford asked, sounding as though it were a matter of the utmost indifference to herself.

"No, not immediately. We go in quite the other direction, to London."

"What for?" Loo asked, with all the familiarity of an old friend.

"Business. Your business as it happens, brat. It has to do with my guardianship of you."

"Are you looking for someone to take care of me?" she asked eagerly. "I was hoping you would give me a Season, but ought we not to wait till next year, because of being in mourning?"

"It has nothing to do with presenting you to society, this year or next."

"If you are looking for a chaperone, you needn't bother. Claudia is the one I want."

"Miss Milmont?" Thoreau asked in wide-eyed disbelief. "It is not the custom for one young unmarried lady to set up as chaperone to another, delightful though the idea sounds."

"Don't be such a sapskull, Loo," Gabriel exclaimed.

"Claudia is not *young*. She is old, and it is only because her mother wants to go on being young forever that she is dressed up in such youthful outfits, isn't it, cousin?"

Claudia's lips quivered, and she swallowed a mouthful of cream. "That—that is not exactly what I said," she disagreed in a strange voice, while her cheeks crimsoned alarmingly.

"It is so, and you said you would love to be my chaperone, don't you remember? Sir Hillary will introduce us to the pink of the *ton*, and we will both marry great titled gentlemen. If it is only that you haven't yet put on your caps, why there is nothing to stop you from doing so. Sir Hillary can buy you some in London."

"And a gray wig to complete the effect," Sir Hillary added.

"We don't want her to look *too* old or no one will have her, even a widower. Claudia has more or less decided on a widower with a family, so that she won't have to bother having any children."

"Indeed!" Sir Hillary said, staring at the pair of them. "That sounds a fine practical notion."

"Yes," Loo went on calmly. "Since we can't lay eggs like the birds, you know, and have the whole litter over with at once, it saves being confined every year."

"Shut up, Loo!" Gabriel shouted, with a fearful glance at Thoreau, who usually objected to such unseemly talk from Miss Beresford. But Hillary was sitting, sipping on the dreadful coffee with an impassive face, looking at Miss Milmont rather than Luane.

"Mind your manners, cawker," he said, without even glancing at Gabriel. "What else have you and Miss Milmont decided?" he urged Loo on, in an easy, agreeable manner.

"You must know it is all a farradiddle," Miss Milmont explained, still pink around the ears, the last of her blush to dissipate.

"Another inhabitant of Fair-Speech?" he asked. "Lady Turn-about, in fact."

"You know it is impossible! I would never be allowed to be Loo's guardian. I am much too young."

"How old are you?"

"Twenty- . . . Never mind. I am too young for that, and have no experience along such lines."

"Ah, well, *twenty* is too young. I hoped when Loo put your age as 'old' you were at least a quarter of a century."

"Surely twenty-five is still too young?" Claudia asked, with a newly awakening interest. By the time the year of

128

mourning was up, she would be twenty-five, and how she would love to be Loo's chaperone!

"It is rather young for a single lady," Hillary agreed. "But in any case you are only twenty, and I cannot believe Loo would wish to delay her debut five years. Or is it a widower with his family already grown *you* have in your eye too, brat?"

"Oh, no, *I* am young enough to have my own brood. But aren't you older than twenty, Cousin?"

"A little older," the embarrassed girl confessed.

"Don't be impertinent," Hillary cautioned Luane.

"Well, *you* asked her how old she is."

"And did not question her reply. I doubt very much Mrs. Milmont would give her consent in any case. There is just a certain something about a daughter acting the chaperone that takes the bloom off her mama. And we have already spoken to Miss Bliss about the position. I have some hopes, however, that Miss Milmont may be allowed to play propriety for one day. I want to take you to London with me, Loo, and am hopeful Mrs. Milmont will allow her daughter to come along. Gabriel comes too. We would have to leave very early in the morning to get there and back in one day and still have time for a little sight-seeing. The trip takes three hours, more or less. If we can leave at eight, we will be there by eleven, and if we leave London at four, we can be back here by seven—just getting dark. Will you agree, Miss Milmont, if your mother gives her consent?"

"I would love it of all things," Claudia answered, glowing radiantly. "But I doubt mama . . ."

"Leave mama to me," Sir Hillary told her, allowing a small smile to lighten his face.

"Why am I to go with you?" Loo asked.

"Don't ask embarrassing questions," Hillary chided her. "How else can I make an excuse to take your cousin along?"

"You are a complete hand, Sir Hillary," Loo laughed. "As though you want to take Cousin Claudia."

"I trust your good nature will overlook that solecism,"

Sir Hillary said to Claudia. "The girl is totally lacking in graces."

"She has an awkward habit of blurting out the truth," Miss Milmont agreed, laughing also, but too happy at the anticipation of the trip to take offense at anything.

"She is no mind reader, however," he objected mildly.

"What sight-seeing shall we do?" Luane asked eagerly. "Will you take us to Astley Circus? Will it be open?"

"I doubt your chaperone will be interested to see the horses perform," Sir Hillary replied in a disparaging tone.

"I should adore to see them!" the chaperone corrected his misapprehension immediately. "I *beg* mama to take me every year, but she says it is underbred. She *did* let her housekeeper take me to Madame Tussaud's once— oh, years ago, just shortly after papa died. But we ought not to be so merry when we are in mourning."

"Ah, well, if our lack of breeding is to lead us to Astley's, it can't be expected we shall observe any laws of mourning. Your mama intends keeping it mum among her cronies, and no one will know you in any case. Gab and I shall slip off our armbands, and we'll never be taken for a party of mourners."

"It seems wicked to be having such a good time when we ought to be sad," Miss Milmont said, but in no very firm manner, and she allowed herself to be overridden by the others.

"Let's ask Aunt Marcia now, cousin, so that the matter can be settled," Loo said, hopping up from the table.

"It is not yet ten-thirty, and mama never rises before noon."

"Wake her up," Loo directed immediately.

"She is mad as a hornet to be wakened early. That will only set her jaw against the plan. It is better to wait till she's up."

"Let *me* put it to her," Hillary said.

"You won't want to wait so long," Claudia pointed out. "I'm sure *you* could cut a wheedle with her, but it might be two hours before she comes down."

"I am flattered at your confidence in my wheedling abilities, but there is nothing to do outside on such a day as this. We'll see if we can find a few chips to set a fire in the Crimson Saloon and be comfortable there. I wish to speak to Miss Bliss, too. *She* will not lie abed till noon. In fact, she is surely up and about somewhere already. Do you think you might ask her to see me, brat?" Hillary asked Loo.

Luane went to get Miss Bliss and, when they came down, the others had removed to the Crimson Saloon. No chips were in evidence, however, and as Thoreau's idea of pulling a couple of legs off one of the rickety chairs was vetoed by an outraged Miss Milmont, they all sat shivering in the gloom and chill.

Miss Bliss carried a long, rectangular wooden box in her hands and, when she had said good-day to the gentlemen, she handed it to Sir Hillary. "This is your chess set."

"It isn't, you know. She left it to you," he reminded her.

"To dispose of as I see fit. I see fit to give it to you. It was her intention. Besides, I don't play chess."

"The temptation is too strong to resist," he said, accepting the box. "I own I have had my eye on it for years. Thank you, Blissful." He smiled and kissed her cheek, then opened the box, and set the carved pieces on the board, admiring each as he did so, and trying to encourage the others to find them as beautiful as he himself did.

"They are much finer than grandpapa's," Claudia told him. "He has a set with the black pieces carved in wood and the white in mule bone. He is a very good player. At least, I think he is; he always beats me."

"Do you play chess, Miss Milmont?" he asked with interest. "But how felicitous! Our long vigil till your mama comes down is taken care of. Will you be black or white?"

"I know the moves," she replied, which fell upon his ears dolefully. He had suffered through many fifteen-minute games with players who 'knew the moves' and nothing else about the game. Still, there was nothing else to do, and they sat down at a buhl table and chose their colors.

"You be white. That means you have to go first," she told him.

"You know that, too!" he praised her. "And here you let on to be an amateur."

"The horses are beautifully carved," she commented, viewing the knights.

"Yes, the *horses* are generally referred to as knights," he began his instruction. "And these big pieces with the crosses on top are our kings." His shapely hand with its long, slender fingers pointed out the pieces. "You know, I collect, that the object of the game is not to whisk as many of my pieces as possible off the board, but to place my king in check."

"Yes, I know that," she assured him. "These little crowns are very nicely done, aren't they? They are my favorite pieces, for they can hop all over the place."

"And the little crowns are called queens," he continued.

"That's right. The oval with a slash is called a bishop, I remember. They go sidewise. Grandpa doesn't talk much when he plays, but he is very good."

Hillary advanced his king's pawn to the fourth square. Claudia followed with the same move. He was unsure whether she was following him from ignorance, or did it with intention. He advanced his black knight, and when Claudia countered by advancing her queen one space forward to protect her pawn, he felt the stirring of hope that she knew what she was doing. When she had, within the space of ten minutes relieved him of one of his 'horses,' as she persisted in calling the knights, and a pawn, which she called by its correct name, he was alerted to danger and settled into the game with enthusiasm.

"I believe I can switch my little tower and move the king two spaces over here," she said, castling with a doubtful glance at her opponent.

"Yes, but I don't see why you are doing it."

"I see that bishop you have over there in the corner, waiting to slide out and take me," she replied. "Those bishops are the plaguiest things. Grandpapa is always finishing me off with them."

Sir Hillary had failed to observe this fact himself, though he didn't mention it. "You play much faster than Aunt Sophie," Luane remarked. She and Gabriel were watching over their shoulders.

"And much better," Hillary murmured.

"Grandpa hates waiting forever for me to make a move. Check, madame," she said.

"What?" Hillary shouted.

"I told you you have to watch out for these sliding bishops," she warned. Then he saw her bishop attacking his queen. "See, he's way off there, a mile away, but with a clean field to swoop down on your little crown."

"You are not obliged to point out when you have my queen in check," he said.

"Am I not? Well, I wish I had known that. Grandpa always tells *me*."

"It is a courtesy merely."

"I wouldn't have bothered to be courteous. Still, it's an even duller game when the crown is off the board," she remarked, stifling a yawn.

"I trust you don't mean to doze off on me entirely," Hillary said with a lazy smile.

Despite Miss Milmont's yawns and lackadaisical manner of moving her pieces while chatting over her shoulder to her cousin, it was the most enjoyable game Sir Hillary had played in years. On the stroke of twelve Miss Milmont pointed out to him that he was floored, for he couldn't move his king *here* because of her pawn, or *here* because of that sneaky old bishop in the corner, or *here* because he hadn't thought to move his own pawn, or *here* because of the rook, which she called a tower.

"Check and checkmate in fact," he declared, incredulous at being beaten by a mere girl, and one besides who wasn't half paying attention.

"Grandpapa always says, 'I've got you now, Missie,' when I can't move my king. I daresay we don't play it properly."

"You do your grandfather an injustice. If he has taught you to play this well, you don't need the fancy jargon to go with it. We will have a rematch very soon, Lady

Turn-about! You and your 'knowing the moves.' Fair-speech indeed! You conned me properly."

"You should have tipped the board like Aunt Sophie," Loo laughed.

"I didn't notice she had me checkmated. It was the bishop hiding in the corner."

"I didn't get many of your pieces off," Claudia consoled him. "See, I only have three pawns and one horse and one little tower, and, of course, your crown. It was the crown that did you in."

"And I cautioned *you* against going after pieces. You've gammoned me, Miss Milmont. Ah, here is your mama."

Mrs. Milmont came striding in, all smiles to see Sir Hillary come to call on her so soon. Her vivacity at his dinner party had paid off handsomely. "Sir Hillary, so nice of you to come," she said, advancing and holding out her hand. "Has my little girl been giving you a game of chess? Dull stuff, Claudia. I'm sure Sir Hillary is bored to flinders."

"*Au contraire*, darling. Beat to flinders. This is a very clever little girl you have here."

"Naughty boy, you are funning. What a charming time we had last night. We must return the favor and have you to dine here one evening. I shall speak to Jonathon about it. He is locked in his study, poor fellow, trying to make heads or tails of Aunt Sophie's jumbled accounts."

"An unenviable task, but it is you I wish to see, not the captain."

"Let us be seated," she said, leading him with great condescension to a sofa a little removed from the others, who regarded the tête-à-tête eagerly, trying to read by signs the outcome of Sir Hillary's proposal.

"I have to go to London tomorrow," he began. "Some business to do with Loo. She is coming with me."

"How unpleasant for you," she commiserated. "Just the worst time of the year, with the roads full of potholes, and very likely it will pour rain, as it is today."

"I hope not, but in any case, what I want to ask you, darling, is whether you will be so kind as to loan me your little daughter to accompany us. Company for Loo on the long trip."

"Who will chaperone them?"

"I will undertake to look after them both. We do not mean to remain overnight. Gabriel will look after the girls while I transact a little business. It will be an outing for them. I felt you would be depressed to be showing little Claudia such a flat time on her annual vacation. I am sure it has bothered you no end," he added with a considerate smile.

"To be sure it has, for we usually have such a gay time, seeing all the sights and shopping and so on. But it seems a little irregular—for the girls to go with no female escort."

The name Miss Bliss, though unspoken, hovered in the air between them.

"I am Loo's guardian, and will be happy to stand *in loco parentis* to little Claudia for one day. Say she may come. I will take good care of her, I promise you. And if the weather turns bad, the girls can stay at my place—it is staffed year-round, and Gab and I will put up at an hotel. Though we shant go at all if the weather looks unpromising."

"I can see no harm in it. If *you* undertake to look after them." Her real regret was that she could not insinuate herself into the carriage, but with Mr. Blandings' arrival pending, she didn't dare leave. Jonathon could not be counted on to issue the invitation without her here to nudge him into it.

Pleased with his easy success, Sir Hillary remained chatting for a quarter of an hour to reward Marcia, regaling her with a string of anecdotes of the *ton*, largely apocryphal. She was delighted to be reaching such an intimate footing with him and had already formed the plan to make Jonathon, by prayer or price, invite him to dine while Mr. Blandings was at Swallowcourt.

Miss Bliss rose to glide from the room, and Sir Hillary went to intercept her. "I wanted to have a word with you, Miss Bliss," he said. "Did you think I had come begging for the chess set, when I asked for you? I had, of course,

135

but having invented a pretext for my visit, I am determined to present it."

He walked with her to the door, and they chatted a while. Something to do with Luane, Marcia assumed, and ignored them. A small package was handed into Miss Bliss's care, and she went immediately to her room to dispose of it. Sir Hillary returned to the Crimson Saloon and began putting the chessmen in their niches in the box.

"I have bad news for you," he said to the girls as he did this.

"But she was *smiling*! I made sure she said I could go!" Claudia said in a disheartened voice.

"She gave her permission for the trip to London. The bad news is of my own devising. I am making a stipulation regarding the trip. You must promise me you will not go digging up Aunt Sophie tonight."

They had forgotten about it in the excitement of the trip, but once it was called to their minds, it seemed a steep price to pay, even for a trip to London.

"And let Jonathon walk off with my necklace? How *can* you suggest such a thing, Sir Hillary?" Luane demanded.

"He will not do so."

"You can't know that."

"We'll compromise," Claudia intervened. "We'll bear watch on Jonathon tonight, and if *he* doesn't go after the diamonds, *we* won't. Will that serve as well, Sir Hillary?"

He considered it a moment. "One slight handicap occurs to me. Bearing watch on Jonathon all night will play havoc with your rest. You won't close your eyes till dawn, and we mean to leave at eight. And I might just mention that when I say eight, I mean eight, not eight-thirty or nine-thirty or any other hour that suits you. If we are to have a decent visit, we must make an early start."

"I am usually up by seven," Claudia told him, "and shall make myself responsible for having Loo ready too. But about staying awake all night, I daresay we would be a trifle pulled by tomorrow. Still, we can't leave him an open field. Even seeing the horses at Astley's isn't worth that."

"I suggest another compromise then," Sir Hillary began. "Jonathan is working on his accounts. I'll ask him over to Chanely with me, and offer to give him a hand with them. It's a bad day; he'll be in no hurry to return. A snug dinner, a couple of stiff belts of brandy, and I can persuade him to remain the night."

"He might agree to it," Luane said. "Then *he* can keep an eye on *you*, while *you* are keeping an eye on *him*."

"Just so—we hold each other in check," Hillary agreed.

"And he'd never tackle it in the broad daylight, so while we are gone tomorrow the diamonds will be safe," Claudia added. "So everything will be fine till tomorrow night."

"You girls never give up," Gabriel said with a weary sigh.

"I hope we are not quitters!" Loo turned on him. He had managed to reinstate himself in her good graces during the morning by talking enthusiastically about the projected trip to London, but this reminded her of what a quitter he had turned out to be, and she sneered at him.

"I'll take the whelp home before these two come to cuffs again," Hillary said aside to Claudia. "Are you quite sure you want to chaperone this hoyden of a girl? I cannot think it would be a pleasant task."

"It wouldn't be so unpleasant as trying to knock reading and arithmetic into my cousins' skulls," she replied.

"You act as tutor?"

"Yes, they, too, live with grandpa. Their father was papa's brother, and since my grandfather is becoming gouty, he is leaving the running of the estate to my Uncle Gerald. I keep out of mischief by trying to teach them."

"No pleasant task, from that frown," Thoreau remarked.

"It's not so bad when they will settle down to work, but usually they are blowing holes in their desks with winkies—salt peter and a candle you know—or throwing the ink and books at each other, or me, or bringing mice or badgers into the schoolroom. They are hard to control as their mama doesn't like me to hit them. However, they mean no harm. They are not *bad* boys, only high-spirited."

"They should be sent away to school."

"Grandmama is afraid they wouldn't receive a proper religious education and has convinced their father to have them educated at home. But they will be soon getting into Latin and Greek, and I have some hopes they will hire a tutor before I am quite done in."

An angry scowl greeted this remark, and fearing she had in some manner revealed herself as the lazy, spineless creature she was so often told she was, she took her leave of him.

Jonathon was not too reluctant to exchange the drafty, dusty study in which he labored for the gracious warmth of Chanely, and if anyone could make heads or tails of these scrambled accounts, it was Sir Hillary—as clever as an accountant with figures. The eagerness with which he snatched at the invitation even gave rise to the suspicion that he had been looking for an excuse to go to Chanely. Within ten minutes he was out the door and did not return to Swallowcourt that night.

Chapter Eleven

Sir Hillary was out in his estimation if he thought he would be kept waiting by the ladïes. They were from their beds at six, had dressed, eaten, and done all that was necessary before seven-thirty, save throw on their bonnets and pelisses. They therefore had an impatient wait for the appearance of Thoreau's traveling carriage and team of four. Miss Bliss had risen early to see them off, knowing Mrs. Milmont would not be on hand.

"Everything all right?" Hillary asked her when he was admitted to the house.

She nodded quietly and slipped into his hand that same parcel he had given her the previous day under the pretext of taking his hat.

"We've been ready and waiting this age," Loo told him.

As promised, the gentlemen had removed their armbands, and it was a merry party that set out for the metropolis. The ladies did not look precisely fashionable, but in their best bonnets and pelisses, they were at least respectable. Gab and Loo sat on one side of the banquette in the carriage, and Claudia and Thoreau on the other. Both girls found it exceedingly pleasant to have a sheepskin rug beneath their feet, a snug blanket over their laps, and satin squabs to cushion their backs and heads.

"What luxury!" Claudia marveled. "This seems a positively decadent carriage."

"We have more debauchery in store for you," Hillary promised. "Hot coffee in this wicker basket you see here on the floor, and some scones, still warm from the oven. I had my cook make them specially this morning, in case the crumbs at Swallowcourt were not sufficient for two growing girls."

"Sir Hillary always does things in style," Luane informed her cousin. "He doesn't often exert himself, but when he *does* take you anywhere, you may be sure he will not stint."

"Thank you," Hillary said with a quelling look at his ward, who smiled sweetly back at him.

"Let's eat, before everything gets cold," Loo suggested. Whatever they had managed to find to eat at Swallowcourt did not appear to have dulled their appetites, for every drop of the coffee and every bit of the scones was dispatched within twenty minutes.

Settling back amidst the pagan luxury, Claudia said to her companion, "I take it you talked Jonathon into staying the night? I didn't hear him come home."

"He's still sleeping, or was when I left. The accounts are in such a state we were up till midnight trying to make any sense of them. Old Sophie was a dreadful rackrent. If Jonathon had known the way she was letting the whole place go to ruin, he would have been justified in having in the authorities. An entailed estate is subject to minimal maintenance. I mentioned it to him more than once, but he was afraid it would turn her against him. I never thought he had much hope of getting anything more than the estate."

"It seems a pity, and he can't sell it either since it's entailed."

"Nor rent it, unless he brings it into some sort of order. It was really very bad of Sophie to serve him such a trick.

140

I wonder if she had in her mind to do more for him when the rest of the will is read."

"The diamonds, you mean? Is that why you're bound and bent Loo shant have them?"

"I'm not bound and bent Loo shant have them! And it isn't the diamonds he'd get if he got anything else. I only want to keep you two gravediggers out of Bridewell."

"If *you* would help us . . ."

"Shall we speak of something else? I had hoped to escape the whole saga of the Beresford Diamonds for this one day."

They spoke of other things—of what they were to do that day first, then carefully Hillary steered the conversation to a more personal vein. What were Claudia's grandparents like, and her uncle and aunt, the children. How did she amuse herself at home, and did she go to many parties? How did she usually pass her holiday with her mother? A picture emerged of a dreary existence under the thumb of an austere grandmother who was dead set against frivolity, and a grandfather under the cat's paw, though of more lenient tendencies himself. The yearly holiday with Marcia sounded equally boring. Always in the late winter—the worst time of the year for any gaiety in the city, chosen, of course, to keep the girl's age a secret. He also asked casually when her father had died and, a few moments later, how old she had been at the time. When London was reached, he had a pretty accurate picture of Miss Milmont's age and circumstances and a confirmed dislike of her mother.

The interest of all the occupants of the carriage turned to the scenery as they entered the city, and Gabriel said, "You're going out of your way, aren't you, Uncle? I thought we would be going downtown."

"We'll stop at my place first to freshen up," he replied, as they continued through the fashionable West End. Claudia recognized the district, but was not very familiar with it as mama lived farther south in Belgrave Square.

"Another Palace Beautiful!" she said as the carriage pulled up in front of a mansion done in the Palladian style, brick with columns in front. "Do you live here too?" she asked Sir Hillary.

"I spoil myself," he admitted. "Your grandmother would have a poor opinion of me."

They alighted, and he said to his driver, "I'll leave this team here. Hitch up the other and have the carriage ready in an hour."

They were admitted through double oak portals by a butler, and the ladies were shown upstairs by a maid.

"Sir Hillary must be very rich," Claudia said in an awed voice to her cousin, when they had been left alone in a large, handsome chamber.

"He has a lot of Consoles or something that seem to make one very rich," Loo told her. "Aunt Sophie has them, too."

"What can they be?" Claudia asked in perplexity.

Luane shrugged her shoulders and pulled off her bonnet. "I wish I could stay here when I come to London, but as Hillary is a bachelor ... But what a pair of gossoons we are, cousin! We ought to get busy and find him a wife."

"Does he not have anyone in mind? He seems very old to be still a bachelor."

They brushed their hair and splashed water on their faces and hands as they talked, turning aside from time to admire some ornament or piece of furniture.

"He's thirty-two. He has a new flirt every year," Loo said. "I've met some of them when he brings parties to Chanely, but he never brings the same girl twice."

"I expect they are very pretty."

"Diamonds of the first water, Gabriel calls them. Shall we go? He hates to be kept waiting."

"Yes, let's, or he'll get snarky again." The two scampered down the long staircase. "He told the driver not to come back for an hour," Claudia said. "What can he mean to do here for so long?"

"His man of business might come here to save going into the city."

They discovered when they went below that the hour was to be spent much more pleasantly than that. A fine

142

luncheon was laid, awaiting them in a small dining parlor. "This will save time," he explained.

"I thought we'd get to eat out at an hotel or restaurant," Loo pouted.

Claudia could not think any hotel would provide a more sumptuous repast than that awaiting their pleasure—roast fowl and sliced ham, a raised pigeon pie, and side dishes of vegetables promised a pleasant break in the day.

"Don't worry, brat. I didn't forget your cream buns," Hillary said, and she was satisfied with that bribe.

"Did you send word ahead we were coming?" Gab asked.

"Yes, my cook is at Chanely, and my housekeeper had to make the meal by herself. I didn't want to leave it to chance."

Loo engaged Gabriel in a discussion of their schedule, and Claudia sat stunned in consideration of this elevated style of living. When she and grandpapa went to the city for a visit, they usually took a boxed lunch, and grandpa told her not to mention to his wife that they stopped for an ice or pastries and coffee.

"By the way," Hillary said aside to Claudia, "I told your mama a whisker that I kept two chefs. You might not mention what I just said. It would set me down a peg in her eyes."

"Of course, you wouldn't want to risk *that*!" she quizzed him.

"No, I mean to remain on terms with her if I can."

"You might even induce her to come to one of your London parties, if you butter her up sufficiently," she said, smiling.

"I have quite resign- . . . *decided* on it."

"I can't think why you should have *resigned* yourself to anything of the sort."

"Can you not, little Claudia? Then I have not been making myself as clear as I thought I had."

"What—you cannot mean it! Do you *really* intend to make me Loo's chaperone?"

"Yes, that is my intention."

143

"Surely I am not old enough."

"You've aged a few years since yesterday, when you were twenty."

She was unoffended. "I have no experience along such lines. Oh, I should love it, of course."

"You're not going to do a Lady Turn-about on me, I trust?"

"It will not serve. You know it will not, and it is unkind of you to raise my hopes so."

"Don't raise your hopes too high. I have some nasty strings attached to the scheme."

"You mean to move us both in with mama, don't you?"

"No, my wheedling powers are not so enormous. But what an undutiful daughter you are, to consider living with your mama a nasty string."

"I didn't mean that! I have always wished she would let me stay with her, but she wouldn't have us. Not even *you* could arrange it."

His eyes hardened. "As it happens, that was not the stipulation I had in mind."

"Miss Bliss? But she would not be nasty in the least. I like her excessively."

"You fatigue your poor little brain to no account. I shall reveal the whole of my fell scheme in due time."

Despite his warning, she went on belaboring her brain. "If you mean to hire Miss Bliss—well, in fact, you already have—then I see no place for *me* in your scheme. Unless I could be Loo's abigail. I could handle that very well, if mama would permit it. But she wouldn't, not in London at least."

"It seems strange to me you should be interested in being a *servant* to your niece, or indeed to anyone." His face was taking on its angry aspect, and Claudia did not continue the matter aloud. "Try this pigeon pie," he said a moment later. "You will be back at Swallowcourt for dinner, you know."

She accepted a large wedge of it and other treats, and though Sir Hillary succeeded in diverting the conversation to other channels, her thoughts were still half on trying to decipher what plan he had in mind.

At the end of half an hour they had been fed and got back into their bonnets and pelisses for the beginning of their sight-seeing. Thoreau was to leave them for half an hour to attend to his business, while Gabriel took the ladies to stroll along Bond Street and see the shops.

"I expect you will want some blunt," Hillary said to Luane. She held out her hand, and he folded some bills into it.

"Look, cousin, we are rich!" she said, showing the money to Claudia. "I shall buy you something, too, so you can save your guinea."

"Did your mother not think to give you some money?" he asked Claudia.

"I have some money," she replied, embarrassed.

He did not, of course, enquire how much, but he was pretty sure the guinea was the extent of it. Again Claudia looked at him and wondered why he had that hard look in his eyes.

"Shall I buy my caps?" she asked, to ease the strain.

"No, take my advice, and buy yourself some heathen luxury," he replied, his expression softening. Then he turned on his heel and left, to get back into the carriage.

Loo found a shop carrying her favorite coconut rolled in chocolate and cream, and another that purveyed all manner of "toys" for ladies. There she bought a hideous pair of paste stars for dancing slippers which she did not own and a chicken-skin fan for her cousin. With a guilty conscience and a streak of practicality, she then went to a clothing store and bought a pair of woolen hose to ward off the chill blasts of Swallowcourt. With wealth left to spare, she got Miss Bliss some wool, and a new red bridle for her horse.

Claudia looked in vain for a heathen luxury worth a guinea, and finding none, got some muslin to make handkerchiefs for grandpa.

When Sir Hillary left the group to attend to his business, he made only one short stop, at Hamlet the Jeweler's at the corner of Cranbourne Alley. He asked for Hamlet himself and presented to him that same packet given to him by Miss Bliss, some hours before. The contents were examined carefully by the jeweler and, when Thoreau returned the parcel to his inner pocket, he wore a satisfied smile. He went to meet the others for the matinee performance of the horses at Astley's Circus.

Gabriel was still child enough to be delighted by the show, and man enough not to care to show it. He smiled quite condescendingly at Loo when she grabbed his arm and said she was sure the lady with hardly any clothes on was going to fall off the white horse, for she was standing up and at a canter, too, without even holding on.

The day was mercilessly short. They went for a drive in the carriage to see Buckingham Palace and Westminster Abbey from the outside only—there was no time to go inside. At four they had to depart, and it was with a forlorn sigh and a last look out the windows that they took their leave of London.

Luane had to open her parcels and show her guardian how wisely she had invested her money. He winced at the paste stars, shook his head at the fan, and smiled at the woolen hose. "Not completely given over to dissipation, I see," he congratulated her. "And what sybaritic indulgence have *you* been squandering your guinea on, Miss Milmont?"

She showed him her muslin. "Oh, for your caps," Loo said.

"Just so, and with the remainder I shall get blue ribbons, to match my eyes," she prevaricated.

"To seduce the widowers," Hillary nodded. "Tell me, is it a necessity that the gentleman be a widower, or would an elderly bachelor do?"

"A bachelor would not have a ready-made family," Claudia pointed out.

"I happen to know one who has."

"Then he cannot be a very proper person, sir, and I am surprised you speak to me of him."

"What a nasty mind you have, little Claudia. There are other ways to acquire a family than to sire them yourself. All it takes is a death in the family, and a bachelor may find himself saddled with a couple of brats."

146

"I didn't think of that," she confessed, chastened.

"It's pretty clear your mind was straying where a young girl's mind has no right to be. I'm shocked at you," he charged with mock severity.

"It comes from reading of so much lechery in the Bible," she replied.

"Yes, there is nothing like the Bible to pervert a pure mind," he agreed, and the subject was allowed to drop.

They stopped at Hornchurch for tea, and were back at Swallowcourt at seven-thirty, only a half hour later than planned. The gentlemen descended from the carriage, and as Hillary sent the driver around to the stable, it was assumed they meant to come inside for a while.

Luane bustled in first, eager to tell of her marvelous activities, but she was greeted by a captain pacing up and down the Crimson Saloon, with a full budget of his own to be disclosed, and an irate Mrs. Milmont, willing to help him. Before the visiting gentlemen had their curled beavers and capes bestowed, they were hauled into the Saloon.

"You've gone too far this time, Thoreau," Tewksbury charged. "I've had the constable at my door—*my* door! threatening to take against *me* because of them wild beasts you've had set to watch Aunt Sophie's grave."

"It cannot be illegal," Thoreau replied calmly. "Fletcher would not have done it if it were."

"No, and if you and Fletcher hadn't done it, the dogs wouldn't have gone chewing up the vicar's brat. Well, I wash my hands of the matter. Told him *I* had nothing to do with it, and he must see you and Fletcher. If there's to be a legal action and damages and so on, it won't come out of *my* pockets."

"It is impossible to take out what is not in," Thoreau agreed. "The vicar's boy—was he badly mauled?"

"They've had the sawbones sent over—and *that* will come out of your purse, too."

"I thought at the time it was a barbarous idea," Marcia added her two groats.

"Strange you didn't express your thoughts; you are not

usually so reticent, Marcia," Thoreau said in an ironic tone.

"How badly was the boy hurt?" Loo asked, as her guardian's question was not answered.

"How the deuce should we know?" Jonathon snapped. "The constable said he was bitten badly."

"Bronfman was not to let the dogs run loose. I can't believe he let them consume the boy entirely. It is likely no more than a nip," Thoreau said, tossing his cape on a chair, and throwing his hat on top of it.

"Well, whatever they did, the constable says he's getting an injunction to have the dogs called off, and he's going to see you tomorrow—and the vicar, too."

"Thank you for the warning," Hillary nodded. "I shall have my purse ready. Well, well, how exciting. Perhaps we should have stayed home, eh, girls? Always in the wrong place at the wrong time. See what an adventure you have missed."

"Are the dogs still there tonight?" Miss Milmont asked, which brought a resigned sigh to Thoreau's lips.

"Yes, Bronfman wouldn't leave without Sir Hillary telling him so, but he's keeping the dogs on a short leash," Jonathon answered.

"Oh." Her monosyllable was despondent. "But they will be gone tomorrow night?"

"Positively," Sir Hillary assured her. "We can't have them eating up any innocent child who wanders through the place. One would think they took their meals at Swallowcourt."

"What's that supposed to mean?" Jonathon asked, on the defensive.

"Exactly what you think," Hillary replied. Then he turned to Mrs. Milmont. "You see I have brought your little girl back safe and sound, as I promised. And you forgot to give her pocket money. A regrettable oversight. She couldn't buy the ribbons for her caps."

"Caps? What nonsense is this? My little girl won't be putting on her caps for decades yet, and I am sure she had plenty of money, if she wanted to buy some ribbons."

"I daresay she could have got both the ribbons and the muslin from her guinea if she had shopped wisely."

"Why, I bought her ribbons in Malton just the other day."

"Don't pay any attention to him, mama," Claudia said. "He is only funning, you know." She then directed a quelling stare on Sir Hillary.

He turned aside to her and said in a low voice, "I forget myself. My intentions will not prosper if I rattle on so heedlessly. And besides, I have something of much greater interest to discuss than your caps."

He then turned to the group and cleared his throat. "*Attention, s'il vous plaît!* Have you been into your cellars yet, Jonathon? I hope they yield something better than that inferior sherry usually served. I have an announcement of some significance to make. It really calls for champagne, as it regards diamonds."

"Eh?" Jonathon's eyes nearly started from his head.

"Yes, you heard aright. It involves the Beresford Diamonds, or to be more precise, Diamond, in the singular."

"What, just one?" Jonathon asked sharply.

"That's what I said. Just one. Yes, you are looking at an heiress," his eyes turned to Luane, who was looking as much mystified as the others. "One of the stones in the necklace you were given was the genuine article, brat. The biggest one too, that great egg that hangs off the front of the necklace."

"I'm rich!" Luane shouted and clapped her hands in glee.

"How did you find out?" Jonathon asked.

"The same way you did, I fancy. I happened to notice the cut on the glass case where they are kept. I was sure it was not there before, and it occurred to me it was the sort of incision a diamond might make on glass. It was but a step to wonder if the diamond that cut it was not in the case, and by trying the stones, I discovered which one it was. How fortunate for Loo that it was the largest one. I took the necklace to Hamlet today, and he confirmed my theory. So your old Aunt Sophie didn't do so badly by you after all, Loo."

"It is a mistake," Mrs. Milmont said. "She didn't mean to give Luane a real diamond."

"I think she did," Hillary contradicted. "The wording of the will was rather peculiar as I recall, said the contents of the case 'exactly as they are now are' or 'stand'—something of the sort—were to go to Loo. And I don't see how the switch could possibly have been made accidentally."

There was a good deal of general discussion, argument, and angry cries; but eventually the news was accepted as true and irrefutable, and the request for wine was repeated by Sir Hillary.

It was not champagne but Madeira that was produced, and with everyone having to re-assess his or her plans, there was a little silence while they sipped. Then little groups broke into excited chatter anew.

"The dogs will be gone tomorrow night you say?" Jonathon asked Hillary.

"Yes, Captain, you'd do much better to wait till tomorrow night to go after the necklace," Thoreau informed him nonchalantly.

"Nobody said anything about going after the necklace."

"I really didn't expect to be told in so many words."

"It was Gab that went digging her up the very night she was buried, you might happen to remember."

"Yes, but *he* hadn't seen the scratch on the glass case. We mustn't be too hard on him. It was very quick of you to have noticed it, by the by. When did you first perceive it?"

"Don't know what you're talking about," Jonathon insisted.

"No one is listening; we might as well be alone, and I promise you *I* shant tell a soul. Was it when Loo threw the necklace down in a fit of pique the day the will was read? It must have been then. So it was that rather than your awareness of the inner steel lining in the coffin that deterred you from having a go in the graveyard that first night. I thought your surprise quite genuine when you heard of it the next morning. You didn't see the glass case again till the night of my little dinner party—oh dear!

And that, of course, is why you koshed poor Miss Milmont on the head, knowing she wore a fortune in diamonds. And here we accused the girl of imagining the whole, or alternatively *you* of going after her emerald ring. But what prevented you from making the snatch that night? Did someone disturb you? My servants have no consideration, I fear."

"Don't be so foolish," Jonathon said.

"It is foolish of me to expect a confession, when the evidence is all circumstantial. But how well it hangs together! You made the deuce of a mess in my study, Jon. Didn't you know I never keep anything valuable in that safe? And I am quite angry with you for hitting Miss Milmont. That was ungentlemanly in the extreme. But I see you dislike the subject, and who shall blame you? Let us speak of other things. Did my servants give you a good breakfast? I hope so, and I hope you didn't waste too much time looking for the necklace while I was gone. I thought of telling you I had it with me, but then I said, no, let him have his little fun. He will be missing the excitement of making plans to thwart Boney, and this is the very thing to divert him. I took the precaution of leaving the necklace with Miss Bliss last night and picking it up this morning, in case you decided to try sleepwalking."

"Look here, Thoreau . . ."

"You may call me Hillary."

"How do I know you don't plan to go after them tonight? For all I know you could stop at the graveyard on the way home and tell Bronfman to leave."

"I could do that, but I shant."

"How do I *know* you won't?"

"You wound me, Jonathon, so untrusting. Let us see now, you *could* keep an eye on me by inviting me to remain the night, as I invited you last night."

"So that's why you did it."

"Well, I didn't think you'd be going to the *graveyard*, for you thought the whole necklace was genuine, but I wasn't sure you wouldn't be breaking into my house again, and to save my locks I asked you, after first removing the necklace here."

"What about young Gabriel?"

"What about him? If I am to stay, you'll have to find a bed for him, too. Or would you prefer to come to Chanely again? Still another 'or' occurs to me. We could just make a gentleman's agreement to wait till tomorrow night, if you wish. I confess I am tired after so much driving and would like to have a night off."

"A verbal agreement aint good enough."

"Seems a pity to disturb Fletcher to have it done up legally," Thoreau said, smiling lazily.

"I aint that big a gudgeon."

"Aint you, Jonathon? You fooled me. What is it to be then? You at Chanely or myself and Gab here? You'll have to feed us too. We hadn't time to stop for dinner."

"We've waited dinner for the girls. I suppose there's enough for you and Gab, too."

"I doubt it severely, but Loo has a bag of candies we'll take from her if we find ourselves too ravenous. Are we to remain then?"

"Yes," Jonathon decided, and it was settled.

The dinner was no better than Thoreau's worst fears—stringy mutton, lukewarm potatoes boiled to a pulp, carrots and turnips, the whole topped off with bread pudding. There was plenty to go around for the extra company, as no one took very large portions.

When the gentlemen joined the ladies in the Crimson Saloon, Sir Hillary went to Miss Milmont's side and said, "Are you too fagged for another game of chess?"

"You took the set home."

"So I did. Pity. How about whist?"

She covered a yawn with her fist and said, "I am a little tired from the trip. Is it true you are to remain overnight?"

"Yes, do you mind?"

"Not in the least, and it will be an excellent time for us to dig up the diamonds, while we are all in the same house. We shant have such another opportunity."

"And you are too tired for a game of whist! There is no understanding women. Also you seem to have forgot ten to cut myself and Gabriel out of this adventure some time ago."

"How can you be so spiritless?" she asked with contempt.

Goaded at this charge, he added, "Well, I promised Jonathon that *tonight* I shant go in any case, and I think he means to lock my door."

"It will be better to wait till the dogs are called off. I wonder if they hurt the little boy very much."

"I hope not. More frightened than hurt, very likely. I shall go to see him tomorrow."

"Well, it seems we have all called a truce till tomorrow. I must own I am grateful for it. One is always fagged after a trip."

"We'll talk tomorrow. Go to bed, Claudia. You look burnt to the socket."

"I shall, but not before I thank you for the wonderful day. It was marvelous, from beginning to end. Thank you."

"Sleep well." He blew her a kiss as she turned to take her leave of the others. Marcia observed this with a sharp narrowing of the eyes, but when she strolled casually up to him to try to sound him out, he excused himself with a yawn and went to his room.

Chapter Twelve

On Thursday, spring pretended to be coming at last. A balmy breeze wafted through the ill-fitting windows, and the damp chillness of Swallowcourt was alleviated somewhat. Outside the sun shone, and a brave beam or two penetrated the dusty fenestration to pick out a tarnished bowl on a table, and the dusty surfaces of heavy furniture.

"This promises to be a pleasant day," Sir Hillary remarked, taking his place at the table beside Luane and Claudia. Gabriel was there before him, and they were joined shortly by their host.

"Just coffee for me," he continued. Gabriel was either braver or hungrier. He tackled a plate of eggs and a muffin with apparent relish.

"Did everyone sleep well?" Thoreau continued. "Luane and Miss Milmont, I observe, are bright-eyed and bushy-tailed and full of schemes, as usual. Jonathon, have you been to the village yet to enlist the smitty's help, or do you plan to attempt opening the casket with a file?"

"Don't see why you keep harping on that," Jonathon replied in a surly tone.

"It is the reason I spent a highly uncomfortable night on a lumpy mattress and unaired bed, and the reason I am drinking mud this morning instead of coffee. As it is uppermost in all our minds, I see no point in avoiding the subject. But *you* are the host, captain, and I bend like a reed in the wind to your wishes. We shall speak of other things. I plan to bid you farewell as soon as I have drunk my coffee. I repair to Chanely to await the constable and the vicar, pursuant to which I must see Fletcher. What are you ladies to do?"

Doubtful hunchings of the shoulders indicated their lack of plans, and Jonathon had a suggestion to put forward. As it was no longer eligible to court Luane, the inheritor of only one diamond and the tiara, he spoke to her bluntly.

"If you've nothing better to do you might get Sophie's junk out of her room. Don't see why I must go on sleeping in that nasty little yellow room, when the best bedroom is empty. Mean to say, *she* aint in it any longer, though it's full of her stuff."

"Why should *I* clean it for you?" Luane asked. "Have a servant do it."

"You forget, brat," Sir Hillary said to her, "Aunt Sophie's personal effects were left to you."

"Poo, what do I care for her musty old gowns and letters a hundred years old. Throw them out."

"It might be worth your while to have a look," Gabriel suggested. "She had that quite valuable traveling case in wrought silver with her combs and mirror and brushes."

"Oh, and a sweet set of cut glass perfume bottles. I *do* like them," Loo added, brightening to consider these acquisitions.

"Daresay they're part of the furniture, if we was to take it to law," Jonathon said.

"I think not," Hillary contradicted.

"What of her costume jewelry?" Claudia asked. "Her watch . . ."

"Will you help me, cousin?" Loo asked Claudia, and it was agreed.

Thoreau and Gabriel left them to their chore and went

155

to Chanely to confront a humble constable, shaking in his boots to tackle Sir Hillary Thoreau, and apologizing a dozen times for his task. He was set at his ease, told the dogs would be called off that same day, given a glass of small ale, and sent on his greatly relieved way. The vicar had still not arrived at ten-thirty, so Thoreau and Gabriel harnessed up the curricle to drive to Billericay, first stopping at a shop to pick up a toy for the wounded boy. The boy ran out to meet them when they reached the vicarage, pointing proudly to a small plaster on his leg, "where the dog ate me." The matter was handled in a trice, with good will on all sides, and a refusal by the vicar to let Sir Hillary pay even the doctor's reckoning, as he was coming to give Martha, the vicar's wife, a look-over anyway. She was increasing again, one of the annual rites of spring in Billericay, as regular as the flowering of the trees or the lengthening of the days.

Sir Hillary made another stop before going to see Fletcher. Something in the window of Miss White's Drapery Shop attracted his eye. As Gabriel had already been sent off to the sweet shop while he talked with Fletcher, he did not hesitate to go in and purchase what had attracted him. Miss White raised her eyebrows and wondered who Sir Hillary should be buying a shawl for, with his mother cold in the grave and never a sign of a sweetheart. Wasn't for his housekeeper, for it was miles away from her birthday, and she wouldn't be wearing such a lively shade either. Very odd the way he had looked at it and said, "Yes, that will suit her admirably" with *such* a look in his eyes.

The parcel was stowed in the curricle before he went on to see Fletcher. The contretemps was explained to Fletcher—old news to him by now. They agreed that not only the dogs but Bronfman himself should be dispensed with.

"It has troubled me, I confess," Fletcher said. "She did not specify in the will that the grave was to be guarded. Indeed, I rather suspect her intentions to have been otherwise, though she did not say that either."

"She was certainly inviting mischief," Sir Hillary said.

"Indeed it seems so," Fletcher agreed blandly.

"I must tell you, Fletcher, I have had Luane's necklace to London for examination by Hamlet the Jeweler," Hillary said next.

"So soon?" Fletcher asked, surprised. "Well, and what did you discover?"

"You must know what I *discovered*, but what I *told* everyone is that the large pendant stone is a genuine diamond. I thought that stuck as close to the truth as I could possibly do. Captain Tewksbury already had his suspicions. She wished us to believe Luane received only a set of paste stones, and I have varied from Sophie's wishes as little as I felt feasible. We must now sit tight and see what transpires."

"Dear me, this promises to be very interesting," Fletcher said, with a meaningful glance at his caller.

"I didn't feel it just to give Gabriel the edge over the captain, strong though the temptation was," Hillary continued.

"You have acted in the best interest of all parties—the *fairest* interest that is," Fletcher corrected scrupulously.

"I hope I have. You don't feel this deception on our part invalidates the will?"

"Certainly not. So long as all parties are under the same belief, there is no advantage or disadvantage accruing to one more than the other. The will stands. There is no question of that."

They took a formal leave of each other, and Thoreau went to join Gabriel.

While this business was being transacted, Luane and Claudia went to Aunt Sophie's room to begin the unpleasant chore of sorting out the belongings of their dead relative. Two crates were hauled to her room, one to hold utterly useless items such as gowns in tatters from age, and the other to contain goods to be sent to the poorhouse in the village. Those objects that she wished to keep, Luane set aside on the bed. The silver traveling case, a gold and nacre inlaid dresser set, the perfume bottles, and a few bits of jewelry were laid there. Luane soon found yet another carton to be necessary, to hold things too good to give away, and not suitable for herself to use.

"I'll haul this lot to Maldon or Billericay and sell them," the practical miss declared, tossing a sable-lined cape into the box, where it jostled with kid gloves and slippers, a morocco leather stationery set, and some rather ugly figurines. "I wouldn't be surprised to get ten pounds for them."

"That's a good deal of money," Claudia said. "I wonder if I might sell my cracked Sèvres vase."

The chore was unappetizing and dusty, but by noon it was done, and Claudia raised the much more interesting point of digging up the diamonds. She was utterly stymied at Luane's reply. "I don't need the necklace now. She didn't mean it for me, and it would be illegal to steal it. Sir Hillary would only make me give it back to whoever it really belonged to after the year is up, so I shant bother digging it up."

"But what of our adventure?" Claudia asked, disappointed.

"It's over, unless you want to dig it up for yourself," Loo told her.

"No, I don't want it. But only think, Loo, if the pendant is worth ten thousand pounds, the rest of it is worth forty thousand!"

"Ten thousand is enough," Loo answered. "We can live on that, if needs be. That will give us five hundred a year, along with whatever Gabriel earns."

"You could live much better on the interest of fifty thousand!" Claudia pointed out.

Her cousin hunched her shoulders and dismissed the topic. "Now how shall I get all this junk to the village? Gab must take me."

There was no mention of Claudia accompanying them, and she felt not only disappointed at the sudden termination of the adventure but rejected as well.

"I wonder if they mean to come back this afternoon," Loo asked aloud, but really of herself. "I think I'd better ride over to Chanely and see Gabriel." She hopped up, but still made no offer to her cousin to accompany her, so

Claudia went belowstairs to admire her cracked vase. From the window she saw Luane canter down the hill to Chanely, and her heart sank a little. Loo didn't return for luncheon, and she made a dull meal with her mother, Jonathon, and Miss Bliss.

At Chanely, Luane had to wait for only a short while before Gabriel and Sir Hillary arrived. Immediately she had greeted them, her guardian sighed and said, "I suppose you are come to engage our help in a digging expedition."

"No, I've given up on that, but I have come for your help and Gab's. *You*, Sir Hillary, I want to sell my big diamond at once and invest the ten thousand in the funds, and Gabriel must take me to the village to sell all Aunt Sophie's old junk, which Claudia and I have been sorting through this morning."

"Impossible!" Sir Hillary exclaimed, and Gabriel said, "All right," at the same instant.

It was to Hillary that Luane turned a wrathful eye. "Why is it impossible? You have the stone. I never mean to wear it and would like to be getting my interest on the ten thousand pounds. It would be enough . . ." She looked to Gabriel, but broke off her speech in midsentence.

"I am to *hold* it for you till you are eighteen, or married, whichever comes first. Permission was not given to sell it. And it would not be easy to sell in any case. People with a whim for a ten-thousand-pound jewel don't grow on trees, brat."

Luane listened, a furrow wrinkling her brow, then she said, "But it didn't say in the will you could not sell it for me. You were to be in charge of it—which could as well mean in charge of selling it and investing the money in something secure."

"That is not the way I interpreted it."

"I shall ask Mr. Fletcher."

"He will confirm what I've said. Till the year is up, the stone cannot be sold."

"But it's *mine!*" she shouted, stamping her foot and falling into a strong spasm of anger. "Why will you be so miserable and selfish?"

Thoreau looked bored and sat down. "There are other reasons about which you know nothing, brat, and I have no notion of enlightening you any further, so pray don't pester me."

"You're just afraid Gabriel will marry me if I can get my hands on the ten thousand," she charged.

"If he has a brain in his head, it would take more than ten thousand to induce him to marry a spoilt child like you."

She fulminated and turned to Gabriel for a refutation of this charge. He was looking sheepish and replied, "He's only funning, Loo."

"Are you a *man*, Gabriel, or are you a boy?" she asked coldly. "Do you mean to let him insult me in this manner?"

"It's no insult," Gab parried.

"Oh! You hateful dog. You needn't think I would marry you if I had a million pounds, and so I tell you to your silly face."

"You could do better than this cawker if you had a *million*," Thoreau agreed pleasantly. "But you haven't; and you haven't ten thousand, either. You have a diamond, which I am holding and shall continue to hold till the year is up."

"Or till I marry! Well I *will* get married, so don't think it! Don't think I *won't*, I mean," she corrected angrily.

"Take a look in the mirror, hoyden," Thoreau suggested. "Next time you come courting Gab, you might wash your face and run a comb through that mat of tangles. You look like something the cat dragged in." With this uncompromising speech, he arose and sauntered towards the door. In the doorway he paused and turned around.

"Did Miss Milmont not come with you?" he asked.

"No," she snapped, hurrying to the mirror, where she viewed a pink face with only a tiny smear of mud from her gloves under one eye, and a few wisps of black hair dislodged by her ride.

"Pity. She would have enjoyed this dramatic scene." He smiled sardonically and left.

Gabriel's first thought was to reinstate himself, and to

160

this end he said, "I'll be happy to take you to Billericay to sell Aunt Sophie's stuff."

It was a step in the right direction, but he had to be punished for not standing up for her, so she said, "Oh, Billericay! That is nothing. They wouldn't give me a quarter what it's worth there. I could drive the gig to Billericay myself. If you don't mean to take me to Maldon, you might as well forget it."

"Maldon then," he allowed. "Will you stay to luncheon, and we'll drive up to Swallowcourt afterwards to collect the junk?"

A repast at Chanely was always a welcome treat, and she agreed with great condescension to remain. At the table, Thoreau very largely ignored the pair of them, only nodding in agreement when Gabriel outlined his plan to drive Loo to Maldon, then adding, "You'd better take my curricle, or you'll not be back before dark."

"Yes," Gabriel agreed readily, for he much preferred taking the reins of Sir Hillary's grays to poking along in the closed carriage.

When they got to the stable, however, Loo recalled the size of the carton she had to transport, and recommended the closed coach instead. "I'd better ask uncle," Gabriel said.

"What a child you are!" Loo scoffed. "He said you might take me, and he won't want you pulling the springs of his curricle with huge boxes weighing a ton. The stable boys will tell him why we had to take the coach instead."

He was already in too much disgrace to argue and was persuaded to take the carriage she recommended. Claudia saw the carriage pull up to the door of Swallowcourt a little later, and hopped up eagerly thinking it might contain Sir Hillary as well as the younger couple. She was let down to see only the two emerge, but still had some hopes she might be asked to join them for the trip. Her hopes were dashed immediately.

"Will you help me load Aunt Sophie's boxes into the carriage?" Loo asked. "Gab is taking me to Maldon to sell the things."

"To Maldon! How nice. You'll have a lovely drive," Claudia said, with a hopeful smile.

"Yes. You come upstairs too, Gab," Loo answered unthinkingly. "You can take the big box for the poor people. I'll get a footboy to help you."

They struggled with boxes, and as they were put into the coach instead of on top, which would have taken more time, there remained no room for Claudia. She waved them off and walked sadly back into the house. It was rather a fine day, she decided, looking out at the few rays of sun that still lingered, and she went for a pelisse to have a walk around the grounds. She had been out for perhaps a quarter of an hour when she saw Sir Hillary's yellow curricle coming up the road and hurried her steps towards it in case he shouldn't see her. She thought she must be quite out of shape, for her heart was beating dreadfully from her haste. Quite thumping in her breast, in fact. Her hustle was rewarded. Hillary saw her and drew rein.

"Taking the salubrious air, I see," he said when she had approached him. "I made sure my coach had been stolen to make room for *you* on the trip to Maldon."

"Stolen?" she asked. "You mean Gabriel took it without your permission? That was very bad of him."

"Yes, but I reckon I know where to lay the blame. It was the brat's idea. Will you hop up with me and I'll drive you back to Swallowcourt?" He put down a hand and she was lifted up, with his help, to the seat of the curricle.

"What a wonderful view you get from here," Claudia complimented him. The parks looked finer, the sun brighter, the whole world a changed place from this perch beside Sir Hillary.

"Yes, I made sure I was doing Gab a favor to lend him my open carriage. Now why the deuce did he go and take the closed coach?"

"It would be because of the boxes—two large crates and a little box of trinkets besides. It would not all have fitted into this little gig. Open carriage, I mean," she corrected herself, feeling it might be an insult to call such a wonderful conveyance a 'gig.'

"That's the reason, I suppose, but he ought to have asked me. I might have wanted the coach myself. In fact, I did."

"Are you going somewhere, too?" Claudia asked, fearing her afternoon was yet to prove a dull one.

"Only back to Chanely, but I hoped to take you and Miss Bliss with me. Mrs. Robinson is pining for a coze with her old crony. They usually get together once a week at my place or Swallowcourt for a good chin wag."

"I'm glad. It must be lovely to have someone of your own age and interest to talk to once in a while."

Hillary felt a familiar stab of pity for the forlorn creature at these words. "I make no claim to your green years," he replied, "but I hope our mutual interest in chess will induce you to come back to Chanely with Miss Bliss and give me a game. We can all three squeeze into this gig for the short drive without too much discomfort, I think."

Claudia noted with relief that he himself called his fine carriage a gig. "Oh, yes. Or I could walk if it's too crowded," she offered.

His pity was rapidly turning to anger at whoever had given this young girl such an opinion of herself, that she should walk, while a housekeeper and a man drove. "Nonsense," he said gruffly.

They arrived at Swallowcourt to pick up Miss Bliss and were in some danger of having Marcia Milmont add her hefty frame to the overcrowded curricle, till she recalled that Mr. Blandings might arrive during her absence. The three managed to squeeze into the curricle without an excess of discomfort and executed the short drive down the hill to Chanely, while Sir Hillary entertained them with a description of Luane's visit.

"Why don't you sell the diamond for her?" Claudia asked, which he had rather feared she would. He gained a reprieve from replying by Miss Bliss's intervention.

"I wouldn't do anything of the sort till the year is up," she said firmly. "It may be Sophronia means to give Luane the rest of the necklace to go with her goose egg if she still has the big diamond. She's a deep one, old Sophronia. Selling off the diamond might be just what she was afraid of. You are right to make her hold on to it, Sir Hillary."

"That's what I thought," he agreed.

"She sounds positively *wicked*," Claudia announced. "Trying to lead everyone's life, and she isn't even alive to see it."

"Oh, I don't know. I sometimes imagine I hear her cackle in the house yet," Miss Bliss replied.

"You have a wild imagination, old girl," Hillary laughed, though a little shiver ran up his spine as he remembered that strange echo in the graveyard, when Gab had managed to wrest the wooden coffin open and been confronted with the steel box inside.

Miss Bliss was taken to the housekeeper's room for their weekly chat and dissipation of two glasses of very good sherry, and the chess board was set up in the main saloon for the others.

"Now," Sir Hillary said, rubbing his hands and admiring the carved pieces, "I must keep a sharp eye on the plaguey bishops today, and make sure you don't steal my little crown. Will you be white or black?"

"I am usually black. Grandpa likes to go first."

"So did Sophie. You were black the last time. Be white this time."

She agreed and moved her black knight forward first. Sir Hillary kept careful note of every move she made, hopeful of learning something, if he could not beat her. But Miss Milmont appeared to pay only a cursory attention to the game and was more interested in talking. "I have some good news for you, Sir Hillary. Luane has given up stealing the diamond necklace. We don't mean to go digging up Aunt Sophie any more."

"Sad news for *you*, little Claudia," he replied, noting that her next move was to advance her white knight. "She mentioned it to me."

"Well, aren't you relieved? It bothered you no end

when you thought we were going to go after the diamonds again."

"It doesn't matter," he said, his major interest clearly on the game. "Would you like some wine? Do have some of this Madeira. If I could manage to make you tipsy, I might beat you yet. Why did you advance your queen's pawn?"

"Good gracious, I don't know. You have to move something to get the game started, and that leaves me a nice long shoot to the right here for my black bishop, if your queen or somebody should wander unsuspectingly into my line of attack. Next I'll move the king's pawn and give the white bishop a clear field."

"I see." He noted this strategy, and warned himself to keep clear of her two curst bishops. He poured two glasses of Madeira, and they played on a while.

"I suspect we are leaving a clear field to Jonathon and mama and Mr. Blandings. Do you plan to stop *them* from taking the necklace?" Claudia asked.

"Purge your mind of diamonds if you can. We are going to relax this afternoon. My only immediate plan is to win this game."

She advanced her knight and took a pawn. "This fellow is in my way," she warned, and he was set to scouring the board with his eyes for attacking bishops and crowns.

"That was foolish of you, little Claudia. You are just exchanging my pawn for your own," he said triumphantly, lifting her pawn from the board.

"I was hoping you would fall into that obvious trap," she replied, scooting her queen forward and lifting his knight from the board.

"Damnation! It's not fair for you to keep gabbling away to me and ruining my concentration."

"You're just like grandpa. He always grumbles, too, if I say a word while we're playing this silly old game. You'd better not move that pawn you're giving the eye, or you'll put your own queen into check. And I shant warn you this time either."

"You just have," he said, pulling his hand away from the pawn.

"It's not much fun once the crowns are gone. I should have you stymied within five minutes."

"There is nothing so foul as a poor winner. A poor loser I can comprehend, but a poor winner is repugnant. There," he said, moving his rook's pawn. "I don't think I can get myself into any trouble with this move."

"No, nor me either, for I see you hope to take my black knight with that innocent looking little pawn. I am not such a flat as that. And if you try to take me with your horse, you are leaving *your* horse at my crown's mercy, you see."

"It is kind of you to point out all my likely errors, but I'd like to try my own skill, if you don't mind. Drink your wine and get bosky."

She sipped the Madeira, and finding it quite nice and sweet, she tipped the glass back and drained it.

"I didn't mean you to take me literally, Claudia," he said, smiling at her.

"Not *little* Claudia this time?"

"You are no longer a little girl, are you?"

"No, and I wonder that you keep calling me that odious name. It is a term of contempt, I think, like your calling mama darling."

"It is nothing of the sort," he argued, refilling her glass. "It is only that I have heard your mama call you 'little Claudia' for years past numbering—that is, for several years."

"Ever since I *was* little, very likely," she laughed. "Your bish . . ."

"What?"

"Nothing." She looked around the room, then back to the board, where he had put his bishop in front of her rook, so she whisked the bishop off on him.

He clenched his fists and howled. "How do you manage to chatter like a magpie and drink and still beat me all hollow? Now leave me alone, and let me concentrate."

She sipped her wine with a smug smile on her face and in absolute silence slid her bishop sideways to pick up his knight.

"I don't believe it! I *saw* that pest of a bishop not two

seconds ago, and was determined he wouldn't get me. What did I do wrong?"

"You moved that pawn; that has been all that stopped me from taking your horse these past three moves, for *it* would have taken me, till you moved it. I was going to warn you, but you asked me not to."

"Ha! Well, I've got you this time, for my rook can move sideways as well as forwards, and I'll just shoot him across here and have your bishop, since you think you're so smart."

"Oh dear! I like my bishops so much. I shall have to rush this pawn to the finish line and turn it into a bishop. There! Now I'll have my bishop back, if you please."

"I'm outclassed," he said and drank his wine to revive him. "That is the simple fact of the matter. I'm outclassed by a green girl that doesn't know the time of day."

"You'll pay for *that* piece of poor losing, Sir Hillary," she vowed and turned her full attention to the board. "I'll have your queen within four moves, and then it is but a moment to put you in check."

"Fair speech, ma'am. We'll see about that."

"There'll be no more fair speeches from me. I leave you to the mercy of your own stupidity." On this condemnatory phrase she clamped her jaws shut and made good her boast of relieving him of his queen, in not four moves but three.

"There—*now* who is a greenhorn?" she asked in gloating accents.

He stared at the board in perplexity. "Shall we continue this uneven match to its inevitable conclusion, or shall I just admit defeat and start anew?"

"We'll finish it! It is such fun when I see you can't make a single move to save your king's skin. Don't rob me of my simple pleasures."

The game was over shortly after this contretemps, and Sir Hillary firmly reassembled the pieces for another match, muttering to himself as he did so. "It's the pawns I'm not paying enough attention to. It's a mistake to underestimate the pawns."

"The mistake is in underestimating the opponent, little Hillary," she said smugly.

"*Little* Hillary!" he gasped.

"I observe *you* do not take the description as any compliment."

"I am six feet tall!"

"It was more an intellectual description," she admitted, laughing at him.

"I will beat you at this game, Claudia Milmont, if I have to move you into the house, bag and baggage, and bolt you to your chair to do it."

"In that case, I think you must give us a fire. It is a trifle chilly in here, is it not?"

"Yes," he said promptly with a smile. "That is, *I* am not chilly, and we won't want a footman clattering round the grate, but I shall get you a shawl."

"What are you doing with a lady's shawl in the house?" she asked, rather impertinently.

"It is one of mama's," he replied, and shouted out the door for a footman to bring the new shawl that was on the parson's bench in the hall.

"How convenient!" Claudia remarked, thinking it odd that his mama's shawl should be so handy, when she had been dead for a number of years.

A very beautiful rose-colored shawl with a long fringe was brought in, and Sir Hillary arose to arrange it around his guest's shoulders.

"How lovely!" she said, running her fingers over the soft wool. "It looks brand new. Your mama cannot have worn it much."

"No." He stood back to admire the effect. "She hardly wore it at all. She found it too bright after she had bought it and put it away. It is more suited to a young girl. In fact, you may as well keep it, for there is no use for it here."

"I couldn't do that."

"Why not? Do you dislike it because it belonged to a person who is now dead? The fact is, mama never had it on at all."

"No, it isn't that. I wear Aunt Harriet's old blue shawl

at home all the time, and she is dead, but it is not proper to take such a gift from a stranger."

"A stranger?" he asked, dumbfounded. "Upon my word, I thought we had got past being strangers a long time ago."

"Oh—acquaintance is what I meant, of course."

"Connection is the word you are grasping for, Claudia, and it is quite unexceptionable to take a small gift from a connection."

"Is it?" she asked doubtfully. "It is lovely, and I should like to have it, but I am in mourning, and it wouldn't do, being such a nice shade of rose."

"As you wish. It will make a cozy blanket for my hounds."

"Sir Hillary! You cannot mean to do that with it! It is much too fine, and brand new, too. If only I weren't in mourning . . ."

"You don't plan to mourn forever for an aunt you scarcely knew, I shouldn't think, but it is up to you, of course."

"It seems a terrible waste to make a dog's blanket of it," she admitted, and from the proprietary manner in which she snuggled into it, Hillary thought she had decided to keep it.

"You should wear brighter colors—when you are out of mourning, I mean. They suit you very well," he said, admiring her fashion.

"I would love to," she allowed shyly, "but I have three gowns already, and they are all dull colors, so I shant be wearing anything so bright as this for a long time."

"Is three a magic number?" he asked.

"Of course. One for best—for Sundays and so on, and one for second best—for going to the village, and one for the evenings at home. Plus a couple of gowns for working in the schoolroom, of course," she added.

"I see," he replied, as though she were explaining some matter of which he was totally ignorant, though he had a good idea of the number of gowns belonging to his friends.

"Your mama has more than three gowns, I think."

169

"Mama leads a different sort of a life from me. She is very sociable and has dozens of lovely gowns."

"A Feigning Woman, in fact?" he teased.

"Sir Hillary! Have I induced you to have a look at good Bunyan's book? Where else did you hear such a phrase?"

"Nowhere else. I have been scanning it, as you guessed, and I don't think *you* have much in common with his Feigning Woman."

"More than I like to consider. 'Sin is very sweet to my flesh,' as Hope says to Christian."

"Idiot!" he laughed indulgently. "What sins can you possibly have committed?"

"It is a matter of coveting," she explained. "I *want* all the good things of the world, and I want them now, like Passion, instead of waiting for them in the next world, like Patience."

"There is nothing so demoralizing as an excess of Patience. Your friend Passion sounds much more interesting. If a little judicious coveting is your worst transgression, you are out of gunshot of the Devil. I see nothing sinful in a pretty young girl wanting a few gowns to show herself off to best advantage."

"Show herself off! You see, you do think it bad, even if you are too polite to say so."

"Not in the least. Only consider how fine God has decked out the peacock."

"Well, but He didn't deck the wren out so finely, did He?"

"No, but I wouldn't be a bit surprised if He liked the peacock better. Everyone else does. Don't strive to such a pitch of godliness that you have no human passions. No pride, covetousness, lust, anger—well, I forget the rest of 'em but I daresay you don't."

"Gluttony, envy and sloth," she reemed them off without a second's hesitation. "No danger, I have them all. I think grandma is right, and I'm tainted in the blood."

"Good God! What nonsense is this?"

"Or at least six of them," she said, in a considering mood.

"Which one do you figure you're lacking?" he asked with interest.

"Not the same one as you," she replied enigmatically.

"But how intriguing, little Claudia. Have I managed to escape one? Tell me which. I made sure I had the whole lot."

"I don't think you're a glutton," she allowed.

"What a flattering tongue she has! And yourself?"

"It is time to begin our second game if we're to finish before Gab and Loo get back."

"We needn't finish before they get back. I would much rather consider our many vices—and our single virtue apiece, since you say we have one. *I* lack gluttony, and as to *you*. Now let me see, you have admitted shamelessly to covetousness; you are an acknowledged glutton, proud as a queen I think, beneath that humble facade you wear . . ."

"And the greatest sloth in the world. I hate work."

"Dear girl," he said with a winning smile, "are we working our way around to finding your young body to be without a trace of lust?"

"Why should you think that? I am as lusty as anyone."

"I was thinking more of lustful, as it is sins we are discussing."

"What we were discussing actually was my single virtue, and the one I meant was pride. In spite of what you think of me, I am not proud in the least."

He looked unconvinced, but admitted he was happy to hear it was only pride she was lacking. "I have enough of that one for both of us. And you have been making a shambles of my pride with your mastery of this curst chess game. There, I shall be white this time, and set this little horse out here for you to steal away on me. Come along, take it before I change my mind."

She moved queen's pawn and ignored his taunting. "Sir Hillary," she said after a moment.

"Yes, darling?"

Her eyes narrowed at this term of endearment, or possibly contempt, though it had not quite the same tone as he used to her mama. "Were you serious when you said you thought I might be Loo's abigail? You haven't spoken to mama, or she would have said something to me. Do you think it a feasible plan?"

"Would you really like the job? She is a rare handful, you know."

"I don't doubt she is, but it would be such fun. The thing is, if you are serious, you ought to say something to mama now. My holidays are half over, and once I am back in Devonshire, there will be no getting away."

"It is just a trifle early yet."

"What difference can a few days make?"

"No difference, but still I must wait a little."

"Is this just talk to amuse me? If so, it is cruel," she said wistfully.

"Hush, Claudia. I'm thinking."

"About my position?"

"About your queen."

This callous response set Claudia's hackles up. "Talkative, of Prating Row. Did you come across him in your reading, Sir Hillary?"

"Shh!" He held up one shapely hand and quite ignored her question.

"He seems to be a pretty man. Notwithstanding his fine tongue, he is but a sorry fellow," she quoted at him.

"Sorry." He moved his queen sidewise at last. "Now what were you saying?"

"Nothing. Nothing at all."

"Don't sulk. You said something about a sorry fellow, so you must have been talking about me. What was it?" he asked, diverting his mind from the game.

"I was just mentioning one of Bunyan's characters."

They played on, but for Claudia the charm had gone out of the afternoon. He had no intention of making her Loo's abigail. She would go back to Devonshire in a week, and resume teaching her cousins. Luane would stay at Swallowcourt till Sir Hillary allowed Gabriel to marry her, and that would be an end to the whole thing. The game dragged on for over an hour, with Claudia winning again. Shortly after its end, Miss Bliss rejoined them.

"Are the youngsters not back yet?" she asked.

"They were going to Maldon," Hillary explained. "In the closed carriage it will take them all afternoon. We shant wait dinner for them. They can eat later if they don't stop along the way."

Miss Bliss nodded and looked at Claudia. "What a lovely shawl," she said. "You didn't have that on when we came, did you?"

"No, it was a little chilly, so Sir Hillary loaned it to me."

Miss Bliss shot a quizzical glance at her host but didn't press the matter. They went in to dinner, and during the meal Sir Hillary beguiled Claudia back into a good mood. She had never really believed she would be able to live with Luane. It was all nonsense, of course, and Sir Hillary must think her a fool to have taken his little joke seriously.

After dinner, Miss Bliss suggested they be getting back to Swallowcourt. "I thought we might as well wait for Loo, and I could take you all back together," Sir Hillary replied.

"Gabriel must have taken her home," Claudia replied.

"I thought they would stop here. Well, it will be the curricle again then, ladies. Ready for the squeeze?"

They professed themselves ready, and when Claudia put on her pelisse, she laid the rose shawl aside and prepared to leave without it.

"You are forgetting your shawl," Hillary reminded her.

She looked at Miss Bliss, feeling foolish to take it in front of her. "It belonged to Mrs. Thoreau," she explained to the housekeeper.

"I've seen it on her," Miss Bliss lied gamely.

"You are thinking of mama's mauve shawl, Blissful," Sir Hillary intervened. "I was telling Claudia earlier that mama never wore this one, for she thought it was too bright."

"Yes, yes, I remember now, it was the mauve one I was thinking of. This would be the one you told me you had put away in a cedar chest."

"Yes," he said curtly and ushered them out the door

before Claudia should enquire how it came to be sitting in the hall.

Though she did not make the enquiry, the fact occurred to her and its being untrue discovered by the simple expedient of sniffing it. Not a single fume of cedar was discerned. She felt she had been conned into accepting a gift under false pretenses and was pleased rather than offended.

When they reached Swallowcourt, Hillary said he would check to make sure Gab and Loo were there before stabling the curricle. He was informed by the shuffling butler that there hadn't been a sign of them, and everyone was becoming worried as it was now dark.

"I'd better drive down the road and see if they've had an accident," Hillary decided. "Will you like to come with me, Miss Milmont?"

She pointed out, "If there has been an accident, you will need all the space in your gig."

"Very true. Always thinking ahead, like a good little chess player," he replied. "I'll be back to let you know what has happened. If that cloth-head of a Gab has broken my horses' knees, you will want to have a bed ready for him. I'll likely beat him to a pulp."

Claudia went to her room to dispose of her rose shawl before mama should see it and ask questions. As she folded it with great care, she noticed a little white tag on the back. She saw it was the merchant's ticket, and her eyes widened to see what a shocking sum Mrs. Thoreau—or someone—had paid for it. She sniffed again—not a trace of cedar aroma, and the ticket too looked very new. She wondered whether Sir Hillary had not bought it himself for the sole purpose of giving it to her. And *if* he had, *why* had he? It was a singular mark of attention, too, that he had asked her down to play chess with him—quite enough to turn a simple girl's head, till she remembered how fond he was of the game. Yes, really he had not wanted to talk of a thing but the game, and it was only because she could play better than he that he asked her. But it was very odd about the shawl.

She went downstairs and found her mama and Jona-

174

thon seated in the Crimson Saloon playing cards. Miss Bliss had not returned belowstairs.

"Has any company come while I was away, mama?" Claudia asked, knowing her mother was on tiptoe for the arrival of Mr. Blandings.

"Not a soul, and I might as well have gone to Chanely with you as not," her mother replied angrily.

"Who was you expecting?" Jonathon asked suspiciously.

"No one," Mrs. Milmont snapped. "Why should I be expecting anyone?"

"Seemed to me you both sounded as though you expected somebody to be arriving."

"No such a thing. It is only that Mr. Blandings knows I am here, and if he happened to be going to London from Marcyhurst, he might pop in to say 'how do you do'," Mrs. Milmont admitted. "Tell me, Claudia, what did you do all afternoon at Chanely?"

"We played chess."

"Played chess!" her mother scolded. "Was there ever such a slow top as this girl. Such a fine opportunity to make yourself agreeable—not that Sir Hillary is not a good deal too old for you, of course—but there is no need to bore the man to distraction. What had you for dinner?"

Claudia enumerated a list of appetizing dishes that made Marcia wish more than ever she had joined her daughter for the feast.

"*We* had mutton again," she complained. "We must do better than that, Jonathon, when we return Sir Hillary's hospitality."

"You forget he was here last night to dinner."

"Don't be a ninnyhammer," Marcia said sharply. "It would do you no harm to be on terms with Sir Hillary. You will be looking to make a good marriage now that you are a man of property, and you might meet all the heiresses at his London mansion if you buttered him up a little. Now that you have this property, you are not so ineligible, for even if it is a shambles, no one need see what it looks like. If you nab a girl with a good dowry, you can bring the place to rights."

This called to Jonathon's mind that Miss Milmont had

a fine dowry, of unspecified proportions. Luane wasn't worth bothering about with her one little diamond, but someone had to get the load of blunt, and who was to say it wouldn't be Miss Milmont. "Would you care to give *me* a game of chess, Miss Milmont?" he asked.

"I have already had two games today," she pointed out.

"Dull old game anyway," he replied, relieved. "Would you care to see how I've arranged Aunt Sophie's room, now that I am moved into it?" he plunged on, having decided to amuse her in some manner.

She didn't look much interested, and her mama playfully slapped him with her fingers, saying he was a naughty boy to be trying to lure little Claudia away alone with him. "Run along and have a look, Claudia," she added, now that she had given Jonathon a hint that he was to be naughty. It was hard getting such an unwise daughter settled.

"Very well, but let's hurry back," Claudia said, "I want to be here when Sir Hillary brings the others back."

They went upstairs, and she observed a room unchanged from the morning but for the captain's brushes and personal paraphernalia decorating the dresser in place of Sophie's, and his polished boots standing in the corner, instead of Sophie's sewing basket.

"It's very nice," she said, but without much enthusiasm.

"I've moved the clothespress over a couple of feet, you see to make room for this chair with the hanger built onto the back. Be dandy for hanging up my jacket at night. Saves rooting around in that big old clothespress. Found the chair in one of the guest suites. Always liked those chairs. Clever idea."

"Very clever. Shall we go back down?"

"This room is really very fine," he continued. It was the best furnished room in the house. "Pretty good window hangings, and a new curtain to the bed lately, I think. I like the golden satin cord draws on the window curtains. A touch of class, you know, that twisted satin."

"It's very elegant. You must be quite comfortable here. It is a pity the rest of the house is in such decay."

"As to that, a couple of thousand would put it into shape. Your grandpa—does he live in a good style in Devonshire?"

"The house is fine, but grandpa is a bit of a skint with his money. He saves a great deal," she replied.

Such tidings were music to Jonathon's heart. The girl must be worth a bundle. "And you've lived with him like a daughter, as you might say?"

"Yes, I am considered a daughter, since he has none of his own. Grandpa and I are very close."

"The devil, you say." Every phrase she uttered raised her to a higher pinnacle of eligibility. "He will make some provision for you before he goes, no doubt."

"Yes, some provision will be made for me," she agreed, and thought it none of the captain's business that the likeliest provision was for her to remain on with his son and his wife, as a teacher to their children.

He said no more as he piloted her back to the Crimson Saloon, but he kept a firm hold on her elbow all the way down the stairs, as if afraid she might slip through his fingers. Still Sir Hillary had not returned.

"Wouldn't surprise me too much if the pair of them had slipped off to tie the knot," Jonathon said. Money and marriage were at the top of his own mind, and Gab might have thought a single diamond worth marrying.

Claudia stared at him in horrified fascination. "Do you mean they might be getting married?" she asked.

"Why not? She's a devilish hurly-burly girl, been hot for Gab ever since she landed in here, and does just as she pleases with him, too. Wouldn't surprise me in the least."

"Mama, do you think it possible?" Claudia asked.

"Certainly not. We are all in mourning, and besides, Luane is a minor. They would require a special license."

A commotion at the door diverted their attention. Claudia dashed to the hall to see the pair of miscreants, looking like two puppies caught with their paws in the bacon bowl, being led in by a scowling Sir Hillary.

"Thank God, you're back!" Claudia shouted, running to her cousin and throwing her arms around her. "We were so worried about you! Jonathon thought you were run off to be married. What on earth happened to keep you so late?"

Luane looked sheepishly at her guardian, and said, "Nothing," in a small voice.

"Well they might be ashamed to own up to their conduct," Hillary said. "We shant regale the whole company with the tale, but I shall tell you before the others join us, Claudia, and you decide how much of it is fit for the others' ears. They drove to Maldon and sold Aunt Sophie's stuff . . ."

"Oh, and I got fifteen pounds, Cousin!" Loo inserted, rallying from her shame, "for they took the whole lot, the old black gowns and all, that I planned to give away. Only fancy that. And you should have sent your old cracked vase with me, for I daresay I could have got a guinea for it. I swear the fellow was a Johnny Trot, wasn't he, Gab?"

"He hardly looked at the old clothes," Gab reminded her. "It was the silver-chased traveling case and that little opal pendant on a golden chain that he gave you the money for. I didn't know you meant to sell it. It was worth more than he gave you, I think."

"You sold Aunt Sophie's opal pendant for fifteen pounds?" Hillary asked, his anger mounting.

"It was only a trinket," Luane defended herself. "It cannot have been valuable, or she would have had a replica made."

"It was worth a lot more than fifteen pounds! A beautiful thing," Hillary said aside to Claudia.

"Poo, it was a dark old thing," Loo asserted.

"Yes, a *black* opal is likely to be dark. So that explains the wonderful bargain you drove with the Johnny Trot at the shop. What else did you give him?"

"The rest of it was just junk," Gabriel answered. "I made her keep Aunt Sophie's hunter watch, Uncle," he offered as a palliative, and he handed the watch to his guardian.

"I'll put it away, before she exchanges it for a cream bun," he replied, sticking it into his pocket.

"But this transaction cannot have taken you so long," Claudia said. "What has kept you till this hour?" It was nearly ten by this time.

"What must the gudgeon do but go spending her untold wealth the minute she got her hands on it," Sir Hillary resumed his tale.

"What did you buy?" Claudia asked, with more interest than censure.

"All sorts of things, but Sir Hillary is keeping them for a punishment." She tossed her head at her guardian to accompany this speech.

"A green straw bonnet with coquelicot ribbons is the *pièce de résistance*," he informed Claudia. "Quite appropriate for a Christmas comedy at Covent Gardens. The rest is of a similar inappropriateness for a young girl in mourning. And how you came to permit that piece of folly, Gabriel, passes my comprehension."

"She hadn't meant to wear it right away, uncle," he explained.

"Not now or ever, if she wishes to continue under my protection."

Claudia gave her cousin a silent, sympathetic look.

"To get on with their spree," Hillary continued, "it was already coming on dark when the shops closed and the money was gone . . ."

"I still have ten whole pounds left!" Luane charged righteously.

"Then they thought it *might* be a good idea to head for home, which they did," Hillary said with a warning look at Luane.

"That is not so very bad, Sir Hillary," Claudia began soothing him in a conciliating manner.

"Oh yes, *that* appears to be the one sensible notion that occurred to either of them during the entire day. They did not quite complete their journey, however. What must they do but come nine-tenths of the way home, then stop at Billericay, where they are known to everyone, and hire a private parlor for a midnight dinner."

179

"I expect they must have been very hungry by that time," Claudia said.

"I expect they might have contained themselves during the two more miles and eaten at home. I can imagine what is being said around the village, the two of them hiring a private parlor, and with Aunt Sophie not yet cold in her grave. Using *my* carriage into the bargain, as though I had given such behavior my sanction. Well, you had better marry the wench after this piece of imprudence, Gabriel, for you have certainly ruined her reputation."

"We left the dining room door wide open," Gabriel countered.

"It was closed when I entered the inn."

"We only closed it because we recognized your curricle drive up," Luane told him. "Before that it was open the whole time."

"With half the village gazing in amusement at that frightful red and green hat that is more suited to an actress or lightskirt than a young girl in mourning. I don't know what you were about to allow her to act so, Gabriel."

"She didn't put the hat on till after we were in the private parlor. Just trying it on, you know," Gabriel explained.

"I wonder she didn't pull off her gown and change that too, in sight of all her admirers."

"No, I only changed my hat and gloves and reticule," Luane said. "Oh, the sweetest little beaded reticule, Claudia. You will love it. I would have got one for you too, only I bought the blue for myself, and the red was a trifle garish."

Claudia smiled her thanks for this nonexistent present and turned to Sir Hillary, who was shaking his head in helplessness at his charges. "The horses are all right, are they?" she asked, as that had seemed to be his chief concern when he went after them.

"Yes, they failed to put them in the ditch somehow. I have left the carriage standing outside and must go. You tell the others what you think sounds not too bad, Claudia."

"Mayn't I have my parcels before you go?" Luane asked.

"Certainly not! I have no wish to look across the aisle at church Sunday and see that red and green bonnet. And you, Gabriel, will go back to Cambridge tomorrow."

"What about *me*?" Luane asked.

"Well, what about you?" Thoreau demanded.

"My reputation is ruined. You said Gabriel must marry me."

"You must both show some signs of maturity before that time."

"Tomorrow is Saturday, uncle," Gabriel pointed out.

"I am well aware of it. In that manner you won't have to travel on a Sunday and will be back in time for classes on Monday. You hadn't planned to hang on to her skirts for a month, had you? We'll get rid of you before you cause us any further embarrassment. And you'd better show me a good report at the term's end, or I'll hire you a tutor and you'll spend your summer with your nose in a book."

"May I leave after lunch, and come and say good-by to Loo in the morning?" he asked.

"You'll leave early," Sir Hillary answered, unmoved.

"It only takes five hours to get there. We can easily be there before dark if we leave around one."

"*We* are not going, pup. *You* are going post."

"Oh," was all Gabriel replied to this, with a hang-dog look at Luane.

"What time does the post leave?" Claudia, hoping for a reprieve.

"Around eleven, I think," Gabriel told her.

"Surely, Sir Hillary, you will allow him to come to say good-by to Luane. You cannot be so cruel as to forbid that," Claudia coaxed.

He felt much inclined to forbid it, but when Claudia said, "Please," in a pleading tone, he changed his mind. "Very well. Come on, Cawker. Time you were in bed." He grabbed Gabriel's sleeve and turned him towards the door.

Gabriel smiled at Luane in an apologetic way, but she was scowling at Sir Hillary and didn't see him.

"Good-night, Claudia," Thoreau said, ignoring Luane completely. "Don't waste too much sympathy on this pair of whelps. You will be changing your mind about wanting to be Loo's abigail. I'll come with Gabriel tomorrow and help you prevent their falling into some new scrape."

"Good-night, Sir Hillary," she replied. She was not happy with his highhandedness and refused to honor him with a smile.

"Are *you* angry with me too?" he asked.

"You are a little hard on them."

"Pudding heart!" he laughed at her. "Some abigail you'd make to the hussy. She'd bear-lead you as she does this cawker. Don't let her convince you I am quite the monster she will make me out. I'm not, you know."

"Oh, no."

"Good-night again," he said, and took her hand as though to shake it, but instead he raised it to his lips. Then he turned and left.

"He is trying to jolly you into being on his side," Luane said the minute the door was closed. From the moon-struck look on her cousin's face, she feared he was succeeding, too. "He always takes to being gallant with ladies when he means to bring them round his thumb. He was such a tyrant, cousin! He wouldn't let me finish my apple tart and hauled Gabriel right up from the table by the collar and shook him. I was *furious*! And Gabriel doesn't stand up to him in the least, just as though we were doing something wrong to stop for a bite to eat, when we were both *famished*."

"We'd better let the others know you're back," was her reply.

"You tell them. I'm tired," Loo said, and ran up the stairs to her room.

Claudia did no more than stick her head in at the door and tell her mother Luane was home but had gone to bed already. Then she went up the stairs after her.

"Tell me all about it," Claudia invited, throwing herself on to Loo's dimity-covered bed.

"I wish I could *show* you all the lovely things I bought, but, of course, that old stick of a Hillary won't let me have them and will likely cast them into the fire, for he doesn't like me to look too attractive in front of Gabriel. Such a sweet bonnet—a great high poke right past Gabriel's head, with the gayest red ribbons. I looked a very dasher in it; everyone was turning to stare at me."

"I thought you only put it on after you were in the parlor."

"Well, I put it on in the carriage before we went into the inn, for how would anyone see it otherwise? I hope what he said about my being a hussy won't put you off from wanting to be my chaperone."

"He has no thought of that. He has already hired Miss Bliss. I had hoped I might be an abigail for you, but he didn't mention it to mama at all. It was just talk."

"That sounds just like him. You notice how he said Gabriel would have to marry me, *then* said we were both too immature. He always pretends he is going to do something nice for you, but it never happens. He was afraid to let Gabriel come to see me alone tomorrow, for fear he'd offer for me. That's what all his coming to see *you* is about. And now he is trying to turn you against me too, by calling me a hussy."

"He didn't mean it; he was just angry."

"Poo, what has *he* got to be angry about? *I* am the one who was bilked out of my nice black opal, only because he didn't tell me it was valuable before I sold it."

"He had no idea you were going to sell it."

"I wouldn't have had to if he'd sell my diamond as I *begged* him to. Only think of the injustice of it—I am *rich* and can't get my hands on a penny because he won't let me. And there is no reason why Gabriel must leave tomorrow either. Lots of people travel on Sunday now. Sir Hillary does himself, and it is all fudge that he doesn't want Gab to travel on Sunday."

"Grandpapa never travels on Sunday, except to church, of course."

"He is just afraid I will get Gabriel to offer for me if he is allowed to stay over another day, and I should too, if I had my ten thousand pounds. I got him to admit as much today. He said anyone could live on five hundred a year."

"You have your ten pounds anyway. Or did Sir Hillary take that, too?"

"No, for it's still in my old reticule, and he forgot to take it."

They talked for half an hour, with the younger girl castigating Sir Hillary as the blackest of villains, while the elder tried to excuse his faults. Luane began yawning, and then Claudia realized that she too was tired. Just before she left, she said, "And we are never to dig up Aunt Sophie again? I am sorry about that."

"If you want an adventure, I imagine Jonathon is going digging tonight. Gabriel thinks so, but it is illegal, and he will have to give the diamonds back in the long run and likely go to jail too."

"It wouldn't be any fun with Jonathon. I'll go down and say good-night to mama before going to bed. Goodnight, cousin."

Chapter Thirteen

It had been a long day and an eventful one for a young girl accustomed to no excitement at all, but still it was not over. When Claudia returned to the Crimson Saloon, mama's visitor had arrived at last, and Claudia was reintroduced to Mr. Blandings whom she had met briefly at Bath some years ago. She did not remember that he was so big, so black of hair and swarthy of face, so loud of voice, so altogether common. Or perhaps it was only that two years ago she had not been comparing him to Sir Hillary Thoreau.

"So this is your little girl," he said, arising and pumping Claudia's hand which he held in a viselike grip. "Don't take after you—but she wouldn't, of course."

This statement reminded Claudia that for the duration of the man's visit she was to be on her guard against being mama's daughter, as well as being her true age. A sharp nod from her mother told her she better not forget it.

"She is a Milmont through and through," Marcia decreed, to give some explanation to Jonathon for her

185

lover's peculiar statement. "But how comes it, Mr. Blandings, you were so late in coming? I made sure you would be here a couple of days ago."

"There's the bad luck of it, my dear. I wasn't in London when your note arrived. I'd gone off to Hampshire to give a mortgage on a nifty little property—at ten per cent too. I make it a point to pace out every acre before I give a mortgage on it. There's no saying it won't end up being mine, for ten per cent is the worst you can do on a mortgage, as against five per cent in the funds. With luck, the fellow will default, and the whole lot will fall into my hands. Much good it would do me if it turned out to be a swamp or a bog. Pace every foot of it out myself. Yessir, Jeremy Blandings didn't become the Trump of Mortgagees by buying a pig in a poke. And how did your business fare, my dear?"

"Mr. Blandings, I am not here on business!" she objected.

"I mean the will, of course," he explained, surprised at this obtuseness on the part of his beloved, whose mind usually kept pace with his own financial reckonings. "Did she leave you anything of account?"

"This is no time to talk of such things, when we are in deep mourning," she replied, with a sanctimonious face, from which avaricious eyes peeped out. As she spoke, she unconsciously fingered her rope of pearls, which were usually to be seen around her neck.

"Left you the pearls I see," he answered.

. . "Yes, and Claudia got that fine emerald," she answered. She had made her obeisance to propriety in mentioning that they ought not to discuss such things, and now felt free to go into all the details. "Show him the ring, Claudia."

Claudia held out her hand. "The mischief of it is she has managed to get it shoved on to her finger and can't get it off," Marcia added.

To the utter amazement of Miss Milmont, mama's suitor pulled a jeweler's glass out of his pocket and stuck it into his eye to examine her emerald. He dragged her to the lamplight to do this, twisting her finger this way and

186

that to get the best view. "A poor light. I'll have a look in daylight tomorrow. I can't see any flaw in it. It's a good deep color—and large. Fifteen carats, I make it."

Claudia's amazement gave way to amusement, and she could scarcely keep from laughing aloud. She found herself wishing Sir Hillary were there to share it with her. "I didn't realize you were in the jewelry line, Mr. Blandings," she said.

"I turn a penny where I can," he admitted carelessly. "Many of these old families that are mortgaging their places are happy to sell off their unentailed heirlooms to help raise the wind. That's why I carry this little lens with me. You never know when someone will want to sell a ring or a jeweled piece of some sort. Picked up a dandy little bracelet from this chap in Hampshire," he said to Marcia. "You will like it, my dear. Diamonds and sapphires."

"Mr. Blandings! What will my daughter—my—Claudia think, to hear you talk so. She will think I am in the habit of accepting gifts from you, and you know very well I have never taken a thing."

"That's very true. You will never accept so much as a rubbishing little diamond or ruby or a thing. I picked your stepmother up a dandy little masterpiece by a feller called Rembram or some such foreign handle, to hang over her rose sofa." He added aside to Marcia, "Where you mentioned you wanted a little picture to hang in the corner, my dear. And what does she do? She refuses outright to accept it—a mere trifle—and I had to hang it in my pantry, for my saloon walls are crammed as full as a picture gallery. Not an inch of wall to spare anywhere."

"I didn't care for the scowl on that old lady's face, Mr. Blandings," Marcia said playfully. "If you want to get me a picture I would like, you must get a nice Gainsborough, or a Reynolds, and not give me a dark picture of a homely old malkin with a broom in her hands. Not that I would accept it, of course," she added firmly.

"I was told Rembram was a good investment," he assured her.

Jonathon had been auditing this conversation and now

spoke up. "Did you call Claudia Marcia's *step*daughter?" he said to Mr. Blandings.

"Yes, so I did, and it was very bad of me, for I know she likes to call her her daughter. She told me so dozens of times."

"Well, she *is* her daughter!" Jonathon announced, rather angrily.

"Yes, yes, so she is," Mr. Blandings agreed imperturbably, and Claudia began to suspect for the first time that Mr. Blandings might have more of the true gentleman in him than she first thought.

Her mother, she observed, was jiggling in her seat in embarrassment and, to smooth over the pass, Claudia said rather quickly, "When did you turn from your metal work to general business, Mr. Blandings?"

She could not have posed a question more likely to divert him, for he was justly proud of his accomplishments. She sat through a long speech outlining his rise to fortune from two years spent—wasted, he insisted—in a parish school through his apprenticeship to an ironmonger; his gradual but steady rise to assistant manager and, eventually, owner of the establishment; his inventions that bettered the production and profit of iron; and the amassing of his first fifty thousand, at which time he figured he was ready to sell out and set up as a man of property. But time had hung heavy on the hands of a man used to work and, bit by bit over a period of only a few months as it turned out, he had become completely involved in mortgages. He was now worth, he told her proudly, one million pounds, give or take a couple of thousand, and known throughout the country as the Trump of Mortgagees.

"How interesting!" she exclaimed, impressed at his wealth and title.

"Oh, yes, could buy and sell half the titles that look down their knife-sharp noses at me. But I don't care for rubbing shoulders with the nobs, except in the way of business. I'm no good at scraping a leg, or twirling about on a dance floor, or doing the pretty with the ladies. I'm a plain man. A country squire is what I'll be happy to be, if

I can talk a certain little lady into being my missus," he said coyly with a smile in Marcia's direction.

"Well, my dear," he went on, "what was it you wished to consult with me about?"

Marcia looked at Jonathon and at Claudia and replied, "We'll discuss that in private, Mr. Blandings, if you please."

"Ah, I have stuck my foot in my mouth again," he said, unoffended. "As you wish; we'll discuss it later. Tell me, what happened to that great diamond necklace of your sister's? The Beresford diamonds you called it, if I mistake not. Who got it?"

"Nobody. It was buried," she told him.

"Eh?" He shook his head, and actually stuck a hairy finger in his ear to ream it out, for he could not believe he had heard aright. "Thought you said it was *buried*," he laughed at his own folly.

"So I did. She had the diamonds buried on her body, and the corpse is sealed in a metal coffin."

"That's a bad business," he shook his head. "Become crazed, the poor old lady. You'll be having the will contested then."

"No such a thing!" Marcia fired up. "We can't even say she's crazy, for if we do, we won't get the money, which is to be given out in a year's time, but there are *conditions*. Miss Bliss thinks one of the conditions might be that if anyone tries to have her declared insane, that person won't get any of the money."

Mr. Blandings considered this matter and shook his black head again in consternation at such unbusinesslike goings-on. "That kind of monkeyshines is what I don't hold with. If you mean to give a person a thing, give it to her. To be giving with one hand and holding back with the other is a mealymouthed way to do a thing. The pearls were given outright, were they?"

"Yes, the pearls are mine, and the emerald. That is, the emerald is Claudia's, of course."

"This is a mischievous business. Those diamonds won't be in the earth above a fortnight. It wouldn't surprise me if someone has snatched them already."

"Sir Hillary Thoreau—he's one of the executors . . .", Marcia began.

"Is *he* in on this business?" the Trump enquired.

"Yes, he's a connection of Sophie's. He hired a man with a gun and two dogs to guard the grave."

"That was well thought of. With Thoreau in charge, this matter might be straightened out yet. A good head on him."

"Yes, well, the dogs bit a little boy, and the constable made him call them off, so the diamonds are just sitting there waiting to be taken." Marcia then remembered that she was discussing in public what was for Mr. Blandings' ears alone, and she sent Claudia off to bed. Jonathon, she feared, she would have to hint away, but he had matters of his own to attend to and rose and went off with Claudia.

"You have hit the nail on the head, as usual, Jerry," Marcia said, reverting to his first name when they were alone. She also moved from the frayed petitpoint chair to the lumpy sofa beside him. "The grave is unattended, and someone will certainly steal the diamonds. Now, who has more right than her own sister to them? Tell me that."

"No one, my love. She should have left them to you. I made sure she would."

"And so she shall, for *you* are going to steal them for me."

From long practice in using his brain in business, Mr. Blandings was about three steps ahead of his beloved and not in the least surprised at her command. He demanded to know precisely all terms of the will, and upon discovering that the bulk of it was not to be read for a year, he put his heavy foot down and told her severely he would not go digging up a coffin and stealing a rubbishing set of diamonds he could buy without missing the price. "If it's diamonds you want, my little minx, you know where you might get them without disturbing the dead."

"Yes, but someone will surely take them, Jerry, and it does seem a shame for them to go to Luane Beresford, or the captain."

"If Thoreau is in charge of the operation, you may be

sure they won't be stolen without being discovered. He's a bright lad."

This called to mind his brightness in discovering that the great stone in the replica was in fact a real diamond, and she told Jeremy about that.

"Only the one stone?" he asked.

"Yes, the rest are paste. Till then the captain thought the whole set was genuine, which is the only reason he didn't dig up the grave sooner."

"How long has it been that he's known the difference?"

"Sir Hillary discovered it in London and told him only last night."

"He couldn't have made arrangements in time to make a go for it last night then, but if there's any fiber in the fellow at all he'll be making his bid tonight. And the other Tewksbury fellow as well—Gabriel, is it you call him?"

"Certainly Gabriel will, for he dug her up the very night she was buried, only he discovered the steel lining and couldn't steal the diamonds."

"He sounds a proper wide-awake young rascal. And Thoreau let him off with that, did he?"

"I fancy Hillary knew all about the steel box from the start, but you can see what sort of people we are dealing with. They will stop at nothing to steal my dear sister's necklace, and if we don't get cracking, Jerry, they will beat us to it."

This blatant hypocrisy on the part of his beloved amused Mr. Blandings very well. There were many things about Marcia Milmont that he admired. Her charms, though they had ceased to cause distress in most quarters, were not too ripe for his taste. Her gentility, thin as it was, was above his own. She was a gentlewoman, and he had determined when he was seventeen years old to marry one of those rare mortals. He came in contact with many of them these days, but till he had clamped his sharp black eyes on Marcia, he never met one he felt comfortable with. She admired his business dealings—was nearly as delighted as he himself was when he turned a good bargain. She would lend tone and cachet to his establishment without boring him to flinders. The fact that she was a liar, a conniver, and a schemer would add spice to life. Take that business about letting on young Claudia was her stepdaughter. As though Sophie would go leaving an emerald ring to a girl no blood-kin to her! And in short, he was as close to being in love with her as it was possible for such a hardheaded man to be with anyone, and he was determined to win her by any means necessary. He was not besotted enough, however, to stick his neck into a noose for her or anyone else over a trifling necklace.

"It's a rum set-up," he remarked. "But Thoreau aint about to let anyone waltz off with the trinket, my love. You upset yourself for nothing. Now, I see you forming a pout at me, naughty puss. We can't have that. I'll tell you what I'll do, and you approve it. I'll talk to Thoreau tomorrow and see how the land lies, but in the meanwhile I'll set myself to guard the grave for you. If the captain or the other young sprig comes creeping up, I'll give 'em a taste of the old home-brewed. In the dark they won't know what hit 'em. The stones won't be stolen this night, I give you my affydavey, and you may lay your pretty head easy on your pillow."

"But it is such an excellent chance to steal them, with the dogs gone, you know. There is no saying he won't ship in a squad of dragoons or some such thing by tomorrow to guard them."

"The dragoons have better things to do with Boney cut loose." He essayed a pout himself to bring her round. "Seems to me you want any diamonds but the ones *I* offer you. If it's the set of the stones you like, I'll have them duplicated from the replica."

"Now Mr. Blandings," she chided. Jeremy became Mr. Blandings when she pretended to be angry with him, as well as when they were in company. "You know it would be improper in me to take such a valuable gift from you."

"Wouldn't be improper for you to take them from your husband," he slid in.

A day seldom went by that the subject didn't arise be-

192

tween them. Marcia loved Jeremy's wealth nearly as much as he admired her gentle birth, but she loved even more to move in the *ton*, and a Cit, even a solid gold one, would lower her a peg in the eyes of her lofty friends, she feared. It was the sole impediment to their union. For herself, he might have been born in a stable for all she cared, so long as he had clawed his way up to a mansion. "It is early times yet to speak of that," she replied.

"Early times for a young thing like *you*," he rallied energetically, knowing his role to a т. "You forget *I* am a man of three and fifty. We have known each other over two years. How long do you mean to keep me dangling at your apron strings, eh?" He slid an arm around her plump shoulders as he spoke, setting her old heart all aflutter. He was absolutely the *manliest* man she had ever attracted.

She pushed his hand away in an arch manner that did not discourage him entirely. "Now you are just trying to distract me."

"Turn about is fair play. You have been driving me to distraction these four and twenty months."

"Oh, Mr. Blandings! How you do run on. I am sure you never give me a thought from one day to the next."

"And *I* am sure I am not sitting here in this drafty old shack because you bade me come. Say we do the thing, old girl, and I'll shower you with diamonds."

He grabbed her hand and squeezed her fingers. "What a famous emerald-cut diamond, big as a lantern, I have got tucked away in a vault, waiting to be put on this little finger," he said, undeterred and unfooled by her protest. "Had it of the Duke of Welbourne. He's all to pieces, you know. Got Skye mortgaged to the hilt, and they do say his heir is bringing in the bailiff to look into the running of it."

"Do they indeed?" she asked. Their lovemaking was often interrupted by *on dits* of this sort, with neither of them finding it at all irregular. "And he trotting through town in a different carriage every day, and the duchess queening it over everyone as though she were loaded with blunt."

"Bellows to mend with the pair of them. I could foreclose on his Leicester hunting lodge tomorrow if I had a mind to, but there's no saying he won't come around, and there's no point getting on the west side of him."

"Very true. He stands to inherit from his uncle, Sir Bartholomew Rankin, and *he* might pop off any day."

"Yes, there's a mort as knows the value of a pound, old Rankin. Has the first penny he ever made, I daresay. But about *us*, Marcy dear."

"Now you mustn't pester me, Jerry. I am in deep mourning for my dear sister and can't think of a thing but her. You mean to stand guard over her grave tonight, do you?"

"I'll guard it with my life."

"And you'll talk to Thoreau tomorrow and see what you can worm out of him?"

"That I will, my girl."

"I suppose I must be satisfied with that then. I daresay you are fagged and will want a little lie-down till it is time to go to the graveyard."

"No, no, I will be better relaxed sitting here with you, imagining we are together at Marcyhurst—married."

"I declare, Jerry, you have nothing on your mind but marriage."

"Not a thing in the world. Did I tell you I got ten per cent for the mortgage in Hampshire, my love?"

They sat bickering and cooing and gossiping for an hour, and when Jonathon stole past the door half an hour later, he was interested but not much surprised to see them sitting hand in hand.

She's going to land that old bird yet, he thought to himself. Be rich as a nabob. As he put a shovel and a file into a canvas bag and set off for the graveyard, it occurred to him that the sole person to inherit the nabob's fortune when he passed on was Claudia Milmont. Old Marcia was too old to give her new husband a son and heir, and the only possible person to get the blunt was Claudia. She also stood to inherit God only knew how much from her grandfather. Wasn't a bad-looking woman in the least, and once the world caught on that she was such an heiress, there'd be every rake and rattle in town trotting after her. By Jove! What a lucky thing it was that *he'd* discovered her first. Have to make up to the girl and get things settled before she left. He hardly thought it worth his while to bother with Sophie's diamonds, but still, they'd tide him over till he married Claudia and became a millionaire.

He left his mare tethered to the iron paling that set the graveyard off from the surrounding countryside and walked quietly to Sophie's mound. He thought, as he approached it, that the headstone had already been erected, for there was a tall straight slab just at the head of the grave. This was a curious affair; he made sure the price of the stone must come out of his own pocket. That will of hers—cursed document—must have made provision for it. As he got pretty close to it, he was surprised to see a soft red glow that became brighter, then receded again to a faint spark. The hair on the back of his neck rose, and an involuntary shiver shook him. He stopped, stared, and felt the panic rising in his breast.

"Good evening, Captain," the glowing spark said, and he dropped his canvas bag on the ground with a clatter.

A form—a shadowy bulk, detached itself from the memorial slab and approached him with the spark dancing around in front of it. "Sophie!" he screamed and turned tail to flee.

"Yes, I came to commune with her spirit," a suave voice replied, and Jonathon stopped abruptly.

"You!" he charged.

"As you see," Sir Hillary answered and took a long draw on his cheroot, causing the spark to glow brightly.

"What the deuce are you doing here?" Jonathon asked angrily.

"I have just explained my presence. I am come to blow a cloud with the dear departed. That is, *she* is not smoking, of course, but I brought my favorite chair to sit by the graveside. The ground is damp and chill, and I felt I would be more comfortable with a chair. A pity I had not thought to bring two. Most remiss of me. I *do* apologize, for I had a pretty good notion you would come to pay her your respects as well. But you have brought something— what is it that made such a racket when it fell just now?" He advanced and picked up the clanging canvas bag. "Garden implements, I take it? Yes, I am sure you were about to plant some bulbs or flowers at the graveside. I had the same idea, but decided to wait till daylight. Do you think she would like daffodils? And some snowflakes, perhaps, to give her a bloom early in the season."

Panic was replaced by anger and a smidge of embarrassment in the captain's bosom. "Don't try to bam me you came here to smoke."

"Surely you can see for yourself I *am* smoking. Sophie never minded in the least. Even in her sickroom she often invited me to light up. I never did, of course, but it was kind of her to make the offer. Would you care for a cheroot, Jonathon? I brought half a dozen with me; I was unsure how long a vigil I would make."

"I don't smoke."

"Bully for you. I hope you are not about to warn me it is a filthy, disgusting habit, as nonsmokers are so fond of doing in that revoltingly self-righteous way they have. I am very well aware of it. But then I don't drink to excess, or gamble at all except in a spirit of sociability, and I know you wouldn't have me perfect. There is nothing so vulgar as an excess of perfection."

"You don't have to worry about that!"

A low, amused chuckle escaped Thoreau's lips. "I find you almost tolerable at times, Captain. Really, you are not at all so bad as people say. Shall we get on with the gardening? I will be quite happy to lend you a hand." He opened the canvas bag and extracted a shovel. "Yes, I see you have brought a shovel. You take it and I shall use the spade." Upon saying this, he extracted the file.

"Jonathon, you careless fellow, you have brought a file in error. I can't do a thing with this. Or is it to sharpen the lip of the shovel? Yes, that must certainly be why you brought a file. There can be no other reason. Now, I shall just sharpen up your shovel for you, and you can begin sorting out the bulbs. Ah—where are the bulbs? You cannot mean to say you forgot the bulbs, too, you absentminded soldier. Really, you are beyond anything. I think you might as well go back to Swallowcourt and forget all about your gardening for tonight."

Jonathon stuffed the shovel and file into the canvas bag and replied, "I'll just stick around and bear you company, Thoreau."

"That's downright civil of you, Jonathon. And by the by, I have already told you very recently you may call me Hillary. You hurt my sensibilities to go on calling me Thoreau, as though I were your batboy. Sure you won't have a cheroot? A pity we hadn't thought to bring a bottle, and we might have had a party. Now what is this?" he asked, as he espied yet another gadfly coming to join their party.

"Blandings!" Jonathon said in an angry voice. "I knew he was up to no good and him rich as Croesus."

"He can well afford to give Sophie a few blooms for her garden. In fact, with his blunt, he might set up a greenhouse and swathe her in orchids. Ah, Mr. Blandings," he said, reaching out his hand to shake with Mr. Blandings, who accepted the hand across the grave with all the sangfroid of the aristocracy.

"Evening, Sir Hillary," he said in his usual hearty voice. "Been wanting to have a chat with you about this foolish will of Mrs. Milmont's aunt."

"How clever of you to know just where to find me."

"I had no notion you'd be guarding the grave yourself. Marcia told me you'd hired a man, but he was called off, of course, wasn't he?"

"Yes, the careless soul let his dogs feast off a child. But he is an ex-soldier you know—Bronfman. A military man, like the captain here. They are a heedless company."

"Plans all gone awry, are they?" Mr. Blandings said to Jonathon, but not in a condemnatory tone at all. Almost sympathetic in fact.

"Yes, he came to plant some bulbs on his aunt's grave,

but unfortunately forgot to bring them. You don't happen to have a couple of lily roots on you, I suppose? No, it is too much to expect."

"Where's your nevvie?" Mr. Blandings asked, not diverted by these frivolous questions and remarks.

"In his bed, if he knows what's good for him. Would you care for a chair, Mr. Blandings? Do join our little party. A cheroot?"

"Thankee kindly." He accepted the cheroot and lit it, but ignored the offer of a chair. "Tell me, Thoreau, do you plan to stay the night? If so, I can go back to bed. Promised Mrs. Milmont I'd guard the grave, but if you're here, there's no point in my staying up all night too."

"As you see, I have brought my chair and cigars, and plan to make a night of it. But don't dash off on me. You've just got here, and I enjoy the company. Sophie hasn't a word to say for herself tonight, and I was becoming quite lonesome till Jonathon dropped by."

"Aint legal, you know, Captain, what you're doing," Mr. Blandings warned the captain.

"Surely there is no law against planting flowers on a grave?" Hillary asked, shocked. "One sees them everywhere."

"Yes, yes, I know you fellers always stick together, but the fact is grave-digging is a crime, and stealing diamonds is a crime, and if the captain's caught at it, it will be more woe than wonder," Mr. Blandings pointed out.

"Tell me, Sir Hillary," he continued, "since you've lost the soldier with the dogs, what plans have you made for guarding the grave? Stands to reason you won't be sitting up here every night yourself, and I'd like to tell Mrs. Milmont what you plan, to set her mind at rest."

"Mr. Fletcher, the solicitor, has taken the strange resolution that nothing ought to be done to guard it. The will did not provide for it, you see."

"That's asking for mischief," Blandings stated.

"It is indeed," Hillary agreed. "There is no saying who will decide to go planting flowers on her grave. We will have a regular garden on our hands, and there was no provision for a person to tend them in the will."

Blandings considered this a moment, then puffed on his cheroot, and spoke out in a conclusive fashion. "This boils down to one of two things, don't it?"

"Very likely," Thoreau agreed, "but I don't see what the two things are. Perhaps you will be kind enough to enlighten us."

"I will. A—there aint no diamonds in there to steal, and B—there are, and she wanted them stolen. It's as simple as that, for the fact of the matter is, she didn't make up this zany will for no reason. Or she might have been crazy, but I don't think it myself. Tell me, am I right or am I right?"

"You make it so miraculously simple, you put me to the blush, and Jonathon too, if he isn't blushing already from being caught redhanded. It is surely one or the other, but the question is, which?"

"They're buried all right," Jonathon said. "Loo has the big diamond and a set of paste stones, and the rest of the set is buried right here." He tapped the grave with his toe as he spoke.

"In that case," Blandings stated, "she wanted 'em stolen. And if she was the sort of mort I think she was from Marcia's description of her, she means to avenge herself on whoever steals 'em. Mark my words, Captain, she'll get back on you if you set shovel to this grave. She'll take away Swallowcourt; that's what she'll do."

"Well, she won't, for it's entailed," he countered.

"Is it so? Then in that case, you've nothing to lose, unless you're caught in the act, and I think it's downright crazy of the solicitor not to have the grave guarded. Who's to know you took 'em if you aint caught with them in your hands."

"That's what I thought," Jonathon agreed, happy to be borne out in his reflections by such a downy cove as the Trump of Mortgagees.

"Sophie wasn't quite such a slow top as that," Hillary reminded them. "You forget the money which is not yet accounted for. Its disbursement depends on what happens in the year between her death and the reading of the remainder of the will. Who is to say that the person who digs up the grave does not disqualify himself from inheriting the money?"

"That sounds sensible," Blandings agreed, "but again, unless the culprit is caught in the act, who the deuce is to know *who* took the diamonds? You'll see they're gone right enough, but with you all blaming each other and the possibility of anyone for miles around having helped himself to them, you'll be dished to know who's responsible."

"Precisely why I am come to visit dear Sophie," Hillary pointed out.

"Yes, pretty well, Sir Hillary," Blandings said, "but you don't plan to sit out here for three hundred and sixty-five nights, through snow and sleet and hail, I don't suppose?"

"No, I think I shall be knocked senseless, bound, gagged and blindfolded long before that, and the grave torn open. It is my hope that I recognize my assailant and can place a finger on him. Sophie *must* have counted on me to do it. Whether the diamonds are there or not, she must have planned to take action, posthumously by her will, against whoever opened the grave."

"It'll be the devil of an expense, but you must do one of two things," Blandings informed him.

"I envy you the ability to reduce infinite possibilities to a duo. Tell me my two options," Hillary begged.

"You either hire a set of guards—and I don't mean one or two that can be overpowered, but a half a dozen or so good stout fellows to do the job for you, or else you have the coffin dug up officially and put in a safe place."

"I love you, Mr. Blandings," Sir Hillary said simply. "I always had the notion that there was a simple solution to this Gordian knot, but till you came along with your sword and cut it open, it eluded me. Of course we must have her coffin exhumed and put in some safe, guarded place. I'll speak to Fletcher about it. Tell me, before you go away and take your good sense with you, what safe place had you in mind?"

"Jail," the Trump replied promptly.

A strange, howling noise as of ghostly laughter came around them, and they all stared.

"An owl, very likely," Mr. Blandings said.

"That wasn't no owl!" Jonathon declared, but hesitated to say in front of two grown men what he considered the noise to be.

"You hear that, Sophie?" Hillary shouted into the dark night, and then let out a raucous hoot of laughter. "Jail it is," he said, laying an arm over Mr. Blandings' shoulders. "And serves the old devil right. It's where she belongs for serving us such a trick. I wonder if Fletcher can arrange it."

"Seems to me you well-born fellows can arrange anything you want," Blandings opined.

"If only we could always have your good sense to tell us what we want," Hillary said, smiling.

"I won't have auntie put in jail!" Jonathon objected.

"Hush, Captain, you'll wake the dead," Hillary warned. "You may as well take your shovel and file home and put them away. You won't be planting any flowers at the round house."

"You aint putting Aunt Sophie in jail," Jonathon repeated and picking up his tools, he departed.

Blandings and Thoreau stood looking after him. "He's to be pitied," Blandings asserted.

"I have always pitied him very much," Thoreau said.

"If Swallowcourt was entailed on him, he ought to have seen it was kept up properly. Welbourne's heir is having the bailiff in to look at the way Skye is being run. Only thing to do when you get a fool or a scoundrel running a valuable property into the ground—an entailed property."

"He should have done so, certainly."

"However, he's a fine figure of a man and has a dandy uniform. I daresay he'll marry money, as the saying goes."

"If he don't, it won't be for lack of trying," Sir Hillary told him, and they stood discussing the general state of the world for half an hour. Then, their cigars burnt, Blandings left, and Sir Hillary resumed his vigil at the grave.

From behind a not too far distant tombstone, Mr. Fletcher turned his collar up around his ears, and huddled into the folds of a warm horseblanket, waiting for dawn.

Chapter Fourteen

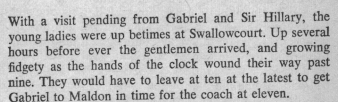

With a visit pending from Gabriel and Sir Hillary, the young ladies were up betimes at Swallowcourt. Up several hours before ever the gentlemen arrived, and growing fidgety as the hands of the clock wound their way past nine. They would have to leave at ten at the latest to get Gabriel to Maldon in time for the coach at eleven.

"He plans to let him say no more than hello and good-bye," Luane said, pink with anger. "If he even lets him come at all, that is. There is no counting on him to do as he has promised."

"He may have changed his mind and decided to let him go tomorrow."

"Changed his mind and sent him off last night is more like it."

Sir Hillary's character grew blacker as the hour grew later, and when ten had come and gone, he could hardly have been worse if he'd stuffed his nephew full of opium and murdered him in cold blood, in Miss Beresford's opinion.

"He won't be coming now," she said. "He wouldn't even let him come and say good-by to me."

"I am sure there's a good explanation for it," Claudia soothed her. "They will both come riding up any minute; you'll see. Sir Hillary has decided to take him to Cambridge in the carriage; that's what it is."

"Well if that's what he's doing, they'll leave by noon. They should be here by now. Come, cousin, let's take the gig and go to Chanely."

This seemed a harmless way to lessen Luane's anxiety, and Claudia was certain Gabriel had not gone off without first coming to see them, as he had promised.

At Chanely they received the bad news from Mrs. Robinson that Gabriel had been up early and eager to go to Swallowcourt, but his uncle had slept in.

"Slept in!" Luane asked. "He *never* sleeps in."

"He did today, and still looked fagged when he got up."

"Out carousing half the night, I suppose, and ringing a peel over us for stopping for a bite of dinner."

Mrs. Robinson did not deign to reply to this calumny, but to cheer the girl up, she told her Gabriel had thought it safer not to go off to Swallowcourt without his guardian because of the rare temper Sir Hillary had been in the night before, and the upshot of it was that Thoreau's valet had had to drag him out of bed barely in time to make the coach to Maldon. They had dashed off at five past ten, and it was nip and tuck whether they'd be in time to catch the coach.

"Maybe they missed it," Claudia suggested.

"If they did, they'll wait for the two o'clock," Mrs. Robinson had the hard job of informing them.

Luane indulged in all the fury of a woman scorned and marched from the room.

"Let's wait till Sir Hillary returns. He will have a message for you from Gabriel—a letter maybe," Claudia said.

"He wouldn't give me a message if he had it, and he wouldn't let Gabriel write me a letter. Is there a letter, Mrs. Robinson?" she asked at the front doorway.

"No, he didn't leave a letter."

"You see," Luane said to her cousin in the tone of one who had suspected the worst all along and could be surprised at no depths of treachery.

They went to the gig and jolted home to Swallowcourt, hardly exchanging a word. Mr. Blandings had left long since with Mrs. Milmont to visit the agent in Maldon, to see if there were any neat little properties to pace out and put a mortgage on.

"I might have gone with them and seen Gabriel off!" Luane wailed. "Everyone is against me!" On this moan she departed from the saloon, to go to her room for a good bout of tears, Claudia suspected. Half-relieved to be rid of her, she took a book into the Crimson Saloon to await Sir Hillary, who she thought would come to them to explain the matter on his return from Maldon. She was in no charitable mood with him. Bad enough he had kept Gabriel from coming, but that he was out carousing half the night himself was a much worse sin. What really capped her ire was that it was none of her business if he had been. She supposed she ought not even to mention it, but she would, of course.

Captain Tewksbury came ambling into the room while she was in the midst of her dumps and seated himself to get on with the courting.

"Your mama and the Trump are smelling like April and May this morning," he told her genially.

"You think they will make a match of it?" she asked with interest. It was a lowering reflection that the captain was more likely to know it than herself.

"Crazy if she don't. Yes, and dashed loose, too, to be sitting around holding his hand if she don't mean to have him. But she will, of course. As cunning as can hold together, your mother," he said, with no thought that this speech might do him a disservice.

"If she was allowing him to hold her hand, it must be settled between them."

"That's what I thought. What do you think of the old boy?"

"I think I could get used to him as a steppapa, do not you?"

"Yes, by Jove, I could," he replied readily.

"You? No, no, I meant did you not think *I* could, for he won't be your stepfather if mama marries him."

"Ha, ha, of course. Foolish of me."

He then rose to strut about the room a little and show off his shoulders and his scarlet tunic. "A fine figure of a man," he commented to bring the subject to her attention, since she seemed mighty interested in looking out the window.

"Yes, he is very big."

"A little stouter than I am myself, but I think the shoulders are about the same size." In this sly fashion he finally got her to glance at his shoulders.

"About the same," she answered listlessly.

"Do you think him handsome?" he ploughed on.

"He is too dark and swarthy for my taste," she allowed, as a vision of Sir Hillary wafted unbidden through her mind.

"You prefer fair men, do you?" he asked jauntily, passing a white hand over his blond curls.

"Not so dark as Mr. Blandings."

"Well, well." This wanton encouragement led him to take a seat beside her on the sofa. "Your holiday is half up," he said, thinking to use the brevity of her stay as an excuse for undue haste in his courtship.

"How I dread to leave!"

"Do you? Upon my word, you are kind to say so, Miss Milmont. I am delighted you have enjoyed your visit so much."

"I have never had such a good visit in my life," she said with real feeling.

"You'll like it much better when the place is fixed up," he assured her, with a wary eye scanning the dilapidation of the chamber.

"A little dust and fraying of carpets doesn't bother me. It is the *people* who have made the visit so enjoyable."

He could hardly believe the soft words of delight she was pouring into his ears. "Good of you to say so," he said and took her hand in his. His eye fell on the emerald, and he automatically added three thousand to her dowry.

"It sinks me to have to think of leaving in a week," she confessed, withdrawing her hand.

"I will have to be leaving myself very soon," he told her, as a preface to getting on with the offer. "I'll be here but a few days longer, for they will be having a tough time getting on without me at the Guards. In these troubled times a soldier's hours are not his own. He cannot always stay where he would like to be, with the people he would like to be with."

"You must dread to leave, when you are eager to set your house to rights," she commiserated.

"A woman's touch is what the place needs," he said leadingly.

"It would be great fun to redo it, but it would require a deal of money," Claudia remarked, looking around the shabby room.

By Jove, if he didn't forge ahead and make his offer, she'd be doing it herself. She shared his feelings on every point. He reached out again and grabbed her hand.

"Are you admiring my emerald?" she asked.

"No, I am admiring your pretty little fingers," he returned smoothly.

"Why, Captain, how gallant you are become!" she laughed and looked once more to the window to see if Sir Hillary was on his way yet. He had, in fact, already cantered his mount round to the stables while they had been talking.

"Are you looking for someone in particular?" Jonathon asked.

"Sir Hillary said he would call on me this morning," she admitted with an involuntary blush.

Tewksbury was already very well aware that he had a rival in Sir Hillary. Hadn't seen him dangle after a girl so obviously in his whole life. Which was another pretty good indication she was well greased, come to think of it. The likes of Thoreau wouldn't be marrying any penniless country wench. And Thoreau knew she would be leaving soon, too. Without further ado, he was on his knees at her feet, pouring out his heart, while she sat in speechless wonder, incapable of imagining what had gotten into him.

Sir Hillary, all unaware, came into the house the back way from the stable, pushed open the door of the Saloon, and stopped dead in his tracks. There on the sofa with her eyes like saucers sat Miss Milmont trying to disengage her hands from Jonathon's grasp, and he, with one red arm outstretched, knelt in mid-declaration. A satirical smile settled on Sir Hillary's countenance, and he stepped in, looking very much as he had on the first occasion Claudia had seen him.

"Is this interruption by any chance untimely?" he asked blandly.

"No!" and "Yes!" came from Claudia and Jonathon simultaneously.

"There seems to be a difference of opinion here, but one always accepts the word of a lady," he said, advancing towards the embarrassed couple. "Pray, don't mind me, Jonathon. Go ahead with whatever you were doing. I seem to be always interrupting you in the middle of your activities, do I not?"

Jonathon gazed at him with open hatred. "I can't very well make an offer in front of a third party," he said.

"You are too shy, my friend. Thinking it necessary to plant flowers by moonlight so no one would see you, and thinking it would disturb me in the least to overhear an offer in form. I don't mind at all. Go right ahead."

"I can't."

"Why not?"

"Because I can't," the captain repeated.

"That is begging the question, surely. Shall I show you how?" Sir Hillary asked. He went to stand in front of Claudia beside Jonathon, who rose and began brushing the dust from his knees.

"I shant bother to kneel, for I see you have made a shambles of your trousers. Standing will do for a re-hearsal, though in a real offer kneeling is all the crack. You take the lady's right hand—so." He took Claudia's hand in his, without once looking her in the face. "You had her *left* hand, Jonathon, the one with the emerald—

lidn't you notice? You take the right hand, unless you are left-handed, in which case I suppose—but never mind, you are not left-handed, nor is Miss Milmont. Next you assume a suitably ardent expression—a mixture of hope, love, and eagerness with something of eternal devotion thrown in if you can manage it, but still firm and manly. Humility has no part in this particular expression. That will come later after she has accepted. I think the facial expression really half the battle. When my time comes, I shall think of a particular trout that has eluded me these several seasons and imagine I am about to land him."

"Now see here, Thoreau," the captain began, noticing a quivering of Claudia's lips that augured ill for putting her into a romantic mood.

"Why must I keep asking you to call me Hillary? Is it so hard to remember? You are impatient for me to get on to the spoken part, I expect. Very well, if you're sure you have appreciated the importance of the expression. You lift the lady's hand—hold still, darling—clear your throat once for effect, and say, 'Miss Milmont—or Jones, or Smith, of course, as the case may be—will you do me the honor to be my wife?' Some recommend an enunciation of one's own unworthiness first, but I intend to avoid that. No reason to point out the obvious. If the young lady has any wit she knows it, and if she hasn't, there is no need to cut the ground from under your own feet. So you make the offer—short and simple—and then you wait. It's time for *your* lines now, darling," he said to Claudia, looking at her at last. It was a quizzical, penetrating glance, deep into her eyes. She was beyond speech.

"Do you need a little prompting, too?"

"No, she don't!" the captain said.

Hillary looked at Jonathon, then again at Claudia. "She does, you know. You can see she hasn't a notion how to reply. We are making you a proposal, darling. That means we are asking you to marry us. *You* must now say . . ."

"I know my part," Claudia told him. "I shall be honored, sir, to accept your kind offer," she said demurely, with the laughter lighting her eyes.

"That's pretty good," Hillary complimented her. "Jus'
a moment's hesitation might have taken that edge of eagerness from the acceptance, but for a first try . . ."

"What makes you think this is my first offer?" she
asked.

"Surely it is your first *acceptance*," he pointed out
"Otherwise you ought really to have said no. But you
have been practicing up to say 'yes,' no doubt, to have
your lines ready for the first man who asked you."

"Oh, you hateful creature!" she flashed out at him.

He bowed solemnly with a flash of his sardonic smile
and replied, "Mr. Talkative, of Prating Row."

"We'll speak of this another time, Miss Milmont," the
captain said and stomped from the room in vexation.

"There—he has given you fair warning this time, darling, and you can be ready with your 'yes' before he has
half the question out."

She was amazed to see he was truly angry, for she had
made sure he was funning the whole time. "Sir Hillary!
You cannot think I meant to accept him!"

The hard look vanished from his eyes so quickly she
thought she must have imagined it was ever there at all.
"Oh, I don't know what you deserve for that performance," she laughed.

"Kean would ask about fifty pounds, but as a good
amateur I wouldn't ask more than the half of such a sum."

"What an abominable trick to play on that poor man."

"Never mind the man. Is that any way to thank me for
rescuing you from your romantic quagmire? Or are you in
the habit of letting him make love to you? I seem to recall
your mentioning it on a former occasion."

"You know I was only joking. He never makes love to
me, but he should have been allowed to make an offer in
peace."

"He will be the better for the lesson, and do the thing
properly the next time."

"Yes, I *do* know what you deserve. A good thrashing!
And I wish he would give it to you."

"I wish he would try," Sir Hillary answered quietly

210

nd, hitching up the knees of his trousers, he sat down beside her.

"What can have gotten into him to do such a thing? I was never so shocked in my life."

"It seems so ungallant to suggest it was anything but your beautiful blue eyes, but the unworthy possibility will keep obtruding in my mind that he mistakes you for an heiress."

"How could he be so misguided? I haven't a penny."

"We have all mentioned that famous phrase 'intervening year' and wondered about its meaning. He has already had a go at Luane; I wonder if he thinks you might do as well, being also a niece. He could be right, for that matter."

"I can't make heads or tails of it. We were just talking about nothing at all, and all of a sudden he was on his knees."

"*Sweet* nothings at all?" he asked.

"What? Oh, you idiot! Of course not. We were saying that we think mama will marry Mr. Blandings. He is come, by the way."

"Say no more!" Sir Hillary said, waving his hands in a graceful way that was always a pleasure for Claudia to behold. "He knows a good thing when he sees it. If it is true your mama is at last to capitulate and have the Trump, then that accounts for his keen interest in you. What an awful thing to say! It is not my own feeling, I think you know."

"It will make no difference to *me*," she replied, noticing but not mentioning the latter part of his speech.

"You will likely stand to come into some of his blunt when he dies."

"He is young, and the healthiest looking man I ever saw. Besides, he won't leave a thing to *me*. He doesn't even know I am mama's daughter."

"I beg your pardon? Do you actually mean she is palming you off as her sister?"

"No, her stepdaughter!" Claudia replied, laughing brightly, but Sir Hillary fell into another scowl.

"You mustn't be angry with her. She dislikes to claim

211

me as her own daughter, for then she would have to be so terribly old. Jonathon very nearly let the cat out of the bag last night. Oh, how I wished you were here, Sir Hillary! It was a famous visit."

"Did you, Claudia? Then I wish I had been here, too. Tell me all about it."

She told him about Jonathon's saying bluntly she *was* Marcia's daughter, adding, "and he never blinked an eye, though I think he tumbled to the truth on the instant. He is so shrewd, Sir Hillary, there is no keeping up to him. Made a million pounds, and with only two years wasted at school. Oh, and the best part, when he was shown my ring, he pulled a jeweler's glass out of his pocket and held my hand to the light, giving its weight as fifteen carats on the spot. I bet he is right, too."

"He's a wonderful fellow. I like him excessively."

"Do you know him quite well?"

"Only in a business way, but he would be quite an ornament to society if he cared to bother. He doesn't, which I think is why your mama is so slow in having him. She'd better step smartly if she wants him. There are a dozen pretty chicks on the catch for him."

"Jonathon says they were holding hands, so I think she must have accepted at last, and very likely he has to get Sophie's diamonds to win her."

"No, he doesn't mean to do that."

"You cannot know it."

"Oh, yes, we had a charming visit last night."

"So *he* was out carousing with you!" she said.

"Carousing?" he looked at her blankly, causing a blush to suffuse her face. "Where on earth did you get that idea? We were merely discussing the case."

"Loo said very likely that was why you slept in so late this morning, and why Gabriel didn't get up to see her. She was mad as a hornet."

"You didn't heed my warning to disregard her slanders against me," he smiled. "I knew how it would be. I couldn't believe my eyes this morning when I came downstairs and saw he hadn't had the sense to go up and say good-by to her while I slept. He thought to bludgeon me

212

into letting him stay till Monday by that ruse, but it back-fired. I hauled him right over to Maldon and put him on the coach. A close-run thing it was, too, to make it."

"Didn't he leave her any message or letter?"

"No, deep into the sulks, and hardly said a word. But you can fabricate all sorts of tender messages to lull the brat into peace. I suppose she's been raising an almighty dust, has she?"

"She went straight to her room, and I must own I was relieved to be rid of her."

"She'll be scribbling him off a blast of a letter, libeling me as the villain of the peace. They correspond regularly. Well, they are as good as engaged, and there can be no harm in it."

"It must be a splendid pastime for her. I love writing my letters to mama. It makes it seem as though you have a friend when you have someone to write to, and some-times they answer you, too."

Every word the girl uttered about her mother threw him into a spasm of anger, but he was aware of the uneven relationship between them by this time, and said nothing.

"And now I will have Luane to write to as well," she finished up.

"Have you given up the idea of being her abigail then?" he asked, surprised.

"*I* given up? It is no such a thing. You didn't mean a word of what you said, and I know it perfectly well. I knew it was just talk."

"Claudia, my dear," he said, a little angry as well as surprised, "that is not a very nice thing to say to me. I know it means a great deal to you, and I have every in-tention of carrying our plan through. You cannot have forgotten, I hope, that I mentioned there were some strings attached to it."

"You haven't mentioned it to mama."

"I shall speak to your mama this very day. And I shall speak to *you*, too, alone, as soon as I have seen her." He arose and began strolling to the door.

"Must you leave so soon?" she asked.

"I can't in good faith eat Jonathon's stringy mutton after the way I treated him this morning. And I can't carry you off with me to Chanely, much as I would like to. I must see Fletcher. More developments in the case. Can I count on you to evade Jonathon's importunities?"

"Yes, I'll run and hide if I see him coming."

"Good girl, and if he finds you, tell him you are already taken, and your lover is a fiend of jealousy."

She looked a question at him. "I wouldn't like to tell him such a plumper," she replied.

He laughed lightly. "With six of the seven deadly sins under your belt, I wonder you should stick at that. And it isn't a plumper, either. When do you think your mama and the Trump will be back?"

"By midafternoon I believe. They left around ten."

"I'll be back around three or four then, to speak to your mother."

"I'll try to cheer Loo up till you get here."

She went with him to the outer door, where he stood with one hand on the handle looking at her, as if he were loth to leave. "Practice your lines, Claudia," he said. He took her hand and raised it to his lips, kissing each of her fingers in a row, then he turned and left, closing the door quietly after him.

She stood a few moments transfixed, before hopping to the saloon to have a view of his back as he rode away. 'Practice your lines,' he had said. The only interpretation she could put on his words was so marvelous she didn't dare think it. It was not possible she had worked that smooth, elegant gentleman up to such a pitch he meant to propose to her. She, a tall, plain, old girl who had nothing to do with style but a craving for it. She went to her room to consider in privacy, with a rose shawl about her shoulders, every detail of their acquaintance. She could find no allusion to marriage but the words he had said before departing. 'Nasty strings' and 'moving her into his house bag and baggage,' being 'resigned' to her mother and the flint-like face he wore every time he heard of her being slighted were not even considered. She dwelt instead on his tall and handsome figure, his noble-looking face, his wo beautiful palaces with their multitude of servants, of he diamonds of the first water he brought to Chanely in ever-changing variety, and was sure she had misunder- tood his meaning. She wouldn't let herself believe any- hing else, for the disappointment of being wrong would surely kill her.

She didn't go belowstairs till Miss Bliss called her for uncheon. Entertaining Loo was completely forgotten, but when her cousin failed to come to the table for luncheon, she went upstairs to get her and received an unpleasant shock. Luane was not in her room.

Chapter Fifteen

Upon her return from Chanely Saturday morning, Luane Beresford did precisely as Sir Hillary supposed she would do—went to her room to write a letter to her dilatory lover, chastising him and his guardian. She did not like writing letters. She knew exactly what she wanted to say, but somehow the words that ended up on her page, much crossed out and very unevenly aligned, did not express her thoughts. Before she had half a sheet filled, she had succeeded only in aggravating her feelings, not giving vent to them. She squashed the messy sheet into a ball, threw it into a corner, and jumped up from her chair. She put her ten pounds in the reticule, donned her riding hat and gloves, and let herself out the back way to go to the stables.

It was eleven o'clock. Gabriel would just be leaving Maldon for Cambridge. On a previous occasion when he had missed the post by a few minutes, Sir Hillary had dashed him on to the next stop—Witham it was. She would hasten to Witham and have a few words with Gab before he left. He would hear the full budget of his uncle's iniquity, and if there was an ounce of pluck in him, he wouldn't stand for it. Just what he would do in the five minutes she might have to see him she didn't know, but she couldn't sit still and do nothing. In her mind she may have realized she wouldn't see him at all, but in her heart and in her fancy she envisioned a passionate meeting.

Maldon seemed a very long way off, and when she reached it, she was much of a mind to turn back, but there she heard the encouraging news that the post had been side-swiped not a mile out of town by a young buck playing hunt the squirrel, and had had to stop and send back to the village for a wheeler. Very likely it wasn't more than a mile ahead of her. With the cheerful prospect of shouting at someone, she urged her mount on to a faster pace. She didn't overtake the post, but various carriages loomed ahead of her that *might* have been it for all she could see through their dust, and in this fashion she got three-quarters of the way to Witham. Then she did see the post and slackened her pace to stay just behind it.

Gabriel, in a deep fit of the sullens, had no notion of getting down to stretch his legs at Witham, and Loo had to go to the carriage and request him to do so. "I have an urgent message from home," she added, to put a good face on it before the other passengers. His astonishment, upon learning the truth, was exceeded only by his anger. How came she to do such a harebrained thing, he asked. Before she could defend herself, the driver was urging Tewksbury to take his seat. Then he realized it was impossible to leave a young lady unattended eighteen miles from home on a fagged animal, and very likely without a penny in her pocket.

"There's another buck here is looking for a seat if you've a mind to wait for the stage," the driver said impatiently.

"Oh, very well," Gabriel replied, and the seat was sold. "I'll have to poke along on the stage now," he said to Loo, who was cheered to learn she would have two whole hours with her lover.

The local inn provided their joint necessities of a place

to converse in private and a meal. With Sir Hillary a good, safe, eighteen miles away, they again hired a private parlor. Money was no problem—Luane had her ten pounds, and Gab too had money from his uncle. An hour passed pleasantly in abusing their guardian, then they went to stroll about the village till the stage came.

"Your horse will be fagged by the time you get home," Gabriel commented.

"I'll just dawdle along and will likely be home before dark."

The word 'dark' made him suddenly aware of the ineligibility of the scheme, and before he was through lecturing her, she had been called a mad woman for chasing after him, even in broad daylight.

"If I had known you only meant to abuse me, I wouldn't have," she returned. "It's clear you wouldn't have done as much for *me*. I suppose Sir Hillary has been running me down to you."

"Certainly not! He blamed me for the whole."

"Then you should be flattered."

"I am, but dammit, Loo, how are you to get back? The whole house will be in an uproar by now if you didn't tell anyone you were coming."

"Nobody will notice. None of them cares a straw about me," she said, letting a whine creep into her voice.

"Sir Hillary will notice."

"Him again! You never think of *me*. I'll be lucky if I ever get home at all this night. I'll likely be waylaid by highwaymen or assaulters of some sort."

"We'll hire a chaise and pair for you right now, before the stage leaves."

She objected to such a foolish waste of money, but when they got to the local stables there wasn't a chaise or pair or even a gig or whisky to be had.

"It will have to be the stage for you, too, then," Gab decided, unsure whether he did the right thing to put an unchaperoned lady on the stage, but very sure he did not wish to face his uncle again that day, in view of the strong words that had blistered his ears that morning. At least, it was a short trip for her. At their next stop at the office of the stage, they met discouraging news. Every seat was booked, and to clinch the matter, all customers were present, as the vehicle was leaving in minutes. The next was at midnight, and entirely inappropriate for a lady traveling alone.

These enquiries ate up so much of their time that Gabriel's stage came and left without his even making an inquiry, and they were stranded at Witham, with only one tired nag between them. In a fit of depression, Gabriel suggested walking home, with the hope that some kind stranger might pick them up.

"*Walk*, and us with nearly thirty pounds between us?" Luane asked in astonishment. "Don't be such a gawk. We'll find a private carriage for rent."

This quickly proved unfeasible. The one gentleman Gab had the fortitude to put the proposition to laughed in his face. "We'll start walking," he told Loo in a commanding tone. "It's only eight miles to Maldon—won't take more than a couple of hours if we hustle. We can rent something there."

"There's a little village half-way to Braintree—only a few miles away. Let's go there instead," she countered.

"It's in the wrong direction. If there's nothing to rent there, we're farther from home than ever."

This detail was quickly talked down as no reason at all, and before he knew what had happened, she was on her nag, being led towards Braintree by himself. Between the mount's slow gait and stopping every time a carriage rumbled past, cloaking them in dust, it was some two hours before they reached the little village, only to discover it boasted no stable at all.

"I guess it must have been somewhere else I thought I saw a stable," she said wearily.

It was now five o'clock. They were miles from home, with no means of conveyance, tired, dirty, and hungry. With Luane, the last named was the first attended to, and they went directly to the only public place—a small, disreputable inn with no private parlor. They ate an unappetizing meal in near silence. Gabriel's mind was roving over the nonexistent possibilities of coming out of the affair with honor, and Luane's was wondering where they should sleep for the night.

"This is the only inn in town. We'll have to put up here for the night," she told him.

"This is no place for a lady." The boisterous company mostly masculine, was becoming interested in the pretty young lady who sat eying them nervously, and began making comments.

"I know it isn't. That huge man with the fierce mustachios is looking at me. You'll have to speak to him, Gab."

Gabriel turned and intercepted a leering look from a man a foot taller and twice as broad as himself, and at least ten years older. "We'd better leave," he said.

She went reluctantly with him, and as they left, a gentleman got up and followed them. Gabriel was prepared for the worst, and was relieved to see the fellow was old, and not so very large. He proved not to be after Luane at all, but only concerned for their safety. After a few polite preliminaries, he gave them some good advice.

"I advise you to go directly to the rectory," he said. "The rector will be happy to put you up for the night. It won't do to put the young lady up at the inn. An unsavory place at the best of times, and on a Saturday night . . ."

The rectory proved to be only a quarter of a mile away, and they had both just enough strength to haul themselves to it and throw their weary bodies on the rector's mercy. All was arranged speedily and satisfactorily. The young lady would sleep with the rector's daughter, and the gentleman would have the spare room. Tomorrow he would escort them to Witham and try for a chaise, or if necessary take them to Maldon himself. It was such a relief to Gabriel that he felt in the few moments between his head hitting the pillow and the arrival of sleep that he had rubbed through pretty well. Given the circumstances, he didn't see what his uncle could charge him with.

After the youngsters had gone early to bed, the rector turned to his wife and said with a sage nod, "There'll be a set of angry parents after that pair of runaways before morning, or I miss my bet."

"They seem very young to be getting married," she answered.

"They do surely, but when it comes to running away and being away overnight, there's nothing for it but to have them decently married. I'll have out my book and brush up on the ceremony. They'll want it done before the young lady is taken home in disgrace. Aye, and wanting *today's* date on the certificate, which I don't hold with."

"Where's the harm, dear?" his wife replied, handing him the book of services to peruse while she sat in happy reminiscence of her own wedding day twenty years previously.

Claudia flew into the dining room all in a flutter when she saw her cousin's room to be empty, but Miss Bliss made little of it. "She's gone for a canter to get rid of her temper. Does it all the time. She'll be in better curl when she comes back."

"I'm surprised she'd miss lunch," Claudia replied.

"She's got her purse full for a change. She'll run over to Billericay and fill up on sweets. She's quite a baby still."

"Does Sir Hillary allow her to ride about all alone?"

"He's only just become her guardian," Miss Bliss pointed out. "Sophie allowed her to ride between here and Chanely alone, and she occasionally sneaked over to the village. Everyone knows her, and it's safe enough."

Claudia was satisfied with this, but after lunch she went to the stables to make sure the mount was gone. She was told Miss Beresford had set off for Chanely, which was along the road to Billericay, but a little later when she had still not returned, Claudia went to her cousin's room. Remembering Jonathon's remarks the previous evening about an elopement, she began to fear that possibility. But the closets held all their customary garments, and on that score at least she could be easy.

As she returned belowstairs, her mama and the Trump

were tooling up to the doorway in a magnificent carriage—black, drawn by four black horses, and escorted by two outriders, though they had only been to Maldon. Such a cavalcade stunned Miss Milmont, and she ran to her mama to compliment her on such high style.

"How grand you and the—Mr. Blandings look. Quite like royalty, in such a carriage. Do you always travel so grandly, Mr. Blandings?"

"No, I usually just jaunter about in a little open phaeton and pair, but I brought my traveling carriage with me, and have no other conveyance at my convenience here. You will be all right, Mrs. Milmont?" he asked with concern.

"Is something the matter, mama?"

"Nothing in the world. Mr. Blandings is leaving. That's all."

"So soon?" She hoped mama had not had a tiff with her wealthy suitor.

"It's oh revwahr, not good-by," he said. "I've been put on to a little property over Chelmsford way—a thousand acres with a mansion on it, that's looking for a mortgage. The terms the agent mentioned sound good, and will be better before the deal's closed or I aint the Trump of Mortgagees, heh, heh. Wish me well, Marcia. I won't be back tonight. It'll be dark, and I won't be able to pace it out when I get there. Tomorrow I'll be up bright and early and into my walking boots. I'll just remind my man to pack them. I never travel without my walking boots. Tell Sir Hillary—well, there's no need to tell him anything. He is taking care of that—er, other matter we spoke of. I must run up and have a bag packed. I'll be down presently, my dear," he said to Mrs. Milmont. "You'll wait and say good-by to me, I hope?"

He nipped up the stairs two at a time, so eager was he to be off snapping up another mortgage, and Mrs. Milmont and her daughter went into the Crimson Saloon to await his descent.

"What an interesting life he leads," Claudia said.

"As to that, he seldom goes to a party, and spends all his time in business deals. I doubt he attends the opera three times a year, though he takes an excellent box for the season."

"He could go to the *ton* parties if he wished. Sir Hillary said *he* would not object to knowing him socially, and as far as that goes . . ."

"Did he indeed?" her mother asked eagerly. "How came he to say such a thing?"

"We were just talking. I told him Mr. Blandings had arrived and the subject arose."

"And Sir Hillary said that? Dear me, if he only meant it, it would make everything . . . But no doubt he was being satirical."

"No, he was serious. He thinks Mr. Blandings an excellent man."

"I had not thought Sir Hillary would take any notice of him."

"He says there are a dozen young girls throwing their caps at him, and once he is married, I suppose he will ease up on his business and lead a more sociable sort of a life."

"What young girls?" Mrs. Milmont asked sharply.

"He didn't give any names, mama. They would not be known to me, you know."

"It's Miss Warren, that's who it is. Mr. Blandings mentioned her name twice recently. Had some dealings with her papa—he was selling Jerry some jewelry I believe. They are all to pieces and would be eager to nab him."

"Very likely she is one of them. I wonder who the other eleven could be."

Mrs. Milmont was entering into a state of high perturbation, to hear of these incursions on her beau's affections. "Mrs. Dorringer is another, mark my word, though she is no longer a young girl, I assure you. Twice she has paid me morning calls, and I was at a loss to discover the reason. I scarcely know the woman, and she is very good *ton*, too. She looked to meet him at my home, bold hussy. Certainly that is what she was at, for now I come to think of it, she asked me half a dozen times whether I was going out, or whether I was expecting any other company. Here I thought it was Jonathon she was after. And wasn't she wearing a new bonnet each time, too, and a pound of rouge on either cheek."

"A man of his handsome appearance and wealth will surely be snapped up quickly enough," Claudia said airily. "It's a pity *you* could not bring him up to the mark, mama."

"*Not* bring . . . you silly chit! He has been hounding me to have him any time these two years. It is only with the greatest effort I have held him at bay so long. Did he not name his country place after me—Marcyhurst? And you heard him say the other night . . . Well, upon my word, I think I must make up my mind very rapidly." She did so in about a tenth of a second.

Claudia quietly excused herself, that they might have privacy to bring their amour to a head before the Trump went dashing off to pace out the environs of Chelmsford.

It was conveyed to Mr. Blandings by a coy smile and a hint that she wished for his speedy return, that her affections were reaching their apogee; and he, no skulker when opportunity knocked, popped the question again as he hastened to the door with his walking boots tucked under his arm. It was settled in the hall, and before he was out the front door he was enquiring whether she would prefer Lady Nolan's emerald cut diamond or the Duchess of Avon's emerald baguette for an engagement ring.

"Both, by Jove. I'll give you both," he chuckled.

"Oh, Jerry," she slapped his arm playfully. "Next you will be saying you want to give me a different one for every day of the week."

"Why not, eh?" he laughed merrily. "We'll decide as soon as I am back. I can't dally, for Curzon is interested in this Chelmsford property, and he is such a flat he will give them a better offer than I mean to do. I think I can screw the fellow up to twelve per cent. I feel this is my lucky day. Tomorrow we'll set the date and all that." He was off, contented that Lady Luck had now favored him in the heart as well as the pocketbook.

Marcia Milmont went up to her room to be congratulated by her daughter, who was accidentally the first to hear the stunning news; and to drop a half a dozen notes to her bosom bows informing each in secret that she had accepted an offer from Mr. Blandings, since he wouldn't be put off any longer.

Chapter Sixteen

It was not much later that Sir Hillary fulfilled his promise to return to Swallowcourt to see the Milmont ladies. He did not speak to the mother, however, as the daughter diverted him from it by telling him in some alarm that Luane had been gone since morning.

"Has anything been done to find her?" he asked.

"Miss Bliss felt she had only gone for a ride into Billericay, but it is four hours now, and she would surely be back. Do you not think we ought to go looking for her?"

"Yes, certainly. Get a bonnet and pelisse, and tell your mother where we're going."

This was done, and within five minutes they were going at a quick pace down the hill to Chanely, thence to the main road. "She wouldn't have done something foolish like run away, would she?" Hillary asked.

"I looked in her room, and nothing is gone."

No trace of her was found at Billericay, even when they appealed to Miss Miller, the queen of gossips, who surveyed the village constantly from her bow window.

"At least she hasn't run away with Gabriel, for he was

on the post by the time she left the house," Claudia comforted her companion.

"Scatterbrain that she is, I don't think she's eloped without a nightshirt. I'll take you home and if she isn't back, go on to Maldon. We don't want the family worrying about two runaway brides."

"Speaking of brides, there is another one, but in no danger of elopement. Mama has accepted Mr. Blandings."

Hillary smiled and nodded. "This will set Jonathon hot on your trail. Remember to avoid him."

"He has something else on his mind. I saw him collecting tools with Tuggins. Very likely he means to dig up Sophie, and he won't have a bit of competition either, for everyone else has dropped out."

Hillary heard this with no great concern and immediately changed the subject. "When do you think your mother will marry?"

"Not very soon, with Aunt Sophie just buried."

"Yes, *she* is a sister. It would be improper for *her* to wed soon."

Miss Milmont ignored this meaningful comment, and drew his attention to a particularly fine stand of willows growing along the creek's edge. Back at Swallowcourt, a second searching of Loo's room brought to light the half-written letter. It was read without compunction by Sir Hillary who said, "She started to light into him by letter but changed her mind. She must certainly have gone after him."

Miss Bliss, when appealed to, thought it unlikely, without so much as a bandbox to hold a change of linen.

"The girl hasn't two bits of brain to rattle together. I thank God she is at least not wearing that green poke bonnet to call attention to herself. I'll leave for Maldon at once and see if I can pick up her trail."

"She has such a head start on you, you won't overtake her tonight," Claudia remarked.

Sir Hillary and Miss Bliss exchanged a worried glance. "The devil of it is I have spoken to Miss Miller of her flight," Hillary said.

"It is as good as announced in a paper," Miss Bliss informed him.

"Looks like another wedding on our hands," Thoreau said grimly. "If she overtook him, and I can't think she would have stayed away so long otherwise, I sincerely hope they find some minister to marry them before nightfall."

"She's under age," Miss Bliss said. "They couldn't even get a special license."

Sir Hillary promised to let them know at once if he discovered anything, but the ladies could think of no means of letting him know if she returned before him. It was learned of a footboy half an hour later that she had been seen on the road to Maldon, and they gave up on any local search.

Sir Hillary's misgivings mounted to alarm as he followed the course of his charges. Their trail was picked up at Maldon and followed to Witham where he learned they had headed north. He was certain they were en route to Gretna Green for a marriage over the anvil. He hastened to Braintree, thinking they meant to hire a chaise there and never even stopped for a moment when he went past the rector's house, where they were ensconced. At Braintree, his most diligent enquiries drew a blank. It was pitch black by then, and his team puffed from the hot pace he had set. As he dined he examined a map, and decided that for some unknown reason they had gone northeast to Colchester rather than due north to Braintree. He stabled his team, rented a nag and set out in the dark for the twenty-mile ride to Colchester, reaching it at midnight.

His thoughts wandered widely—to his own share of blame in not permitting them to marry sooner, to Claudia, to Marcia and the Trump, and to Jonathon. He'd have easy pickings of the necklace tonight. By morning the casket would have been pried open and with no witness. Have to find the necklace in his possession to prove him the culprit. With so much to ponder, the trip passed quickly, yet he was bushed when he reached Colchester. If they were there, they were bedded down at some public inn, disgraced in the eyes of the world. He'd have to see them married before he took them home and pretend the ceremony had taken place a day sooner. Damned fools. The stables were closed, and his enquiries had to wait till morning. He booked a room at an inn and left a call for six the next morning. The rounds of stables and coaching offices took up a good deal of time, and he came to the decision that his best bet was to go straight to Gretna Green and hope to meet them there. With this in mind, he must return to Braintree and get his own fast team.

It was drawing on to noon by the time he arrived, and the first sight of interest to meet his eyes was Gabriel and Luane, straggling along the street, leading Loo's mount. The pair of them looked so bedraggled and in such ill humor with each other that he had hardly the heart to give them the trimming they deserved. When Luane promptly broke into lusty sobs in front of the whole town, he hustled them into an inn's private parlor to hear their story. It was delivered in a disjointed fashion, with each contradicting the other when any allotting of blame arose, which is to say, every minute. But the gist of it was soon discovered, and Sir Hillary breathed a sigh of relief to hear that at least they had found a decent night's lodging. He smiled too at the attempts of the rector to hold on to them till their parents should arrive, and their sneaking away by pretending to be going to church, when they really were setting off for Braintree to hire a chaise to go home. Gabriel was as abject as a whipped puppy, and Loo too tired to fight.

"Now what is to be done with the pair of you?" Hillary asked, more of himself than them.

"I can get on to Cambridge now that you're here," Gabriel offered, to make amends.

"I think not, cawker."

"If you mean because it's Sunday . . ."

"You think I can object to that after the shenanigans you've been up to! You don't seem to realize you've put Loo in the devil of a position—or she has put herself in one. The whole neighborhood knows she's gone, and has a fair notion she's with you. Your having been away overnight together gives rise to the worst possible reflections."

"Do you mean I am *compromised*?" Loo asked, brightening remarkably. "Must he truly marry me now?"

Hillary observed the light in Gabriel's eyes, the whisper of a smile playing on his lips, and the quick but hopeful glance the would-be lovers exchanged.

"I hope you mean to do the right thing by her," he said to Gabriel.

"I will! The old weasel of a rector was hinting he'd do it for us—though why he thought it necessary when he put Loo in his daughter's room—and it was a maiden's chamber, behind his own and his wife's, with no access from the hall—so he can't think I—that is—it was all very proper, uncle."

"Oh yes, *very* proper! It is a pity our neighbors aren't aware of the propriety of the whole escapade. But this coming on top of your little candlelight dinner in Billericay the other evening is bound to set up gossip."

"I shall wear white," Luane said, falling into a careless rapture. "Cousin Claudia will be my bridesmaid, and *you* can be . . ."

"Before you dash off a note hiring St. George's in Hanover Square, I might point out, brat, that it is to be done with the utmost dispatch, preferably before we return."

"I haven't a stitch with me! I can't be married in this dusty old gown I have walked miles in!"

"Oh, lord, and my bags gone on ahead on the post," Gabriel said, remembering his oversight of yesterday. "Couldn't we go home and change, uncle?"

"What a pair!" Hillary shook his head in wonder, but being preoccupied with marriage himself, he was in a tender mood. "One day can make no difference. Claudia will like to be there, too. We'll arrange with our minister to do it tomorrow then, in a quiet way. It will look better if such of the family as is in the vicinity attends, but I can't be your best man, Loo. It will be my duty to give you away. And a relief it will be to be rid of you."

"Jonathon can be our best man. Seems a pity *he* is the best man we can lay our hands on," she said happily.

"Shouldn't we be getting home to arrange things?" Gab asked.

"I'm starved," Loo objected.

"Naturally," Hillary said mildly. While awaiting their meal, he arranged for Loo's mount to be returned to Swallowcourt, and before long the three were headed home in the curricle.

Thoreau felt he should be lecturing them the whole way, but their happy spirits infected him, and they discussed instead plans for the future. Miss Bliss would accompany them to an apartment near Cambridge while Gabriel finished his term. Sir Hillary was losing his excellent excuse to marry Claudia at once, to provide a chaperone for Luane, but was not much dismayed. He had no intention of allowing her to return to Devon to be governess to her cousins, and whipping boy to her fanatical grandmother.

Before they turned up the road to Swallowcourt, Sir Hillary stopped the curricle. "We have all spent the night at Braintree," he announced blandly.

Loo looked to see if his mind had become deranged. She realized he had been acting oddly in permitting the marriage. "That's what we're to *say* to make it look decent," Gabriel told her.

"And don't forget it," Hillary warned her. "The wedding is being performed to accede to your late aunt's wishes. Everyone will think you do it to secure her fortune and will laud your good sense."

"Yes, and the will was so strange that no one will be in the least surprised she made us get married," Loo said smiling.

"Don't count on getting the money though," Thoreau warned.

"Good gracious, we don't need it. I can sell my diamond, now that I'm getting married."

"Five hundred a year is hardly an easy competence, but if you can curb your lust for red and green bonnets, it will keep the wolf from the door," Sir Hillary said and could have said a deal more if not confined by the terms of the will.

"I am as well as graduated, and can find some work," Gab reminded them.

They were rehearsed once more as to the imaginary manner in which they had passed the night, and then went on to Swallowcourt, to be received into the grateful arms of Miss Bliss and Miss Milmont. Jonathon and Mrs. Milmont had taken a run down to Chanely to see what they could learn there and so missed out on the arrival. They had a nice chat with Mrs. Robinson though, pumping her for information regarding the domestic arrangements of Sir Hillary, and Marcia garnered up some new ways of dispensing some of her groom's wealth.

Chapter Seventeen

On Saturday evening, Claudia and Miss Bliss sat together in the Crimson Saloon till after midnight waiting for word from Sir Hillary. When the old clock in the hall clanged twelve, Miss Bliss suggested they might as well retire. They went to bed, but neither of them had any hope of sleeping. They both heard the captain tiptoe from his room and glide down the servants' stairs with his boots in his hand. They also saw him, since the silly clunch lighted his way with a candle, and they both eased their doors open to make sure that it was in fact him. Mrs. Milmont slept through it all.

As soon as the candle disappeared round the bend in the stairs, Miss Bliss crept down the hall to Miss Milmont's room. She had her hair twisted up into a loose knot and a netted shawl around her shoulders. "You know where he's off to!" she warned.

"He's gone to the graveyard, and there is no one to stop him. What shall we do?"

"We can't stop him, but we can follow and be witnesses in court," Miss Bliss announced.

"Do you mean you will come with me?" Claudia asked. "I am so glad. I was frightened to death to go alone."

"I too disliked the thought of going alone," Miss Bliss allowed primly, which brought an involuntary chuckle from Claudia. "We must get dressed at once. I do not plan to wear footmen's trousers at my age. I shall wear my oldest frock and a good warm shawl. And my brogues."

"How did you know we wore the footmen's outfits?"

"Luane carelessly put them in the laundry. I was sorry to see them damp. I was afraid you'd both take a chill."

They parted and within minutes were well bundled up. "I have brought a couple of tallow candles and a flint box, in case it is so dark we need them to make an identification," Miss Bliss said.

"We should have included you in our scheme from the beginning!" Claudia declared.

"With Sir Hillary on hand, there could be no need for my services. But since he is not here, I am happy to lend a hand."

They struck off down the road to the graveyard. Miss Bliss set a brisk pace, and before they had gone half-way, they had to slow down to avoid overtaking Jonathon.

They followed their quarry silently. "There is a short cut here, if you don't mind to hop a stone drywall, Miss Milmont," Miss Bliss said in a low, civil tone. "In this manner we will be there five minutes before him and can seek concealment behind a large tombstone. The monument of Alexander Coughlin is the one I have in mind. Close to Sophie's and offers sufficient width to hide us both."

They scuttled over the wall and wended their way through the tombstones to the spot mentioned. They were no sooner settled than Jonathon loped through the shadows, looking around him for spies. Believing himself alone, he set to work with his shovel, sharp from Sir Hillary's honing the night before.

It took him an age to dig out the grave. "My limbs become cramped," Miss Bliss whispered. "I'm going for a short walk—away from Sophie's grave." She faded silently into the night and was swallowed up by the shadows. She was gone for about ten minutes, at the end of which time Claudia became worried.

When she returned, she said, "This is a strange business." A sound as of metal being filed came to them, and they nodded knowingly. "Mr. Fletcher is here," Miss Bliss went on, her voice pitched low. "He is behind Mrs. McIntyre's monument—the large white cross there to your left. It gave me quite a turn when he spoke to me. He tells me he comes every night, not to *prevent* action, but only to witness it, like ourselves. He wishes us to remain that there may be three witnesses. Poor Jonathon—it must be that the one who plunders the grave is subject to reprisal. One can feel some pity for him. I would warn him, but he would only come back again, and I know Sir Hillary is anxious, too, to have it over with. Ah, there seems to be some commotion at the grave. Jonathon is hauling himself out. Has he the diamonds, I wonder?"

"Hadn't you better light the taper so we can see?" Claudia asked.

"I shall wait for Mr. Fletcher to make his move," she replied.

Before many seconds, Mr. Fletcher advanced from behind the white marble cross, carrying in his hands a lighted lantern. Jonathon dropped his shovel, and some garbled shriek escaped his lips.

"There—you see in the light, he has the necklace," Miss Bliss pointed out.

In the lantern's light, a multicolored sparkle was dimly visible, as was Mr. Fletcher's hand, reaching out for it.

"We are to remain hidden and observe," Miss Bliss said. "It will be more *convenable* for our presence to remain a secret, as we must go on living with Jonathon a while. It could not but be embarrassing for us all."

"I feel wretched! It is so underhanded," Claudia lamented.

"It is regrettable, but we must be guided by Mr. Fletcher, I think. There, Fletcher is leaving, and poor Jonathon's filling in the earth. What a dreary task for him. Our task, however, is over. We may return home now."

Noiselessly they faded away into the night, over the drywall, up the road to Swallowcourt, and finally to bed.

Their late night had one unseen advantage, in that it caused them to sleep in late the next morning, and thus avoid some part of the long, wearying day ahead of them. Sir Hillary's continued absence allowed them to imagine every horrible reason for it. Mrs. Milmont and Jonathon, the latter not visibly changed by the activities of the preceding night, joined together in outlining Loo's likely fate, finishing up by consigning her to a Magdalen house, where the chit belonged.

It was a long day, made longer by the degree of vigilance required to keep well away from a pursuing Jonathon, but in the afternoon he went out somewhere, and when the curricle drove up to the door later, only Miss Bliss and Miss Milmont were on hand to greet it. The latter was at the carriage before they had climbed down, running to pull Loo out and throw her arms around her. She expected to see a face ravaged by its ordeal, but Luane was bright-eyed and laughing merrily.

"You will never guess what, Claudia! I am compromised, and Gabriel must marry me."

Claudia looked to Sir Hillary, who was in despair at his carefully arranged story being so soon exposed. "Let us go inside and explain the *real* story to everyone, to avoid repetitions," he said, frowning heavily at Luane.

Loo's hand flew to her mouth. "Oh, I forgot. We all slept together at Braintree."

"The sooner you forget *that* particular version, the better," Hillary said with a despairing look at Miss Milmont, who knew not what to think.

"You observed it was *Gabriel* who must marry her," he added to Claudia.

Mrs. Milmont was descending the staircase as they entered the house, and it was to the three ladies that Sir Hillary explained the expurgated version of the history of the past day and night, with so many side comments from Lu-

236

ane that he might as well have saved himself the bother of lying.

"We are going ahead with the wedding at once to avoid talk," Sir Hillary finished up.

"What about our mourning?" Marcia demanded at once, not to spike the plan, but only to hear Sir Hillary's views, as she was eager to get on with her own nuptials.

"It was always known Sophie wished for the match," he replied. "It will be thought it is done to oblige her memory, and of course to secure Loo's fortune."

However suitable this excuse might be for the youngsters, it did nothing to palliate the shame of her own hasty union.

"When do you plan to tie the knot, Marcia?" Hillary went on to enquire. "I have not thought to offer my best wishes. I am very happy for you."

"So kind of you to say so, but as to when . . . I do not wish to dishonor my dear sister's memory."

"If you mean to do it very soon, it must be a small wedding, I collect," he replied.

'Very soon.' The words were music to her ears. "And not in London," she added, for her own mind had not been entirely unemployed during the past day.

"Why not be married from Marcyhurst?" he asked. "You and Mr. Blandings could take a family party up there for a week or so and get things in progress. If we all go, there can be no hint of impropriety in it."

'We.' Another word to charm her flintlike heart. "But I am presumptuous to think you mean to include *me* in your wedding party," he added with a smile.

"No indeed! You must always be welcome at my home, Sir Hillary. Mr. Blandings, too, will be happy to have you. Why, you might be best man if you like."

"Delighted!" he returned. "And the captain will give you away, I suppose, if the Guards can spare him another week. He is to be best man at Loo's wedding, for I must give her away."

"And you are to be my bridesmaid, Claudia," Loo added.

"When is the wedding to be?" Claudia asked.

"Tuesday. We were to do it tomorrow," Loo answered, "but Sir Hillary has to get a special license, and I told him we must get new gowns. And, of course, the cook must have time to prepare the feast. We mean to hold the party at Chanely."

"Very wise," Mrs. Milmont said. For one delightful moment she pictured herself too being wed from Sir Hillary's home, but she didn't think her groom would like it.

With so much to discuss, the party sat talking for an hour, till Jonathon returned and was informed of the duties devolved on him. "I'll have to send a note off to London to get leave," he replied. He was thrilled to have two formal occasions to sport his scarlet tunic and, with all the talk of weddings, he hoped Miss Milmont might become infected with the idea.

Sir Hillary tried vainly to get Mrs. Milmont detached from the group to speak to her in private, but her euphoria required a larger audience than one, and she was immune to his hints. At length, he had to leave to set in motion the many chores Loo's wedding involved.

In the excitement, Claudia forgot till after he was gone that she hadn't told him about Jonathon's getting the diamonds.

Mr. Blandings returned in high gig at having paced out as dandy a little piece of land as he'd seen this twelvemonth, and settled a mortgage at twelve per cent. He offered no demur to any plans of wee wifie, as he was already calling Marcia, and agreed to being wed from Marcyhurst. Loo and Gabriel were to go too, as a honeymoon. He went to his room and dispatched a sheet of instructions to his housekeeper for the visit.

Sir Hillary did not return that evening, for the very good reason that he had to drive to London to procure the special license for the wedding. Gabriel was left to speak to the minister, and the ladies to the harrowing but delightful task of arranging their toilettes. Luane was not at all disappointed to have to wear a gown off the rack, nor was her bridesmaid. After toiling over seams to make their own for a few years, they both thought it a rare treat. They were escorted to Maldon for the shopping by the Trump, with wee wifie to oversee the all-important selection of the wares. Luane had received a walloping sum from Sir Hillary, and was intent on spending every penny of it, and even Claudia had such trifles as gloves, slippers, silk stockings, and a charming bonnet showered on her. She had a shrewd (and accurate) idea that the money, though given to her by her mama, had come from the Trump's capacious pocket, and it bothered her not in the least. What she never for one moment suspected was that half her shopping money stayed in her mama's moneybag.

Sir Hillary arrived from London at about the same time as the others returned from shopping in Maldon, and he went immediately to Swallowcourt. His hope of a private interview with Mrs. Milmont was thwarted on this occasion by the presence of the Trump, who dogged her heels as assiduously as the greenest suitor. He even became jealous when he noticed Sir Hillary's attempts to engage her attention. The party remained together throughout the evening. The girls brought down their finery to be admired; Loo asked him a million questions about her wedding feast, her main concern being whether there would be plenty of cream buns. Gabriel got his bride aside on a sofa for a quarter of an hour for a little discreet lovemaking that involved a deal of giggling, and concealed touching of fingers, and coy calling of his beloved by the title of Mrs. Tewksbury. At a fairly early hour, the gentlemen from Chanely left, for it is was, of course, traditional that the bride got to bed early on that one night when she was assured of not closing an eye before dawn.

Claudia went to her cousin's room to wish her goodnight, but in her heart she felt it was good-by. Her cousin and her mama were being married, but her own hopes, pinned on Sir Hillary's enigmatic phrase of two days ago, had withered to dust. Twice he had been in her company, and he had neither spoken to her mother, nor to her, about his plan. Clearly Luane required no abigail now, and clearly he had decided it was unnecessary to marry her. In a bitter mood, she mentioned that it was surprising Sir Hillary was allowing the marriage, after having prevented it for so long. But her old confederate failed her. Luane had nothing but praise for Sir Hillary. A gentle hint that Jonathon wasn't really so bad was blasted when Claudia related the tale of his grave-digging. Even Loo didn't think a husband destined for Newgate would be much company.

"Gab and I will have you to visit us and find a beau for you," she promised airily, but neither girl put much credence in this offer, and it was with a heavy heart that Claudia lagged to her room to consider the old adage, "Always a bridesmaid; never a bride." She had stood bridesmaid to another cousin the year before.

Chapter Eighteen

No one had thought to pray for fine weather for the wedding, and that perhaps accounted for the mizzle that greeted the bride's eyes when she awoke on her wedding day. But the gloom was all confined to the outdoors. In the church, and afterwards at Chanely, it was as merry a wedding as ever took place. The bride looked beautiful, the groom happy, the captain very military, the bridesmaid resigned, and the guests appreciative. With so small a party, and in mourning too, no dancing was held, but in speeches, compliments and good-natured raillery there was nothing more to be desired. Jonathon dogged the side of Miss Milmont, and it took considerable perserverance on the part of Sir Hillary to get her alone for a moment. She was peculiarly blind to his every effort, till he had at last to ask her point-blank if she would come with him to the morning parlor a moment to give her opinion on something he had picked up in London.

Her heart beat a little faster when he carefully closed the door behind them and sighed, "At last," with weary relief.

"You are happy to have them married?" Claudia asked. "It must have been troubling you, since their running away."

"That's not why I lured you in here."

"You wanted to show me something you got in London. Pray, what is it?"

He extracted a small blue velvet box from his pocket, opened it, and held it out to her. On a bed of white satin, a quite large diamond sparkled. Her beating heart went into palpitations. She licked her lips and said, "Is—is it Luane's wedding gift? She will like it very much. My, it must have been very expensive."

"Unlike the Trump, I haven't the knack of picking them up at a bargain, but in this case it made no difference. It has been in the family for some years. I brought it from my bank in London."

"Oh, you mean to give her a family heirloom. I should have thought—but it is very fine. She will surely like it."

"This has nothing to do with Luane. Do *you* like it?"

She looked a question at him, looked again at the ring, and swallowed in discomposure. "Yes, it's very nice," she said, and made no move to take it or even touch it.

"Try it on," he said, lifting the ring from its box and taking her left hand. The emerald he slid off very easily and transferred to her right hand, before pressing the diamond onto her third finger. "Now I have an even worse question to pester you," he said softly, aware of her shyness. "Will you wear it?"

"But why . . ."

"You have forgotten your lines, darling," he said, taking her two hands in his. "I particularly asked you to rehearse them. I made sure you would have them by heart at this late date. Two whole days, and your part is really very simple. 'I am honored, sir, to accept your kind offer' was what you had intended saying, wasn't it?"

"Are you asking me to marry you?" she asked hopefully.

"Good God! Am I doing my part so badly as that? I shall end up taking a lesson of the captain. Certainly I am asking you to marry me." She stared and said nothing for a full thirty seconds. "And you ought really, in kindness, to give me an answer too. It is the custom."

"But Loo doesn't need an abigail now. She's married."

"I had noticed that. You have understood my oblique hints regarding nasty strings, I see. Yes, that excuse for a hasty wedding has been snatched from us. We must find another. I don't mean to wait any six months."

"There can be no need for you to marry me now."

"Claudia!" he said impatiently. "As though I haven't four aunts, two uncles, and any number of cousins that could have taken Loo in. I only left her at Swallowcourt this long to have an excuse for you and your mother to remain. Being an abigail was a pretext. Well, it wasn't even that, for you would certainly not have been her *abigail*, but I thought at first we might have her stay with us till she married, and we could chaperone her. Certainly that was not why I want to marry you."

"Why then?"

"Why do you think?" He grabbed her into his arms and tightened his hold till she was firm against his chest. "Because I have loved you forever," he said into her ear.

"You have not known me for two weeks," she pointed out.

"Not even eleven whole days. About two hundred and fifty-six hours in fact."

"Have you counted them?" she laughed in a quaking voice.

"Did Jonathon not tell you what a keen accountant I am? I have counted every one, wondering what number would remove the taint of a too-hasty offer. Well, actually I didn't count the first five or six. Till you came dripping into my study with your hair plastered to your head, wearing those distinguished moth-eaten trousers, and asking whether I could wield a torch, I was not convinced we should suit. But I see what it is. You are waiting for a proper proposal in form. I shall follow my own advice and go down on bended knee." He released her, drew an immaculate handkerchief from his pocket and shook out its folds.

"Don't be so absurd," she said, taking the handkerchief

243

from his hands, and mangling it between her nervous fingers. He removed the mussed muslin and tossed it aside on a chair.

"It is not absurd to want an answer to my question, however." Of the answer he was in little doubt, but of her ability to utter it, there seemed some question, so he encouraged her by drawing her into his arms again and placing his lips lightly on hers. He was surprised, but by no means dismayed, to feel an instinctive response in her. The fear that her puritanical upbringing might have curbed her natural impulses was removed, and he then embraced her like the confirmed heathen he was.

After several moments spent in this manner, he stepped back and said, "I trust that means 'yes,' darling?"

"Yes! Oh yes! I wouldn't let myself believe you meant to ask me."

"I can't imagine how else you interpreted my heavy-handed wooing. I thought I was being singularly obvious in my attentions for some days past."

"No, you were never obvious. Letting on it was your mama's scarf and . . . and everything."

"Ah, that was foolish, but I *did* want to see you in something other than those grayish things your grandmama selects for you, and you said you like pretty things. So your uncertainty accounts for not having your lines ready. But you cannot have failed to notice my fit of jealousy when I caught Jonathon on his knees at your feet."

"You were very hard on poor Jonathon."

"I wasn't sure what encouragement he had received from you, but I won't be hard on him any more. How soon can you be ready to move into my Palace Beautiful?"

"I am ready now."

He kissed her forehead. "Good girl. Shall we be married first, for the looks of it?"

"Sir Hillary! That is what I meant, of course. You cannot think me so abandoned as *that*."

"And still I am *Sir* Hillary, Lady Thoreau."

"Imagine! Whoever thought I would end up a *lady*?"

"Yes, there seemed a time when you were in some daner of becoming a man, but what I had hoped to convey was that we might now address each other by our given names with propriety, Claudia. Though why propriety should bother us on that one small point I can't imagine, wallowing as we are in the shame of runaways and scrambling marriages."

"We really are a horrid, disreputable bunch, aren't we? I shudder to think what grandmama would say if she knew what I have been up to these past days."

"Your character is not ruined yet. That will come later. I mean to undo all grandmama's good work, you know. Gowns of silk and satin, pagan plays, and operas and balls, and I don't know about you, but I personally plan to burn my copy of *The Pilgrim's Progress*. I give you fair warning of the depths of depravity I have prepared for you, with two Palaces Beautiful to flaunt yourself in."

"I gave them the wrong name. I should have called them Celestial Cities, for they sound precisely like heaven," she said happily, and leaned her head against his shoulder, to be caressed with his fingers.

"Feigning Woman," he teased. Then he took her hand and walked her to the door. "Let us tell mama the good news," he said, with a kindling light in his eyes. "The Trump has been like a dog with a bone and not let me near her to ask her permission."

"Oh, Hillary, what will she say? She will never want to be your mother-in-law and you thirty-two years old!"

"How did you know that?"

"Luane told me in London, when we spoke of finding you a wife."

"Indeed!" he said with a lifted brow, opening the door and striding along to the Blue Saloon, where the others were still making merry. He went immediately to Mrs. Milmont, still holding Claudia firmly by the hand.

"Mama," he said, smiling widely, "congratulate me. Little Claudia has done me the honor to accept my offer of marriage."

Marcia Milmont stared in astonishment, her round face changing from pink to rose as the ramifications of this announcement were borne in on her. None of her reflections

245

were of the sort her daughter feared, however, for the acquisition of a relative from so elevated a social plane as Thoreau inhabited overcame any little disparity between his real age and Claudia's imagined one.

"Hillary! Claudia—my baby! Can it be true? Jerry, did you hear? My daughter has landed the Nonesuch!" She grabbed Sir Hillary's hand, and he feared for an instant she would kiss it. And so she might have done, had she not spotted Claudia's diamond ring at that point and kissed it instead.

"Look at this, Jerry. She has already got a diamond from him."

Claudia blushed for the awful condition of her parent, but as her groom appeared unmoved, she said nothing.

Mr. Blandings took but little note of the news; his interest centered on the ring. Of that he had to make an estimate on the spot. His little jeweler's glass was brought out, and the finger held up to a branched candelabra. "That's a very fine stone," he congratulated the recipient. "Not so large as wee wifie's, but a fine specimen. You could get five hundred pounds for that on the market. Never take a penny less."

Thoreau said they would bear it in mind, and it was for Claudia to assure him she had no notion of hawking it.

"You know where to come if you ever have to," the Trump told her in a low aside with a sly wink.

The general commotion in that quarter soon drew the others around them. With the single exception of Jonathon, everyone else was thrilled at having yet another wedding thrust on them, and the only question to be settled was how soon they could toss a third wedding party in the midst of their mourning.

Mrs. Milmont, forgetting Claudia was only a stepdaughter, began speaking of taking her little girl to live with herself and Mr. Blandings for six months at Marcyhurst, but Sir Hillary scotched that scheme at once. "The devil of it is," he said, "I shall be so busy here finding some place for Gab and Loo to stay that it will be hard for me to get over to Marcyhurst to see her. And, or course, if she returns to her grandparents in Devon, I'll never see her at all."

Such a separation as this held too much danger of a lessening of affection, and the mother at least made no objection to a wedding immediately. "Why, you and Claudia could be married from Marcyhurst too, Hillary. Such fun—two weddings. We might even make it a double wedding!"

"No!" Sir Hillary and Claudia shouted as one. The latter softened her disagreement by adding that she especially wished to be married at Chanely, as Loo had been.

"If you only want an excuse to make it look decent," Loo suggested, "why don't you pretend Aunt Sophie wished for Claudia's marriage, as she wished for mine?"

It was a pretty weak pretext, but no one thought of a better one, and as all parties except the captain were determined to do it as soon as possible, it was decided on. They would all go to Marcyhurst, and then return to Chanely for Claudia's marriage to Sir Hillary.

As an acknowledged fiancée, Claudia now had a little privacy with Hillary, and she told him what she had been trying to find privacy to say for some time. "Jonathon got the diamonds while you were gone," she said as they sat together on a sofa, away from the others.

No disappointment, but rather a smile greeted this news. "Too bad for him," Hillary replied.

"Yes, because he didn't get to keep them. Mr. Fletcher was there and snatched them right out of his hands."

"How do you come to know all this?" he asked suspiciously.

"I was there, too."

"Claudia! You didn't go all alone to the graveyard in the dead of night!"

"No, Miss Bliss came with me. She is a splendid conspirator, Hillary. She even knew a short cut."

At this he laughed aloud. "Blissful is up to anything. And she will need to be, to ride herd on the child bride and groom the next couple of months at Cambridge. They may end up here with us for a while after he graduates. Just till they find a place of their own."

"How nice! They will be our first guests."

With a wary eye at his future mama-in-law, who was smiling on him in a doting fashion, he felt some doubts about that, but said instead:

"Do you know, I had a strange communication from Mr. Fletcher this morning. In the excitement of the day, it slipped my mind, but he said he wished to see us all here or at Swallowcourt tomorrow. Can it have anything to do with Jonathon's grave-digging, I wonder?"

"He won't be put in jail, will he?"

"Lord, no, but the gudgeon has likely cut himself out of any cash in Sophie's will. A pity, for he has lost his heiress, too." He smiled and squeezed Claudia's hand as he said this.

"There is no saying I will ever get any of the Trump's money, Hillary," she warned him.

"That will be a sad blow to me, for, of course, it is the only reason I offered for you!"

She looked closely at his face, to be reassured by his quizzical smile that he was roasting her. "I don't know why you *did* offer. Loo said you usually had diamonds of the first water for girl friends, so you cannot have married me for my looks, and I know I am not at all clever, or anything like that."

"Quit hinting for compliments, Feigning Woman. It is, of course, a chess partner I am after."

Marcia could no longer stay away from the side of her son-to-be, and descended on him to discuss more aspects of the two weddings. As the party was about to break up a little later, Hillary told them of Fletcher's communication, and they agreed to meet at Swallowcourt next morning at eleven. Luane was to remain at Chanely for her wedding night. Already feeling herself a matron, she kindly prepared Claudia a box of sweets to take back to Swallowcourt for breakfast.

At ten minutes before eleven the next morning, Fletcher was at Swallowcourt with Sir Hillary, and five minutes after them Gabriel and Loo arrived in the curricle. The group gathered again around the desk in Sophie's library was as curious as they had been the first time. The captain was the only one greatly discomposed, as he feared some public disclosure of his crime would be made. Any further benefits to accrue to anyone were now in the nature of a superfluous gift, and though Gab and Hillary were quite eager to hear whether the former was to get any money, they did not feel this was the time they would find out. A year hence was the date named.

They were soon disabused of this thought. Mr. Fletcher said in a calm voice that all the events to have taken place in the intervening year had now transpired, and in that case, he had been authorized to read the remainder of the will sooner. "So this is to be the disposition of her fortune," he said. Nerves tautened at the words. The captain especially was pale around the ears, though he sat as tall as any of Wellington's officers. Each person privately figured out that the two events must be Loo's marriage and the digging up of the grave. That great secret had become known within the family circle, as any choice piece of scandal always will. Their surmises were correct, and the all-important moment was upon them.

" 'Upon the marriage of my niece, Miss Luane Beresford to anyone, she is to receive the sum of ten thousand pounds,' " he read. Gabriel was a little disappointed to hear the sum so small, for Sophie's total fortune was thought to be in excess of a hundred thousand pounds. Still, with her diamond it made twenty thousand. " 'And if she marries either of my nephews, the sum will be fifty thousand pounds.' "

"We are rich, Gab!" Loo crowed. She leaned over in her chair and kissed his cheek. There were general congratulations all around, till Mrs. Milmont recalled them to business.

"That leaves another fifty thousand pounds!" she announced.

Mr. Fletcher bowed to her and read on. " 'You will know by now that the necklace buried with my mortal remains was the paste reproduction,' " he read.

The party, with the exception of Sir Hillary Thoreau,

did not know this, and a good deal of chatter was necessary to confirm it. His deception in claiming only the large stone of the supposed replica genuine was explained as adhering as closely to her will as possible after Jonathon had tumbled to it that some part of the necklace was real.

"Well, then, where are the real diamonds?" Marcia demanded.

"The genuine Beresford diamond necklace was given to Miss Beresford in the replica case, and it is hers to keep," Fletcher said.

"Thoreau just told us that," the Trump explained to wee wifie, wondering at her lack of attention on so important a point.

"Gabriel, we are millionaires!" Loo shrieked. "Uncle, you didn't tell me this! And you knew all along I had the real diamonds."

"Not a millionaire," the Trump pointed out. "A hundred thousand is what you've got." Really, the whole bunch of them had gone mad.

"I have known it only since we went to London, but by the terms of her will, I could not reveal it." Jonathon was glaring at Thoreau, and he, feeling very sorry for the captain, said, "Gab didn't know either, Jonathon. There has been no deception but the necessary one that was told to all."

"And we have been scheming all the while to dig up a pair of paste beads!" Marcia exclaimed, the whole truth at last penetrating her whirling mind. "The woman was a monster!" she decreed and would have claimed her insane too, but for the last fifty thousand to be accounted for.

"A cursed rum touch," Mr. Blandings said, rubbing his chin, then he let out a merry peal of laughter. "Ha, she fooled you, wee wifie. And you'd have had me robbing a corpse of a pair of glass beads. Famous! 'Pon my word, I never heard of such a thing."

Silence fell, and every eye turned to Mr. Fletcher for the final clause of the will. "Now for the last of it," he said, scanning the nether part of the page and shaking his head. "To whomever shows the initiative of digging up my mortal remains, opening the wooden coffin, the steel

250

chest, and stealing the paste necklace, I leave the remainder of my fortune, fifty thousand pounds.' "

A hush fell on the room. The first to grasp this outrage was the Trump. "Congratulations, Captain!" he said, rising and going to shake Jonathon's hand.

Jonathon stood, gulping and looking paralyzed with shock. "Me! You mean to say she's rewarding me for digging her up! She was crazed!"

"This proves she was insane!" Marcia joined in at once.

"As shrewd as she could hold together," her bridegroom contradicted her. "A very interesting will, when all's said and done. There's a woman as knew the value of a penny. Anyone foolish enough to let a fortune stay buried in the ground don't deserve to have it."

"But you refused to dig it up for me!" wee wifie reminded him.

"She was a step ahead of us all the way," he admitted, shaking his head at the knowledge that there had existed a mind with more turns than his own. "A rare wonderful old woman she must have been. I wish I had known her. I made sure it was the paste beads she'd buried, and thought it was a trick to punish whoever dug her up, but she was a deep 'un. What we'd have had to do was know she'd buried the paste beads, then go a step further and figure the rest of it. It never occurred to me. Never once entered my head, and I don't figure myself a slow one."

"I was similarly fooled," Hillary admitted. "I thought the test was to see which would show such disrespect as to plunder her grave. But she preferred the man with the initiative to steal to one who would let the diamonds go to waste. Well, it makes a perverse sort of sense."

"Now you say so," his bride challenged him, "but you would never lift a finger to help me and Loo get them."

"*Mea culpa!*" he said humbly. "I was certainly misguided. Loo is fifty thousand poorer because of me."

"No, I'm not!" she said at once. "I didn't plan to dig her up when I thought I had just the *one* diamond! I wouldn't have touched the grave for the world if I'd known I had the whole necklace. I hope I am not greedy. This is much fairer, for really Jonathon was gypped to get only Swallowcourt in such a poor state."

"There may be hope for you yet," Sir Hillary complimented her noblesse.

"She did more than enough for *us*." Gabriel added his pleasure at the outcome.

"And you mean to say I get fifty thousand pounds!" Jonathon said, still not quite able to assimilate so much good news after the fears that had haunted him. "Fifty thousand pounds! I'm rich."

"Congratulations," Hillary said, offering his hand. "I doubt you will believe it, but I am very happy. I have felt from the beginning you were robbed by her letting Swallowcourt disintegrate so."

Jonathon accepted the hand and murmured some acknowledgment of the congratulations. Everyone but Marcia seemed well pleased at the outcome.

"We'll pick up the Beresford necklace if you've a mind for it, love." the Trump whispered in her ear. "I daresay the little lady will be happy to sell it, though we'll get a better price if we aint too eager."

Mr. Fletcher took the captain and Gabriel aside to consult with them as to the manner in which they would like to receive their fortunes—whether in stocks and bonds or cash, for Gabriel would look after Loo's monies. Hillary was asked to help Gabriel decide, and it was half an hour before the whole party gathered in the Crimson Saloon to celebrate.

"All's well that ends well," Sir Hillary said. "The ladies all got a jewel and a husband; the gentlemen a jewel of a wife—with the exception of Jonathon, who may now marry where he likes. I daresay Sophie is pleased as punch to have fooled us all, and Fletcher must be the happiest of the lot to be done with this confounded will."

A strange, eerie sound seemed to come simultaneously from all corners of the room. It was not loud, but perfectly audible—a sound of ghostly laughter. It reached a crescendo, then subsided.

"Shall we all drink a toast to Sophie?" Thoreau asked. "And I trust, old girl, this will be your last performance."

"To Aunt Sophie!" they said in unison and grimaced simultaneously as they swallowed the horrid wine.

HELEN MacINNES

Helen Macinnes's bestselling suspense novels continue to delight her readers and many have been made into major motion pictures. Here is your chance to enjoy all of her exciting novels, by simply filling out the coupon below.

☐ ABOVE SUSPICION   23101-1   1.75
☐ AGENT IN PLACE   23127-5   1.95
☐ ASSIGNMENT IN BRITTANY   22958-0   1.95
☐ DECISION AT DELPHI   C2790   1.95
☐ THE DOUBLE IMAGE   22787-1   1.75
☐ FRIENDS AND LOVERS   X2714   1.75
☐ HORIZON   23123-2   1.50
☐ I AND MY TRUE LOVE   Q2559   1.50
☐ MESSAGE FROM MALAGA   X2820   1.75
☐ NEITHER FIVE NOR THREE   X2912   1.75
☐ NORTH FROM ROME   Q2441   1.50
☐ PRAY FOR A BRAVE HEART   X2907   1.75
☐ REST AND BE THANKFUL   X2860   1.75
☐ THE SALZBURG CONNECTION   X2686   1.75
☐ THE SNARE OF THE HUNTER   X2808   1.75
☐ THE VENETIAN AFFAIR   X2743   1.75
☐ WHILE STILL WE LIVE   23099-6   1.95

Buy them at your local bookstores or use this handy coupon for ordering:

FAWCETT PUBLICATIONS, P.O. Box 1014, Greenwich Conn. 06830

Please send me the books I have checked above. Orders for less than 5 books must include 60c for the first book and 25c for each additional book to cover mailing and handling. Orders of 5 or more books postage is Free. I enclose $_____ in check or money order.

Mr/Mrs/Miss_____

Address_____

City_____ State/Zip_____

Please allow 4 to 5 weeks for delivery. This offer expires 6/78.   A-8

Phyllis A. Whitney

Ms. Whitney's novels constantly appear on all the bestseller lists throughout the country and have won many awards including the coveted "Edgar". Here are some of her finest romantic novels of suspense that you may order by mail.

☐ BLACK AMBER	Q2604	1.50
☐ BLUE FIRE	Q2809	1.50
☐ COLUMBELLA	X2919	1.75
☐ EVER AFTER	P2298	1.25
☐ THE GOLDEN UNICORN	23104-6	1.95
☐ HUNTER'S GREEN	Q2603	1.50
☐ LISTEN FOR THE WHISPERER	23156-9	1.75
☐ LOST ISLAND	23078-3	1.75
☐ THE MOONFLOWER	Q2738	1.50
☐ THE QUICKSILVER POOL	22769-3	1.75
☐ SEA JADE	Q2572	1.50
☐ SEVEN TEARS FOR APOLLO	Q2508	1.50
☐ SILVERHILL	Q2810	1.50
☐ SKYE CAMERON	Q2804	1.50
☐ SNOWFIRE	Q2725	1.50
☐ SPINDRIFT	22746-4	1.95
☐ THUNDER HEIGHTS	22737-5	1.50
☐ THE TREMBLING HILLS	X2807	1.75
☐ THE TURQUOISE MASK	X2835	1.75
☐ WINDOW ON THE SQUARE	Q2602	1.50
☐ THE WINTER PEOPLE	22933-5	1.50

Buy them at your local bookstores or use this handy coupon for ordering:

Romantic Suspense

Here are the stories you love best. Tales about love, intrigue, wealth, power and of course romance. Books that will keep the reader turning pages deep into the night.

- ☐ CROCODILE ON THE SANDBANK—Peters Q2752 1.50
- ☐ DARK INHERITANCE—Salisbury 23064-3 1.50
- ☐ THE DEVIL OF ASKE—P. Hill 23160-7 1.75
- ☐ THE HEATHERTON HERITAGE—P. Hill 23106-2 1.75
  (Published in England as The Incumbent)
- ☐ THE HOUSE BY EXMOOR—Stafford 23058-9 1.50
- ☐ IRONWOOD—Melville 22894-0 1.50
- ☐ LEGEND IN GREEN VELVET—Peters 23109-7 1.50
- ☐ THE LEGEND OF THE GREEN MAN—Hely 23029-5 1.50
- ☐ THE MALVIE INHERITANCE—P. Hill 23161-5 1.75
- ☐ MICHAEL'S WIFE—Millhiser 22903-3 1.50
- ☐ MONCRIEFF—Holland 23089-9 1.50
- ☐ THE NIGHT CHILD—DeBlasis 22941-6 1.50
- ☐ NUN'S CASTLE—Melville P2412 1.25
- ☐ THE PEACOCK SPRING—Godden 23105-4 1.75
- ☐ THE PLACE OF SAPPHIRES—Randall Q2853 1.50
- ☐ THE PRIDE OF THE TREVALLIONS— P2751 1.25
  Salisbury
- ☐ THE SEVERING LINE—Cardiff P2528 1.25
- ☐ STRANGER AT WILDINGS—Brent 23085-6 1.95
  (Published in England as Kirkby's Changeling)
- ☐ VELVET SHADOWS—Norton 23135-6 1.50
- ☐ THE WHITE JADE FOX—Norton Q2865 1.50
- ☐ WHITTON'S FOLLY—Hill X2863 1.75

Buy them at your local bookstores or use this handy coupon for ordering:

FAWCETT PUBLICATIONS, P.O. Box 1014, Greenwich Conn. 06830

Please send me the books I have checked above. Orders for less than 5 books must include 60c for the first book and 25c for each additional book to cover mailing and handling. Orders of 5 or more books postage is Free. I enclose $_____ in check or money order.

Mr/Mrs/Miss_____

Address_____

City_____ State/Zip_____

Please allow 4 to 5 weeks for delivery. This offer expires 6/78   A-18